What Peopl

It's a rollercoaster plot with gorgeous historical detail and fabulous characters. I think people will really take to thoroughly modern [Raya] and her adventures. Magical.

Tania Findlay, *The Sun*, London

An imaginatively written time-slip novel...its underlying message of love, loyalty and friendship is nicely explored and strongly focused. The historical element sits comfortably alongside the modern-day setting and there is enough action to keep interest alive until the end.

The Historical Novel Society, *https://historicalnovelsociety.org*

'[F]ull of adventure, drama, fantasy, history, friendship, self-discovery, [and] humour...The book left me on the edge of my seat and was a real page turner. I cannot wait to read more of Sara's work and hopefully be joining [Raya] and her friends on more journeys.'

Laura Book Blog, *https://laurahbookblog.wordpress.com*

Sara Pascoe has written an actual, genuine, YA novel, and it kicks ass!

Awesome! A real page-turner. Great mix of real detail and zany – but believable – fantasy. A teenager's tale fit for an adult. A must-read.

A fun, page-turner that's thoughtful and refreshing. I loved it!

The book left me on the edge of my seat – real page turner. [There were] fun, loving and unforgettable characters. I cannot wait to read more of Sara's work and hopefully be joining [Raya] and her friends on more journeys

This is one of those YA books that adults will also really enjoy. A great plot full of adventure across time and space, but that also unravels a number of emotional threads as [Raya] goes from being a bristly teenager with an attitude, to someone who can let love in.

Fi Trench, *Amazon.co.uk*

A must read. I read this book in a few days! Even though this book is aimed at a younger reader I wouldn't brush past it thinking it may not be for you. Sara Pascoe has you feeling like you're right there along with the famous witch trials of Essex and you can almost smell the market and spices of Istanbul.

Emma Dixon, *Amazon.co.uk*

This story is amazing. It is as realistic as it is not! It has magic and it has drama, and at the same time it has funny moments, and talking cats and dogs…and it is serious and complex. I believe this is one of those books that people should read at least two times in their life: as teens and as adults.

Marina Boteva, *Goodreads.com*

Harry Potter for punky girls! A great, fun story. Draws you in with well-drawn characters and a plot that takes you on a real adventure, both magical and emotional. [H]ope there are more adventures from [Raya] in the future!

What a refreshing YA novel. Nothing came as predicted and it was a delight from start to finish. The characters were lovable and the writing is so witty yet simple and straightforward! I would recommend this to anyone who is a fan of adventure and fantasy.

Amazing...grabbed my attention straight away...[A] young adult novel but adults will enjoy it as well...full of adventure, drama, fantasy, history, friendship, self-discovery, [and] humour...The book left me on the edge of my seat...unforgettable characters.

SARA PASCOE

Being a Witch

and Other Things I Didn't Ask For

Trindles & Green

Copyright © 2017, 2015 by Sara Pascoe

www.sarapascoe.net
info@sarapascoe.net

ISBN: 978-0-9935747-3-3 (paperback)
ISBN: 978-0-9935747-4-0 (epub)

Published by Trindles and Green Ltd
Loxwood House, 6 Alumdale Road
Bournemouth BH4 8HX
United Kingdom
www.trindlesandgreen.com

Simon Avery, Cover design *www.idobookcovers.com*
Lindsey Alexander, Editor *www.lindsey-alexander.com*
Helen Baggott, Copy-Editor *www.helenbaggott.co.uk*
James Robinson, Book design, *www.wordzworth.com*

For David

Notes for the Second Edition

Being a Witch, and Other Things I didn't Ask For is the second edition of this book.

The first edition was titled, *Ratchet, the Reluctant Witch*, published by Brown Dog Books, Bath, UK, October 2015.

In addition to the new title, Rachel Hollingsworth, the protagonist in the story, has been given a new nickname, 'Raya'.

This second edition is published by Trindles & Green Ltd, Bournemouth, UK. *www.trindlesandgreen.com*

Constantinople or Istanbul?

There have been questions about the correct name for this city when the story takes place, during the mid-seventeenth century.

After the Ottomans conquered it in 1453, 'Constantinople' (or 'Konstantiniyye', the Turkish version) was used on some government documents and coins. And those in the West referred to it as 'Constantinople'. But the people living there and in the surrounding areas called it 'Istanbul', as folks had done since the tenth century. Even street signs said, 'Istanbul'.

Originally from the Greek phrase 'στην Πόλη' '[stin'boli], meaning 'in the city' or 'to the city', the name morphed into a single word. This was reinforced by the popular pun 'Islambol', meaning 'Islam abounds' celebrating its role as the Ottoman capital of Islam. 'Islambol' was also stamped on coins and documents. Istanbul was made the singular, official name in 1923 with the creation of the Republic of Turkey.

Therefore, to be true to the history as I understand it, I let the seventeenth century Ottoman characters in this book call their beloved city, 'Istanbul'. If you've never been to this magnificent metropolis, I cannot recommend it highly enough. I can't wait to return.

Chapter 1

These Boots Are Made for Walking

'Take this, Rachel, in case you need it,' Jake said as he dropped something into the pocket of her cargo trousers. He'd slipped into her room while she was globbing on her mascara. She glanced at his reflection next to hers, surprised how young eleven looked to her now. The sun slashed through the windows this July evening, and the field behind the cottage made a chocolate-box setting. This was one of the nicest foster homes she'd ever been in. But she'd had more than enough by now – it was time to launch out on her own.

'You know it's Raya, you eejit,' she said affectionately. She fished out the items from her pocket: a two-pound coin and a chocolate bar. 'Thanks, mate, but I can't take your money.' She returned the coin but pocketed the Dairy Milk bar. 'Don't mean to be rude or anything, but I've got to get a move on, running late as it is.' She went back to rimming her eyes with black eyeliner – 'war paint' he called it.

They'd only known each other a few weeks, since Jake moved into Angie's too, but as Raya often found with other foster kids, you either clicked or you didn't and that was that. She and Jake got on 'like a gut full of bacteria' in his words, being quite the brainbox. Still, she'd kept her distance. *This is goodbye anyway – I'm out of here.*

The boy gulped and nodded. Raya returned to the mirror and daubed on lip gloss.

'Please don't go, Raya. It's not that bad.' Jake looked down at his feet.

'You'll be fine. Angie's all right, just a bit boring.'

'Yeah, but you show me things, and well…' His lip trembled.

'Hey, don't worry. I'll text you – tell you all about it,' she said absent-mindedly.

'You will?'

She turned and looked him in the eye. 'Yeah, but you can't tell ANYONE.'

'Course I won't.'

She could only worry about herself right now. She was determined to have her own life, at least while she was still sane. Her mum had a 'bad case of schizophrenia' as the social workers called it, which made Raya wonder if there was ever a good case.

Over the last months, Raya had started hearing and seeing odd things. They didn't match her mother's description of schizophrenia – 'like living in your own personal horror movie'. Instead, Raya got simple pictures or sounds: the colour orange when she thought about her current foster carer, Angie; the sound of church bells right before something changed in her life, like getting a new social worker last week. *I'll be happy to miss that circus.*

Raya didn't tell anyone about these things she saw or heard, afraid of finding out she was losing her mind like her mother. Besides, having had a bellyful of being in care, this was one more reason to get out and have a life of her own – while she could.

Tonight she'd meet her boyfriend Tony – he was in foster care, too – at eight o'clock in front of the petrol station. From there, they would sneak onto the train at Earlswood and stay with Tony's cousin in Brighton for a night or two, until they got settled. Raya and Tony had fake IDs saying they were sixteen, only a year and a few months away for Raya, so they could work. Tony could fix cars. She'd get a job in a shop or something. They'd make enough to get by. Besides, Tony told her he had a surprise for her tonight. Maybe it was something they could sell.

'Hey, kids. Dinner,' Angie called from the front room. Raya looked over her shoulder as Jake moped towards the table. A pan of macaroni and cheese steamed. Raya's stomach gurgled. *My luck – figures she'd make my favourite tonight.*

She grabbed her oversized second-hand black leather jacket and rucksack and threaded through the crowded front room towards the door.

Angie, dressed as always in an embarrassingly bright top and leggings, stood with her oven-mitted hands on her hips. Jake slumped into his usual chair. Angie frowned. 'You all right, mate?'

She patted the boy's head with a still oven-mitted hand. He ducked, nodded, but didn't say anything.

At the front door, Raya hoisted on her jacket and swung her rucksack over a shoulder. 'I'm going to Gemma's for pizza and to work on our history project. Remember?'

'Tonight? I thought that was tomorrow.' Angie popped into the kitchen for the salad.

'No, it's tonight.' She had to get going if she was going to get there in time.

Angie put the food on the table and made her way to the door. 'Wait a minute. Let me say goodbye.'

'It's not a big deal. I'll be back in a bit.'

There was a knock at the door.

Perfect – something to occupy Angie and let me slip out. Raya opened the door. It was her new social worker who appeared more surprised than Raya was. Her lumpy jumper was askew and it looked like she brushed her hair with a whisk.

'Oh, sorry,' the social worker said looking up at the name of the cottage. 'I momentarily forgot you live here, um, Rachel. Didn't mean to bother you, I've lost my cat…' She poked behind a bush.

Angie joined them at the door. 'Hi, Miss Braxton, nice to see you.'

Miss Braxton snagged her sweater as she stood up. 'Hi, Miss Reece. I'm ever so sorry to disturb you – my cat's run off again, in this direction. I only live over there.' She gestured towards an old stone cottage with purple trim and a turquoise door. *Figures.* It was beyond the field behind Angie's cottage. 'He keeps sneaking onto the trains heading for London. Thought I'd save myself a trip to whatever train station they throw him off at.'

And SHE'S supposed to sort out MY life?

'Sneaking on trains? That's pretty clever,' Angie said.

Bryony sighed. 'I'll give him that.'

'No, I haven't seen any extra cats around. Have you,

kids?' Angie turned to look at Jake who sat at the table eating. He shook his head.

Oh for God's sake. I can't miss my life because of some dumb cat. 'No, I haven't seen it. But, Miss Braxton – why don't you use your powers to find him, being a witch and all?' Raya gave an innocent smile: didn't believe in all this witching stuff, thought it was a load of rubbish people made up to feel better about themselves. This woman certainly needed to.

'Rachel… we all know Miss Braxton's an "integrator".'

A taxi rumbled past them at the end of the short, unmade road.

Bryony laughed. 'I don't mind the old term. You're right, Rachel, my skills aren't helping at the moment – they're not fail-safe, unfortunately.' She looked behind some more bushes.

Raya felt embarrassed for her. 'Right, sorry. I was just leaving. Bye, Angie. Bye, Miss Braxton.' She had to stop herself from saying 'have a nice life'. She stepped away, but Miss Bryony Braxton, social worker and witch, or the more politically correct term, integrator, grabbed her arm.

'Wait, I just saw something,' Bryony said, squinting into the middle distance. 'I'm only getting flashes, but Raya, don't go…'

Bryony's grip felt like a magnet stuck to her arm. Raya saw multi-coloured swirls. She yanked her arm away.

'Sorry,' Bryony said.

'I'm only off to my friend Gemma's. I'll be fine.' Without giving them a chance to respond, she crunched down the gravel road then ran to catch the taxi.

Chapter 2

Earnest and Innocent

The taxi idled outside of the boarded-up shop on the corner. The driver was putting the car into gear as Raya flung open the back door and jumped in. 'Sorry,' she said between pants.

The driver looked at her through the rear-view mirror and shook his head. 'Only so long I can wait to pick someone up. Where to?'

'The petrol station on the Brighton Road, please. The one past Redhill train station.'

The taxi drove along the narrow country road to the neighbouring town, about a mile away. They were almost there when a police car whooshed past without any sirens on. It all but skidded to a stop on the side of the garage without windows – the shop where she was meeting Tony.

'Drop me here, please,' she said a hundred yards before the garage. She unfurled her sweaty palm, paid the driver and hopped out. She walked quickly but casually towards the edge of the forecourt as two officers leapt out of their car, one with a gun drawn. They slunk through the doors. Bollywood music blared momentarily. The door swung shut blocking all but a few notes of the music.

Raya couldn't believe what she saw. Her heart jumped into overdrive and her stomach leapt into her throat. Tony was standing at the counter pointing a gun at the man behind the till. *A GUN! THIS was his idea of 'doing something for us'? Was he out of his mind?* She wanted to scream, but froze and pretended to look at the newspapers in the boxes outside.

The man behind the counter stood with his hands above his head. A woman, probably the shopkeeper's wife, was huddled into the shelves of cigarettes, crying. The armed officer stole up on Tony like a cat, thanks to the loud music, and pointed his gun at Tony's head. The officer seemed to be talking to him. Tony raised both arms, dangling his gun by two fingers. The officer grabbed Tony in some sort of hold from behind and pressed him against the counter, snatching the gun out of his fingers. The officer whipped Tony's hands behind his back. Chocolate bars flew off the shelves.

A man who had been filling his car with petrol opened the door but stopped in his tracks when he realised what was going on.

'It's plastic,' the armed officer said. He tapped the gun on the counter. 'I'll cuff him, you take statements.'

'You all right?' the other police officer asked the man and woman shaking behind the counter.

The man nodded and put his arm around the woman who sobbed into his shoulder. 'Thank goodness for the emergency call button. Thanks for getting here so fast, officers.'

The confused customer walked up to Raya. His presence felt protective, safe. She stayed next to him. Besides, running would look bad. Real bad.

The officer walked outside and up to the two of them, taking a pad and pen out of his pocket.

'I'll need to take your names and contact details, and I need to know what you saw.'

'I can tell you what I saw, but I don't think she could have seen much,' the man said and nodded towards Raya. He had a country accent and kind eyes. 'She walked up as you fellows were running into the shop.'

'Is that true, young lady?' the officer said.

'Yes, sir. I was on my way to my friend's, Gemma's, to study. Thought I'd stop to buy some crisps. I saw you… stop him.' She didn't have to fake the quiver in her voice. The older man put a hand on her shoulder.

'Do you want to sit down a minute?'

She didn't. She didn't want to stay one more second. It took every fibre of her being not to bolt.

The armed police officer led Tony out of the shop. His hands were behind him in plastic restraints. His cheeks were red, his thick hair flopped over his face with each step. He looked down. The officer put his hand on Tony's head as he got into the car, like they do on television. It all seemed searingly real and unreal at the same time.

'I'll need to take your details in any event,' the officer said to Raya, but she didn't answer.

The other customer nudged her.

'Yes, sorry. Of course.' Before she could decide on fake information, she heard herself telling the officer her real name, mobile number and Angie's address. She was so angry with Tony; for a second she thought about grassing, but then again, how much did she really know about him anyway if she had no idea he was planning this?

After the officer had finished with his few questions, she excused herself, although he insisted she take his card in case she 'remembered anything else'. It would all be on CCTV anyway, he told her.

She walked robotically off the forecourt, forcing herself to maintain a normal pace past two street lights. Then she allowed herself to trot. After another street lamp, she ran, and ran and ran until the world was a blur and all she could hear was the pounding of her own blood. Hot tears streamed down her face. She rushed into Redhill train station, past the closed ticket booth and onto the deserted platform. She jumped off the end onto the grassy bank.

Her Doc Martens beat out a rhythm with the swish of her rucksack against her jacket. She was breathing hard, but well within her capacity.

Two thoughts screamed in her head. *How could Tony do this? And did that social worker really know?*

* * *

After Raya left, Bryony and Angie shared their concerns about the girl. You didn't have to be a witch to know she was up to something.

'It's the worry that gets to me – all the rest I can deal with,' Angie said. She looked through the half-open door at Jake on the couch having finished his dinner. Sounds of television filtered out.

'I know what you mean,' Bryony said. They stood

silent, watching dusk settle over the field between their homes. 'I'll leave my mobile on. I'm sorry I couldn't have been more help.' Bryony started off down the gravel road.

'Oh, I forgot to ask – what colour is your cat? In case it shows up,' Angie called after her.

Bryony turned and gazed at the setting sun. 'He's black and white at the moment, and he's called Oscar. Thanks.' Bryony smiled for the first time Angie saw that evening. Angie thought describing the cat's colour as 'at the moment' odd, but Bryony was already down the unmade road by the time she realised what she'd heard.

After seeing that Jake got ready for bed, Angie placed a garden chair at the front of the cottage and brought a cup of tea and her mobile. It felt like the closest thing to doing something as she waited for whatever might happen. She called Raya's friend Gemma's house and confirmed she wasn't there. Time to call the police. She scrolled through her phone for the non-emergency number when she heard a thump – something fell from the roof over the front door. A large black and white moggie blinked up at her.

Angie startled. 'My goodness, you gave me a scare. Are you that lady's cat, "Oscar"?' The cat wove through her ankles. She bent down and stroked his head. 'You weren't hiding from Miss Braxton, were you?'

'*Wouldn't you?*' the cat said.

'That's a loud meow you've got there,' Angie said.

Oscar looked hard at Angie. *'How about some roast chicken? With gravy?'*

Angie looked at him.

'You don't understand me? Oh man, I LOVE you!' Even though he realised she couldn't understand him, he rambled on, so used to living with witches who could. *'I'll only stay the night – catching an early train to London tomorrow. Only kidding about the chicken, although I certainly wouldn't mind.'* Oscar threw himself at Angie who only heard a lot of meowing. He rubbed side-long against her legs, vibrating his tail straight in the air, making his eyes big.

Angie stepped back, 'All right, all right – no need for a whole song and dance. You can stay 'til tomorrow. I've got bigger problems right now.' She opened the door and he sauntered in. She returned to her phone and was just about to dial the police when a tear-stained Raya trudged up. Angie cancelled the call.

* * *

'Oh, Raya. I'm getting too old for all this.' Angie shook her head. 'I thought you'd run off.' She sounded angry and worried – like she really cared. That was the worst – any whiff of real affection put knots in Raya's stomach. In her experience it never lasted. And getting a taste of what she didn't like to admit she craved only brought up a storm of uncomfortable emotions. *That's it, I'm out of here, one way or another.*

She composed herself and said, 'What? No, I just had a row with Gemma, that's all.'

'Did you, now?' Angie arched an eyebrow. 'Well, it looks like you had a rough time, in any event.' She tried to give the girl a hug, but Raya dodged it, afraid she'd burst into tears, and started towards the door.

'OK then, how about a nice hot bath and something to eat?' Angie said.

A while later, clean, fed and exhausted, Raya tumbled into bed. Her feet bumped into something. She forced her eyes open and saw Oscar sleeping at the end. *Weird, Angie got a cat in the two minutes I was gone? Maybe it's the one the social worker lost,* was her last thought before falling to a sleep laced with nightmares of being chased by the police.

Chapter 3

Barking

The next morning, Jake studied Raya across the table from where he sat munching his cereal. The moment Angie walked out of the front room, he leaned forward.

'So what happened?' He almost hovered off his seat.

'Oh, just didn't work out is all.' Raya yawned for effect, but inside she wanted to tell, and yell, and cry, and run away from herself, if only that was possible. She was terrified the police would tie her to Tony. *If he was capable of holding up that poor foreign couple, even if it WAS a fake gun, I'm sure he'd lie and drop me in it if he thought that would help him somehow.* Just thinking about Tony made everything look a disgusting brown. Another one of those colour-visions; her heart sank further, burrowing into the ground – maybe she WAS going psychotic.

'What do you mean it "just didn't work out"?' Jake brought Raya out of her head, but clammed up as Angie walked in.

'OK, you two – fifteen minutes and you're both off to school.' Oscar came out of Raya's room looking strangely more black and less white than she remembered. He wound around Angie's ankles and meowed, but Raya heard in her head, *'Hey, lady, I'm hungry, if you don't mind. And by the way – I'm more of a poultry man.'*

Oh sweet Jessops – now I'm having proper hallucinations!

Angie went into the kitchen with the cat at her heels. Raya followed.

'Angie?' Raya said. She was shaking. Angie put a bowl with tuna fish on the floor and turned towards the girl.

'Oh, poppet, what's the matter?' She put a hand on Raya's arm.

'I SAID poultry. Oh, that's right – you're not a witch.' Oscar glared at Angie and sniffed at the food. *'Oh well, be careful what you wish for, eh?'*

'Did you hear that?' Raya asked Angie.

Angie's concerned eyes met hers. 'The cat? He certainly is noisy.'

Raya grabbed her rucksack, still packed from last night, and bolted out of the cottage. Her heart hammered, her head pounded. Part of her felt like maybe she could

17

outrun it – the monster that stole her mother. She ran, the thumping of her feet her only anchor. She thought she might rise up and explode, like a big greasy soap bubble. *If only I could.*

The mile run to town helped calm her down. Puffed out, she leaned against the wall of an alleyway, lined with the back doors to shops. She opened her phone and flicked her SIM card into a commercial rubbish bin. Who knew restaurant rubbish stank so? She put her new SIM in and walked around until she found free Wi-Fi. She messaged Tony's friend who ran a squat in east London: 'Coming after all. Other plans didn't work out. Hope that's OK, Podcast.'

Raya used a fake name, one of the few good ideas to spring from Tony's rotten head. Looking back, she could see he knew a bit too much about all things dodgy. At least she was moving forward now and felt better for it – Plan B.

She sneaked onto the train platform without a ticket. After boarding, she made a beeline for the toilet and stood behind the door, but left it unlocked. She held her breath when the conductor tapped, peeked in, then carried on. No use spending any of her hard-earned dosh unless necessary. It had taken months of doing every job she could convince people to give her – gardening, errands for old people, painting fences, dog walking. Anything but babysitting – didn't want the responsibility. After the conductor passed, she locked the door, changed into the dull-grey hoodie she'd brought for the occasion and put on her Goth make-up – thick rings of black eyeliner, great blobs of mascara, wedges of black for eyeshadow and dried blood-red lipstick. *That'll do.* No sense going all out – she wasn't exactly going to a party. She settled into an empty pair of seats facing backwards.

'Is this seat taken?' a grandmotherly woman said.

'Yes, I'm afraid it is.' Raya smiled back. Company was the last thing she wanted.

She logged onto the train's Wi-Fi. Nothing from Tony who had her new number. She wondered if he was in borstal or what.

Why would he think robbing a petrol station was a brilliant idea? If I'd been a few minutes earlier... She realised she didn't miss him as much as she was angry. *Surely the police will go and talk to Tony's cousin. And anyway, I don't even know him – probably a plonker just like Tony.*

Raya stared out the window. Green fields, cows and sheep, houses and ribbons of road receded in front of her. Her phone chimed – a message from Home Girl: 'Hi Podcast, glad you can stop over. Meet me at the shopping centre straight down from the Dagenham Heathway Tube stop. I'll be in the sports shop.' Raya knew what Home Girl looked like from Tony's old Facebook pictures as she didn't risk putting anything new up now. She'd been living in squats for over a year, knew how it all worked.

As the train neared Victoria Station, tall apartment blocks and industrial buildings flashed by. The sky had clouded over. Raya's reflection flickered in the window. She looked younger and sadder than she'd imagined.

* * *

When she emerged from the Dagenham Heathway Tube stop, Raya was surprised how ordinary everything looked. The Heathway was lined with all the typical shops; buses and cars went by, people darted across the road. She realised she'd thought life, everything, would look different somehow once she was free. But it didn't.

No one gave her a second look; she was just another kid with too much make-up, and an unnaturally black 'Atomic' – like the bomb, the name she gave to her hairstyle: shaved on the sides, the rest standing on end. There were a few people in the sports store, but Home Girl was easy to spot. She looked like her photos, except thinner and scruffier. She was handling a pair of multi-coloured high tops.

'Hiya,' Raya said. Her voice sounded meeker than she'd meant it to. 'You Home Girl?'

'Yup. So you found your way all right?'

'Yeah. Finding you was the easy part. It's all been kind of hard going, really, what with the police taking Tony and–'

'Tony was arrested?' She put the high tops back on the shelf. 'I'm sorry. Come on, tell me about it on the way back.'

They walked out of the Heathway Shopping Centre and down the road.

'That's the library. Remember that – they've got computers in there and it's a nice place to hang out,' Home Girl said, nodding to the bright, modern building on the corner where they turned left.

'So, what happened to Tony?' she asked as they walked in matching strides.

'Would you believe it – he tried to rob a petrol station with a GUN and everything.'

'No way! Did you know? Did they try to arrest you too?' Home Girl stared at Raya without slowing.

'Of COURSE I didn't know. It was a plastic gun, anyway – but how stupid, eh? I got there just after he'd done it. For once being late paid off.'

Home Girl snickered, shook her head. 'I am sorry. Sounds horrible.'

Raya dug her nails into her palms to keep from crying as she relived Tony robbing those poor people at gunpoint, even if it was a fake, *and* her almost being part of it. She hunched down into her hoodie. They continued on in silence. There were lots of people out: mums with pushchairs and bags of shopping, businessmen and women, a postman rolling his red, square cart down the pavement.

'That's kind of cool,' Raya said looking at the building on their left. Home Girl followed her gaze to the flats with brightly coloured translucent balcony panels, like sheets of boiled sweets.

'Yeah. I like that, too. I wanted to be an architect,' Home Girl said.

Raya took a good look at her – she was seventeen at most. 'So why not, then?'

Home Girl laughed. 'You in school?'

They walked on, past houses, a shop here and there, then the road curved. Cars passed, a double-decker bus churned out exhaust and noise.

'So, who's in the squat?'

Home Girl looked around. 'Shh. Say "home" or "place", in case anybody overhears.'

'Oh, right. Sorry. Any other rules?' Raya said.

'Not many. The most important thing is don't leave if you're the only one there. If there's no one in it, we could lose it just like that.' She snapped her fingers. 'The only other thing is no open fires.'

'What?'

'When it gets cold, sometimes people try making a little bonfire inside to warm up, but that's just stupid – obviously.'

'Obviously.'

They passed neat blocks of brick-built flats, a patch of green behind a fence, then reached a corner where they turned left, along a larger, divided road. The cars drove by faster. They turned left again along another block of flats and behind a fenced-in, boarded-up pub. About a hundred yards down, Raya followed Home Girl through a break in the chain-link fence. Home Girl rapped three times on the back door to the white box-like extension to the pub. A lock rattled, the door opened and a toothless guy in his fifties smiled at them.

'Hey, Homie. Is this the new recruit?' He walked away before getting an answer. Raya and Homie walked through the kitchen where the tap dripped on a few dirty dishes. There was a new kettle on the counter. They walked into the next room, a large space with a stage at one end. It was dim and smelled of mould and unwashed people. There were bedrolls and sleeping bags in groups of three or more spread around. There were a couple of tables with chairs on the stage. Raya felt queasy – not so much at the grossness of the place, but at the reality of her choices. *So this is it? Either live in an absolute dump or with fake parents who get paid to do it and then spit you out at eighteen anyway?*

The toothless man had settled back down on his bedroll.

'RJ works nights,' Homie said.

'He has a job?' Raya said.

RJ chuckled.

'He's got a corner,' Homie said.

'And it IS hard work,' RJ chimed in.

There were three more people in at the time, two men and a woman. Raya smelled alcohol. She nodded and tried to remember everyone's names. The others besides RJ looked to be in their twenties or thirties. Homie had the most going for her – she wasn't a druggie or an alchy, and seemed pretty smart. It made sense she was in charge.

'You can put your bedroll here, next to mine, if you want,' Homie said.

'Thanks, appreciate it.'

'Best not to mix your stuff up with other people's. Bedbugs, you know.'

Raya followed Homie around while she showed her the toilets, and some sinks where they could give themselves a birdbath. She didn't ask how they managed to keep the water and electricity on in the building. She kept her rucksack on her shoulder. *I guess it could be worse.*

Back in the main room, Homie stopped by a long wall of cupboards. About eight of them had padlocks.

'Here's yours. I'd go out and get a hasp and lock. A key is best. People might watch you do the combination.'

'A hasp?' Raya said.

'The metal parts that let you put the lock through. Oh, and get a few screws. The kind you can't get back out again. I have a screwdriver you can borrow.'

'Good idea. Is the high street the nearest place for that stuff?' Raya said.

'Yup.'

'OK. I'll be back soon,' Raya said, but the look in Homie's eyes told her she knew Raya wasn't coming back. Homie's shoulders slumped; she looked disappointed. *Maybe she'd been hoping for someone near her age.* Raya felt guilty leaving, then felt stupid for feeling guilty. She'd only just met Homie – maybe she saw herself in her. The squat would still be there if it came to that. 'Thanks for everything,' Raya said. 'You've been very kind.' And she meant it.

* * *

'The postcode? I'm sorry. I just moved in with my nan. I'm staying with her while my mum's in drug rehab, and I don't know the post–'

'That's OK. I can look it up for you,' the librarian said, disbelieving but resigned. 'We'll post your card to you in a fortnight.'

'Thanks,' Raya said, then jumped onto her assigned computer, not wanting to waste a precious minute. She got onto Google maps and studied where she was – Dagenham, east London, and the surrounds. It looked like there were more shops and things going west, towards central London. *Surely I can find some work, maybe somewhere that will put me up. Anywhere's better than that place.* It was a little after three in the afternoon and she had an all-day Travelcard. Raya moved the map around on the screen and followed the Tube line west to Barking. BARKING!

Chapter 4

When Feet Obey the Heart

Before leaving the library, she looked up youth hostels. *Oh, that's really cheap. £11.50 per night with free Wi-Fi and brekkie?* She jotted down the address in Lambeth, south London. *Just for one night. I've got £231.64, so that would leave me with... £220.14. I won't eat until tomorrow – I could do that.* The pictures of the clean shower stalls and tidy bunk beds looked like a palace compared to the squat. She wrote down how to get there on the Tube then put her pad and pen back in their zipped pocket.

She smiled at the doubting librarian and left, taking large, happy strides towards the Tube stop. *Maybe it's better without Tony – I can do exactly what I want.* She'd wanted to go back to Barking for a long time but no one would go with her. That was where she was from, where she'd lived with her mum and grandparents when she was little.

Raya laced through the packs of people when she got off at the Barking Tube stop. Guided by wordless memory, she loped past the old building converted into a super-market and down the high street. Even though she'd moved away to Redhill with her nan when she was only five after her grandad died, she'd travelled these streets many times when her brain was still soft, and it had all sunk in without trying.

She turned onto another street of apartment blocks, passed the clock tower, then turned again. When she saw the ordinary three-storey block of flats where she'd lived with her mum, grandad and nan, yearning pummelled her.

The schizophrenia robbed Raya of her mother. Raya didn't remember her healthy, although her nan said she pretty much was until Raya was about three. Mostly, Raya remembered doing the odd things her mother asked her. Like hiding under the kitchen table because the red Formica top would protect them from aliens stealing their thoughts. At times, it was kind of fun, like being in a kids' den with her mum, but those moments would evaporate with the terror etched on her mother's face. Or having to say, 'Butter up, butter down, butter the bread all around,' whenever her mother made her toast or sandwiches to make sure no evil would get into Raya through the food. Once, when Raya giggled while saying the little rhyme her mother smacked her – real fear in her eyes. As a little one, Raya tried to make the world safe for her mother. She was sure her mother would stop worrying about all these things, that it would be OK if only Raya did everything right.

Then, one day, there was a picnic at nursery and Raya ran around swatting sandwiches out of the children's hands and mouths, sobbing and chanting the rhyme, worried all these children would be victim to evil without the pre-emptive ditty. A teacher restrained her with a bear hug until she could stop the choking sobs long enough to explain. This started the ball rolling – social services, and psychiatric treatment for her mum.

At first, they tried to let her mother continue living at home with her parents and Raya. Although the medication seemed to take away a lot of the weird ideas and stopped the hallucinations she also had, her mother did anything to not take it. Part of it was the crummy side-effects, but looking back Raya also wondered if that other world, revealed by psychosis, was the real one for her mother. Who could blame her for choosing fighting aliens and evil instead of just being an ordinary mum? But it still hurt. After about a year in and out of hospital, her mum was placed in supervised housing, where she still lived.

No one knew who Raya's dad was because her mum either didn't know or wouldn't say. Sometimes she'd say he was a famous person, a dead person from history, or even a superhero – more crazy stuff. So her grandparents were given custody.

Raya remembered the smell of cigarettes. Her nan had been a terrible smoker, died of it shortly after they'd moved. That was after her grandad had died.

Grandad.

Tears caught her by surprise. She was suddenly back on his shoulders, her arms around his neck, the comforting smells of car oil and coffee. He'd walk her around the neighbourhood, showing her off to anyone who'd listen. He'd stop in front of the flats before going in, taught her to count with the windows. Theirs was the fifth from the right in the middle row. She was convinced theirs looked that much brighter.

Sometimes, when her nan was at work, and with her mother too unwell or not there, her grandad would take her to the garage where he worked. He'd set her up in a scrapped taxi, with plenty of blankets and lots of toys.

The other workers were always nice to her, bending their grease-lined faces down to check on her, offering her more biscuits than she could eat, sharing their cheese and pickle sandwiches, and giving her very milky cups of tea. She started along the familiar route. He'd died eleven years ago but her heart believed there might be some souvenir, some echo.

She stopped when she reached the grimy building. It was smaller than she remembered. She clenched her jaw and moved towards the mechanic working under a car bonnet. She stood a few feet away until he came up for air.

'Oh, hiya,' the man said, and wiped his hands on his overalls. Raya said nothing. 'Can I help you?'

'I don't know. I mean, I know it's not likely, but does anyone remember Steve Hollingsworth? He used to work here.'

'When was that?'

'Oh, over ten years ago, I guess.'

'Well, in that case let me ask Bob. He might know. He's been here since the dinosaurs.'

'Very funny,' said a small old man, bent over. He came towards them. His face creased into a smile when he saw Raya. She looked away.

'Sure, I remember Steve. A good man and a helluva mechanic. Shame when he passed. Sometimes, he'd bring his granddaughter with him. Cute little thing, blonde hair, blue-green eyes. Called her "Raya", his little ray of sunshine…' He paused and studied her. She recognized him – the milky teas. Her mouth started to quiver. He smiled again.

'Is that you? Well, I'll be! How about a cuppa for old time's sake? I think we have some bikkies. We'll toast your grandad.'

Raya nodded, wanted to say yes, wanted to stay, but couldn't. She felt exposed, preferred to keep the reason for her nickname secret. No one had ever loved her like her grandad did, and she was half sure, half scared no one ever would again. 'Thanks… I'm sorry…' was all she could manage. She turned and jogged across the forecourt towards the road. She didn't know an echo could cut so deep.

Chapter 5
Pavel Patel

On automatic pilot, Raya walked back to the Tube at the start of rush hour and hopped on a westbound train. *Might as well look for work near the hostel.* With everything that had happened, it was hard to believe it was only this morning when she bolted from Angie's house with Jake staring gape-mouthed.

She retrieved her purse from her rucksack, slipped her fake ID and Travelcard into a buttoned trouser pocket, then fingered through the notes in her purse despite knowing exactly how much she had. She plugged her earphones in, put her music on and closed her eyes.

She felt someone staring at her and opened them. 'Agh!' Raya recoiled. A humongous dog with an expressive face stared at her.

A girl and guy a couple of years older than Raya sat across the crowded aisle. The girl, big like her dog, smiled. 'Alfie likes you.'

Raya took out an earphone. 'Hmm, I like dogs, but he's creeping me out – looks like somebody's in there.'

The girl loosened the lead. The huge hound stepped around standing commuters, his gaze locked on Raya's.

'He won't hurt you. He just wants to say hi.'

The dog gave her a sniff, put his heavy head in her lap, and stared up at her. It looked like he was smiling. Raya relaxed and stroked him.

'You know, you shouldn't flash your money around like that,' the guy said. He nodded towards Raya's rucksack on the floor between her feet.

'What? I didn't.'

'You know – when you were counting it before. People can see better than you think,' he said. The girl nodded.

'Oh. Thanks.'

Raya got one of those colours again – everything went an ugly grey-green. She stroked the dog and waited for it to pass. The girl tugged the lead and Alfie stepped back to her. Raya put her earphone back in and turned up the music. She didn't like these two, but the dog was all right.

The recorded voice announced the next stop and the train slowed. The girl and guy got up. Alfie stepped towards Raya.

'Bye, Alfie.' Raya patted his noble head. As the doors opened, the girl pulled Alfie along, the guy grabbed Raya's rucksack, and they bolted.

'Stop them! He nicked my rucksack!' Heads turned. She prized the doors open as they closed on her and charged after them. They'd disappeared into the crush of people. She pushed through, called the dog's name, and yelled for help. Some people tried, but it didn't make any difference. She saw them run down the stairs and darted after them. The stairs opened up to the exit.

It took two tries for her to get her ticket through and by then the three had vanished. Gone.

Raya stepped out of the station and squinted in the glare of the long summer evening. She checked her trouser pockets for her phone and fake ID. At least she had those. She turned around to look at the sign above the Tube stop – Whitechapel Station.

Market stalls lined the pavement in both directions. The shops brimmed with rainbows of clothing, stacks of fruit and veg, electronics, sweets she'd never seen before. Bearded men in long shirts, loose trousers and skullcaps manned the stalls, chatted with each other and drank coffee from small china cups. *Nice staying in your pyjamas.* She felt like she'd been transported to another land. Women in headscarves and veils wheeled pushchairs and carried shopping. School kids darted around. There were university students, arty types, and lots of hospital staff. A little bit of everyone.

She was hungry and thirsty, but now she didn't have any money. She wished she'd kept that two pounds Jake had tried to give her. She'd already eaten the chocolate.

Maybe I should just call Angie. Raya stood by a shop and watched the crowd go by. A woman in tatters with plastic bags on her feet talked to an invisible companion as she rummaged through a rubbish bin. Raya looked away. *Nope. I'm not going back.*

She asked market vendors and shopkeepers if they needed any help. Most said no without hesitation. Some gave her a look of pity. One told her she should lose the spiky hair and heavy make-up.

She went into a toilet in a fast-food restaurant, rubbed off the black circles around her eyes, and flattened her hair spikes with water. Her make-up was gone with her rucksack. But she still had her height. People often thought she was older than she was. She practised her fake birth date so it would roll off her tongue.

After no luck in the market, she ambled along roads of clothing wholesalers; through Petticoat Lane Market;

along Whitechapel Road again; then up to Bethnal Green. Almost all the shops and cafes were closed now. She asked hotels if they needed cleaners. She asked people walking dogs if they needed a dog walker. Most of them hurried away. One old man with an ancient dog gave her a pound.

The evening light stretched on, bathing east London in a syrupy yellow even though it was past eight o'clock. She was exhausted, famished, and her Doc Martens were rubbing blisters. Raya used to think cities looked exciting at night, promising. But tonight the twinkly lights coming on with the dusk didn't beckon, they jeered. She let her eyes unfocus and the rush of people turned into a river of colours.

All of a sudden, she thought: *GO LEFT*. She startled and looked around. She'd never got words like that before. She knew the thought was hers, but it had a different quality, louder, like in all caps. With nothing to lose, she turned left.

Aromas from a kebab shop made her stomach rumble. They smelled like the best kebabs in the world. She stopped in front and considered her approach. A down-and-out stood on the far side of the doorway, devouring one.

If you'd give that dirty down-and-out a kebab, why not me? No – that won't work. Um, sorry to bother you, but I'm travelling up to Scotland to visit my grandmother, someone stole my money and all I have is a pound. Could I buy a pound's worth of kebab meat please? Too long.

'You're right, too long,' the vagrant said. 'By the way, it IS the best kebab in the world.'

'Did I say that out loud?'

The man chuckled. 'Sorry, didn't mean to eavesdrop on your thoughts. Happens sometimes.'

Oh great, another crazy.

'Not crazy – psychic. There is a difference, you know.'

'Right.' She rolled her eyes.

He laughed again, stepped to her side of the doorway and extended a hand. She balked and he stuck his hand in his pocket. The hurt he tried to hide sliced through her.

'I'm Pavel Patel.'

'Oh, hi. I'm, uh, Beatrice.'

'So, you've run away, you've lost all your money and you have no place to stay,' he said.

'You mind-reading again, PATELLA?' This popped out of her mouth.

Pavel wrapped up the rest of his kebab and slipped it into a pocket. 'No, you look like a runaway, that's all.'

Raya flushed, embarrassed by her accidental sharpness.

'He glanced at the clock through the window. 'So, how old are you?'

'How old are YOU?'

'Thirty-eight. I'm only asking because I know some people who run a cafe. From time to time they let people stay in a room above if they help out.'

'Oh, right. Sorry.' And she was. Sometimes she could be sharp, prickly before she knew what she was saying. She felt only kindness coming from this Pavel Patel, and maybe some sadness.

'I'm sixteen.' She reeled off her fake birth date. Her practice had paid off.

He studied her for a moment. 'Seventeen in the autumn, and you can prove it?'

'Yes, sir.' She retrieved her fake ID. It looked much better than she remembered. Much. She held it up and Pavel scrutinised it.

'Now, you don't know me, and you must be careful, but as it looks like you're out of luck – and well, I know what that's like. I can introduce you, and you can decide for yourself.'

Raya nodded. 'I guess I could check it out.'

'In that case, we should get a move on.'

Raya figured she'd go with him as long as they stayed on streets with other people around. The two fell into step, taking long, purposeful strides as they wended their way behind the huge hospital complex. She was sorry not to have had any of that kebab.

I wonder how he got that weird name.

'Oh, that's easy. My mum's Czech and my father's Jamaican, but mixed Indian and black.'

'Could we just stick to regular, you know, conversation? You're creeping me out.'

He laughed. 'Sure, but you have skills, too, you know.'

Raya stuffed her hands in her pockets. 'Whatever.'

A cyclist whizzed by.

Pavel shrugged and resumed his forward march. They continued in silence, past a statue of a woman in an old-fashioned dress, past a small park nestled amongst the city streets where people relaxed and kids played.

Pavel looked at his watch. It was old with a worn strap, but still too nice for the rest of him. 'Come on. We have to hurry.'

Raya trotted to keep up with him.

A bit puffed out, they reached the corner of Commercial Road and Hessel Street. The Cosmic Cafe sign was still lit. Inside were booths, tables and a long counter with padded stools. A lone customer sat at the counter. A man and woman cleaned and sorted things. Raya took a deep breath and caught herself looking to Pavel for reassurance. *Stop it – you don't know him.*

'Nothing to worry about – they're good people. I grew up with them.' When he held the door open for her, he didn't whiff as she'd expected. The two behind the counter and the customer all turned to look.

The man smiled. He was one of those guys who knew he was good-looking. 'Hiya, Pavel. Who's your friend?'

'This is Beatrice,' Pavel said.

The cafe man stuck out his hand. 'Hiya, Beatrice. I'm Ian, and this is my sister and partner in crime, Emma.'

The customer picked up his briefcase and left.

Emma, pretty and slender with a cool short haircut, wiped her hands on the apron over her jeans and T-shirt. She leaned against the counter and extended her hand. 'Hiya, Beatrice. Nice to meet you. Pavel, why don't you go in the back and pick out some nice ones. I'll make a round of teas.'

'Beatrice, you've got to try her muffins. She's working on recipes for her new bakery,' Pavel said, then walked in the back with Ian.

Emma chatted as she made the teas. The men returned talking in that overly jolly way people do when they want to cover what they'd really been talking about. Ian carried a plate of muffins. Pavel and Raya sat at the counter.

Ian and Emma continued to work while Pavel snacked on the muffins, and Raya inhaled hers. She thought about sneaking some into her rucksack, then remembered she didn't have it any more. Emma scratched around behind the counter and came up with a thick turkey and cheese sandwich.

'Thought you could use this.'

'Wow. Thanks,' Raya said.

After a bit more general conversation Pavel said, 'I was wondering if you could use any help. Beatrice here's looking for a job and needs a place to stay.'

Emma looked at Ian, who nodded.

'I'm opening my own bakery soon – not here, in south London – so we could really use the help in the cafe,' Emma said.

Ian stopped scraping the grill. 'You've got ID, to prove your age?' He wiped his hands on a towel and waited.

'Sure do,' Raya said and whipped it out of her pocket and smiled. Ian and Emma looked at it and seemed satisfied.

I don't know if I'd take in some stray with only a fake ID. Raya had studied all this on the Internet. You were legally allowed to leave home at sixteen, but part of her wanted them to be nosier about some kid they were taking in.

Ian and Emma went into the back to get things for tomorrow.

'These two have helped out a lot of folks over the years, especially young people, especially integrators,' Pavel said.

Raya huffed, 'There's no such thing.'

'Really? You know, psychics, empaths, witches – whatever you want to call them, us,' Pavel said.

Raya chased a few sandwich crumbs around the plate. She took a deep breath and held it for a few seconds. There was that social worker seeming to know she was about to run into trouble. *Could that have been real?* This was too much to figure out – made her uncomfortable trying. *Why can't people just leave me alone? Hire me, don't hire me, but stop telling me all this stuff. And besides, I don't know these people. Maybe staying here was a dumb idea.*

She stood up from the counter. 'Thanks for the food and everything, but maybe it's best I get going.'

Emma looked surprised. She put a case of beans on the counter. 'No worries, Beatrice. You can come back if you don't find anything else – see if we still need the help.'

'Thanks,' Raya said as she opened the door. An old-fashioned bell attached to the top jingled. The air from outside, cooler now, rolled in along with traffic sounds. The summer sun bowing out threw slashes of colour between the buildings. London looked big, empty, and lonely. She stood in the doorway, like a cat trying to make up its mind.

Ian slit the case open and shelved the tins behind the counter. 'The accommodation isn't much, but it's OK. It's safe and there's a shower.'

Raya turned back towards the three at the counter. She could have sworn there was a yellow glow around them. She couldn't outrun it, whatever 'it' was – being psychotic or psychic. She was exhausted, skint, and scared. *I guess they don't seem like axe-murderers.*

Chapter 6

The Burnt and the Broken

Over the next few days, Raya learned that cafe work was harder than she'd thought. She hauled bags of potatoes, shifted cases of tins, peeled and chopped piles of onions, lugged unwieldy rubbish to the bins in the alley, waited on customers, and scrubbed pots and pans.

By six in the morning, she was baking with Emma. She was allowed to eat the burnt and the broken, and together they invented new muffins and pastries. Raspberry almond croissants were her favourites so far.

Next she helped Ian with the breakfast rush. The smell of bacon and sausages, both meat and veggie, was like a cloud coming off Ian's grill as he sang to the radio before customers arrived. He was impatient and bossed her around a bit as they hustled to serve customers and make takeaway orders. After lunch, she got a break. Then, after closing they worked together to sort things for the next day. She could eat for free as long as it was leftovers or mistakes. After everyone went home, she often took a walk in the long summer evenings imagining she was looking for a party or a rave which she never found. She usually ended up wandering in and out of the few shops that stayed open. This was not the life she'd imagined.

The first time she was paid, she bought some cheap clothes and a box of the mousiest brown hair colour on the shelf. She decided to grow out the shaved parts on her head. Ian made her take out her face piercings before she'd started.

'Those are unhygienic. You can't wear them while you work,' Ian had said.

'Really? It's not like I rub my face in the food or anything,' she had replied.

She continued to get those weird experiences, and more. Of course, there was the unnerving experience of hearing what that blasted social worker's cat seemed to be saying, but in her head. And in addition to the static images or colours corresponding to certain people or situations, she started getting scenes, sometimes complete with sounds and smells that related to what people, and even animals, were thinking.

She saw a jack-o-lantern, smiling and hollowed out, with no candle in it when a well-dressed businesswoman came in for a latte and muffin.

'Who's that?' Raya whispered to Emma as she wrapped up the woman's cheddar-corn-red-pepper muffin. Emma waited until the bell on the door jingled as the woman clip-clopped out in her heels.

'She owns a clothing company down the road. Lost her kid last year – one of those diseases you're born with. Left her a hollow shell of her former self,' Emma said.

Other visuals included a piano with keys made of cutlery, a liquid telephone, a cackling tree. These corresponded to a musician who had to take on his family restaurant business; a telemarketer with an alcohol problem; and a dog. That made her laugh – picking up a dog's thoughts. His owner, a man who used a wheelchair, told her how the dog hated a tree outside his house that creaked in the wind. *I'm just a visual thinker – that's all. Pictures instead of words. No big deal.*

One afternoon, when Raya was helping Ian scrub the griddle, he said, 'You know, Pavel used to stay up in that room, where you are now, and pretty much did the same job. That was after the accident– ' Ian stopped short. Raya saw an empty, endless dark-grey tunnel; she felt cold and tasted salt. She didn't push the subject.

Then, other odd things began happening. She'd know what people wanted before they opened their mouth or the menu. This happened with new customers sometimes, so it wasn't that she knew what they liked.

When one customer took a particularly long time deciding what to order, and she was getting fed up waiting, she blurted out, 'A mushroom omelette with sweet potato fries and a double-shot latte.'

'How did you know?' the customer said.

'She's our lunch psychic,' Emma said as she served someone at the next table.

'More like lunch psycho.' Ian gave a cheeky grin as he dished up a meal. He might as well have punched her in the stomach; she couldn't breathe. *Tosser!* She ran into the back and burst into tears.

'Aw, come on – where's your sense of humour?' Ian called after her.

'Oh, Ian,' Emma said and went after Raya.

She rested her hand on the girl's heaving shoulder. 'Come on, Beatrice – don't take Ian seriously. He's just taking the mickey. I know he can be a bit of a knob.'

Raya looked up. 'It's not that. I know he's messing around. It's just that… he's right…'

'What are you talking about?'

'I've been getting visuals… visions, I guess – seeing things. I've probably got it, like my mum.' Raya plonked down on a stool. It was a relief to say it aloud to someone.

'Got what?'

'Schizophrenia.'

'Oh, Beatrice, I am sorry. You never mentioned about your mum. But being an integrator is different than having a brain disorder. Why don't you talk to a doctor or someone who can tell you for sure?'

'No!'

Emma took a tray of muffins from the oven. The aroma rolled over them.

'Suit yourself. Well… Ian could do some brain surgery,' Emma said and grinned. She put a tray of unbaked croissants into the oven and ruffled Raya's hair. 'I'll hold you down, and we'll have a dig around that hard head of yours, see if there's anything worth keeping,' Emma joked.

'Shut up. It's not funny. I'm scared.'

'Not finding out isn't going to help, is it? Why don't you at least talk to Pavel? Remember, he's one too – been through it, getting his powers and all.'

* * *

During her afternoon breaks, Raya often took a walk, sometimes to a coffee shop with Wi-Fi. She missed talking to people her own age. She didn't think it was safe to contact any of her friends and she had no interest in contacting Tony. Like a switch, that light had gone out. Then she remembered Jake. She'd promised to keep in touch. He was only a kid, but he was OK.

'Hiya, Jake. This is my new number and email. Everything's cool here. Got a job in a cafe and live in the flat above. Wild part of London, too. You OK? Got to go. R x'

In reality, she lived in a room, not a flat, and the part of London where she was, was more about the hard work life seemed to be than the buzz of party. South Asian shop-keepers, medical staff from around the world, people in the garment industry, harried mums, arty students, tour-ists, people going in and out of the mosques, all teemed on the crowded pavements, lined with a mixture of converted Victorian buildings and boxy modern ones. It didn't give Raya the excitement and wonder she'd dreamt of. When she let herself think about it, it made her feel lonely and a little afraid, if she was honest.

A few minutes later, Jake texted back. 'Wow. Sounds amazing. All normal here. I got to keep that cat, Oscar – kept coming back. Goes everywhere with me, like a dog. J ☺'

She was a little sorry she'd started with Jake; it was as though she'd pulled a cork.

'It's just me and Angie now. You're right, she's a bit boring, but OK. DVD nights are kinda fun, even Oscar watches with us, if it's his kind of film,' he texted.

Boy, he can bang on about that cat.

'And we both got jobs at the Chakmas' shop,' Jake texted.

'Where's that?'

'They opened the village shop – the boarded-up one.'

'Oh.'

'Did you hear? Their petrol station got robbed. The wife couldn't go back there, so they took over the village shop,' Jake texted.

A chill rolled through her. *Is he testing me? Did someone put him up to this?*

'Yeah, heard something about it. What job?' she tried to change the subject.

'It's cool. Angie said it's OK...' and Jake went on and on texting more details about these nice Chakmas, the bloody cat and science magazines than anyone could possibly pay attention to.

Phew. He seems genuine enough – doesn't seem to be spying on me. Another text came through.

'The Chakmas' daughter is an engineer – the kind that builds bridges, like Brunel! ☺' Jake wrote.

O brother. 'Who's Brunel?' Raya wrote back.

'WHO'S BRUNEL? Amazing engineer from the 1800s who built the first tunnel under the Thames with his dad,' Jake wrote.

'So you're working at the Paki shop, eh?' Raya had had enough engineering lessons for the day.

The waitress cleared up the empty paper coffee cup Raya had brought from the Cosmic Cafe. She didn't seem to mind that the cup wasn't from their shop. She wasn't much older than Raya.

'That's racist. Besides, they're from Bangladesh,' he typed.

Easy pickings. 'Calm down. I'm only winding you up,' Raya typed back.

* * *

When Raya returned to the Cosmic Cafe, Pavel was sitting on a stool at the counter. There were no customers. Raya got back to work and they all finished early. Ian put out a pot of his veggie chilli, one of his specialties. Emma brought out some burnt-on-one-side bread rolls and a salad. Ian drew the blinds. With a turn of the key, they all exhaled. *I might not have DVD nights, but these lock-ins are OK.*

'Go on, ask him,' Emma elbowed Raya and nodded towards Pavel.

'You a doctor or something?' Raya said.

'Nothing to be embarrassed about, Beatrice,' Pavel said between mouthfuls. You'd think he didn't eat anywhere else.

Raya didn't say anything.

'Beatrice, what people think of as "psychic abilities", being a witch or integrator, are really nothing more than exquisite access to our own subconscious. Our brains are capable of all sorts of calculations and operations without our needing to be aware of them,' Pavel said.

'Huh?' Raya said.

He tossed her an apple. She caught it.

'See? Did you do the maths? Calculate the rate of the apple flying through the air, the arc, the change in acceleration, in order to catch it?' Pavel said.

Raya shook her head.

'I did!' Ian said.

'Shut up and help me clear up,' Emma said.

Pavel continued. 'I know how weird it can seem when your skills come on – I remember. But luckily for me, there were people in my family with them, so at least I wasn't scared I was going crazy.'

Raya looked away.

Emma set down two mugs of tea then returned to her work.

'Hey, it's OK. Emma told me about your mum. I'm sorry. Schizophrenia can be awful. I can see where it would be confusing,' Pavel said.

Raya crossed her arms, stared at Pavel.

'OK, think of it this way. When someone has a seizure, a fit, sometimes their bodies move all around all crazy like. Right?' He waited for a nod from Raya, then continued, 'But that doesn't mean if you're a naturally talented dancer, you're more likely to develop epilepsy.'

'Still, how can I be sure what's happening to me?' Raya said.

Pavel muffled frustration on his face with a sigh. 'Like I keep telling you, I'm an integrator, I've known plenty, AND I pick it up from you – that you have the talent. And you've been demonstrating it here.' He gestured across the cafe. 'And in a former life– '

'You've been reincarnated?'

'NO! Oh for goodness' sake – no I mean in a former job, a long time ago. Anyway...' Pavel went on to list a bunch of experiences common to schizophrenia. Raya had none of them. She stared at the table, turned her mug round and round.

'What do you say we start regular lessons? I'll teach you how to improve your skills. The better you get, the more these witchy abilities will be under your control, whereas symptoms of schizophrenia aren't. You'll see,' Pavel said.

'And I still think you should go to the doctor – let a medical person sort this for sure,' Emma said. 'I'll book you into the local GP. OK?'

'I agree,' Pavel said.

Raya nodded with no intention of following through. How could she? It would risk blowing her cover.

Pavel continued. 'Meanwhile, we'll do some book learning, too. It's important you understand the science behind all this – what's known so far. To that end, I'd like to start with Rupert Sheldrake's research. Then we'll go over the new physics–'

'Whoa there, mate. I think you're losing our little sister here,' Ian said.

'Our Pavel can't help being a brainbox,' Emma said.

'Or a brain who LIVES in a box,' Raya said, quite pleased with herself. But then realised she'd done it again – been unnecessarily spikey. She felt terrible when she saw the look on Pavel's face.

He stood up. 'Time I'm going, anyway.' He smiled meekly and grabbed the coat unnecessary for this weather and left.

Raya felt the hollow tug of loss and wondered if maybe she did push people away before they could leave her, like a social worker a long time before Bryony had suggested.

Ian and Emma busied themselves with clearing up.

'He'll come back, won't he?' she asked. He has to.

Ian turned away. Emma shrugged. 'You never know with him – not since the accident.'

Chapter 7

Three Knocks

After a couple of very tense days Pavel returned. He waved off her apology and ignored her question about "the accident". 'Hey, you get to be my age, you've seen some stuff, is all.'

Raya began her regular lessons about the irregular. He started with teaching her how to invite the 'sensory messages' – the sights, sounds, smells she received. 'Sometimes they will be simple pictures or sounds. Other times you'll get whole scenes. They can even be like videos playing in your head. Once you have all that down, we'll move onto mind and dream reading.'

'And what about keeping my thoughts to myself? You know, from other nosey integrators,' Raya asked remembering her discomfort at his reading her thoughts when they first met.

He threw his head back and laughed in a way she hadn't seen before. 'Sure. "Thought lock-down" we call it. I'll teach you that, too.'

But first, Pavel taught her the basics of how to be receptive. He taught her to slow her breathing, by counting to five while breathing in, five while holding it, and five exhaling. This, he promised, would allow her to become acutely aware of, well, everything, except 'the noise in her head' – her thoughts. 'Lots of thinking is rubbish. Once you get this down, more things will come to you – you'll see. Eventually, you'll be able to get into this zone without consciously doing the breathing.'

When it was slow at the Cosmic, Raya would sit on a stool at the counter next to Pavel. She'd do her breathing, ignore the chatter in her head (which was a lot harder than she'd imagined), and tell him everything she experienced, from the temperature of the air, the light and colour and shape of things, the sizzle and smells from the grill, muffled sounds from outside.

After a day of this, Pavel said it was time to move on to picking up sensory messages. She practised receiving any messages from customers and also walked around the neighbourhood during the afternoon lull. At first Pavel went with her. 'I don't want you walking into traffic.'

A lot of it still seemed far-fetched, but every so often something clicked. A customer's past played in her head like a video, another's worries about their future came in a series of pictures. And practising these skills gave her something to do during her afternoon breaks besides messaging Jake.

Meandering through east London, other people's thoughts, worries, plans, and hopes breezed through her. And more animals' thoughts. Like the time she found herself staring at a rubbish bin, wondering lots of things about a mouse. She looked around and saw a very annoyed cat glaring at her.

'*Paws off – he's mine,*' the cat said.

At least it didn't scare her this time.

* * *

'Hey, Jake, you'll never guess what's happened,' Raya texted him. She cosied up in one of those oversized chairs in the coffee shop. Her takeaway coffee from Cosmic sat on the low wooden table in front of her. Quiet jazz played and the waitress nodded hello.

'What? I've got something cool, too. You 1st'

'Seems I've got some natural witching abilities.'

'Wow! Really?' he texted back.

Raya squirmed in the chair. Here she was thinking it

was all rubbish – insulting that social worker about it – and now it seemed she was one. She was relieved Jake was cool with it. She knew not everyone would be.

'So, you're OK with it?'

'OK? It's cool! You're my first witch friend. ☺ ☺,' Jake texted.

Raya chewed her lower lip – Jake considered her a friend. She realised she was only entertaining herself with his chats. She took a deep breath.

'I'm honoured to be your 1st! ☺'

'My new social worker's a witch. She used to be yours,' Jake messaged.

'Wasn't that cat hers?' Raya messaged.

'Ya, but likes me better ☺. What witchy stuff can you do?'

Raya told him how she practised reading other people's thoughts, and her experience with the cat.

'It must be great living on your own – doing what you want,' Jake messaged.

Raya thought for a minute before replying. 'It is, but not what you think. Not all fun and stuff. But you feel like you're driving the bus, not just riding on it, if that makes sense?' she messaged.

A few minutes later she got, 'In charge of yourself for once. I'd LOVE that.'

She remembered he had something he'd wanted to talk about.

'You said you had something to tell?'

'Really cool thing at the Brunel Museum.' Jake texted.

'What?'

'A tour of the tunnels he built, first ones under the Thames. They're hardly ever open. They are next week and it's my birthday. Angie said I can't go then cuz it's a school day.'

'Oh wow. That would be so you! ☺ Shame you can't go. The big 1-2, right?'

'Yeah, I won't be a prime number for a whole year now,' Jake messaged.

'You would say that.☺'

* * *

By the middle of the following week, her second at the Cosmic, Raya shot awake feeling frightened and guilty. She'd been dreaming about Alfie, the dog with the Tube thieves. In her dream, they'd been walking together on top of an old stone wall, about thirty feet up. The walkway was five or six feet wide. Another wall rose up at the outer edge, shielding them from whatever was outside the city. This part of the wall was dotted with very small windows, some no more than peepholes. Through them she saw the regular world. It could have been London: traffic; tall buildings; people hurrying.

On the inside edge, there was no wall rising from the walkway. She could see straight out and down across a very old town: cobbled streets; small stone buildings with thatched roofs. Smoke twirled out of chimneys. The wood fires smelled lovely. Horses clip-clopped as they pulled carts. A green, dotted with sheep and a few cows made a swathe inside the wall, circling the town. Talk about your chocolate-box pictures.

Alfie woofed. He had trotted ahead to a corner, where the wall turned left. There was a flat stone area and a break in the outer wall, giving a clear view outside the town. Alfie hopped up and peered over. He said something to Raya, but his words were lost in the wind. She called to him. He turned his head to look at her, lost his balance, and fell over the wall, his frightened eyes the last thing she saw before she shot awake.

The smells and sounds of bacon and sausages on the griddle floated up the stairs. Unable to go back to sleep, she trotted down. Emma hadn't arrived yet.

'What's the matter? You look like you saw a ghost,' Ian said as he put mushrooms on the griddle.

'Not a ghost exactly. Just a creepy dream. Can't stop thinking about it.'

'Hey, can you go get a case of beans?'

'Yeah, OK. Do you know how I can reach Pavel? Ask him, maybe?'

'For the beans?' Ian grinned.

'What I have to live with.' Raya rolled her eyes and she trudged into the back.

'I don't know. You two being integrators and all. Why don't you call him on your mind mobile?' Ian enjoyed his own jokes.

The day passed much like any other, except that the feelings from the dream kept pecking at her. She wished hard for Pavel to stop by. When it came time for her afternoon break, she stayed in. Anyway, with no new messages from Jake for a day or so, there was no real reason to go to the Wi-Fi coffee place today. *Maybe he's fed up with talking to me.*

Dusk painted everything outside a murky sameness. Pavel came through the door. She almost hugged him.

'You OK?' Pavel said. There were two regular customers in a booth at the other end of the cafe. Emma brought Pavel a mug of coffee and a plate of broken muffins. Raya picked off Pavel's plate.

'So, you got it? My sending you thoughts to please come by today?'

Emma smiled. 'He got my text, all right. I couldn't take it any more – you in such a state.' Emma walked into the back.

'You have a mobile?' Raya said. She was hurt.

Pavel looked at Raya. 'Hey, I'm sorry.' He pulled a paper napkin from a dispenser and a pen from next to the till. 'Just don't always trust myself NOT to let people down…' He trailed off as he scribbled. Raya looked at Emma for an explanation, but she shook her head as if to say, 'Don't ask.' The remaining customers paid at the till and left. Raya looked at Ian who nodded. Raya drew the blinds and locked the door. Just as she settled onto the stool next to Pavel, there were three firm knocks on the door.

'They must have left something,' Ian said. But when he opened the door, there stood a police officer, and that social worker witch, Bryony Braxton.

Chapter 8

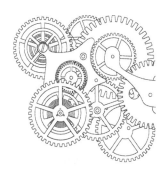

Busted

'Hello, officer, miss,' Ian said, and waved them in. 'What can we do for you?'

Raya looked away then slid into the back.

'Emma, let me do that,' Raya whispered, as she grabbed the soapy baking tray from her.

'Huh? You're acting funny. What's going on?'

'Nothing.' Raya scrubbed hard.

Emma wiped her hands and walked out to the front. Ian and Pavel were looking at something on the counter – photos. Bryony looked over their shoulders.

'Hey, Emma, take a look at these – two runaways, a boy called… what did you say their names were?' Ian said.

Bryony spoke. 'The boy's called Jake Hunter. He just turned twelve, yesterday in fact. The girl, Rachel

Hollingsworth, she's fifteen in a few months – she calls herself Raya.'

'Wait a minute,' Ian said, picking up the picture of the girl.

'Why'd you come here, officer?' Emma asked.

'We looked at the boy's emails and texts. He'd been communicating with this girl, Rachel, who ran away a couple of weeks ago. She talks about working at a cafe here on Commercial Road. You're the third one we've tried.'

'Beatrice, come out here a minute, please?' Ian called out.

'"Beatrice"?' Bryony said.

Metal pans clattered and a door slammed in the back of the building. Ian flashed a look at Emma and tore out the front, the officer at his side.

Bryony slung her heavy shoulder bag down, things tumbled out. 'She had black spiky hair, piercings – the Goth thing, or is it Emo? Can't keep track. Anyway, does that sound like her?'

Emma and Pavel nodded.

'Hmm, I never thought Beatrice fit,' Pavel said.

The three were quiet.

Emma peered out the door. 'They got her.'

The officer and Ian marched a panting Raya back inside. Ian plonked her down in a booth. 'OK, young lady, you've got some explaining to do.' He nodded towards the officer and Bryony.

Bryony scratched around in her bag finally retrieving a notebook and pen. She chewed on the end of it.

The officer took a photo from the counter and held it up in front of Raya.

'Rachel, do you know this boy?'

Raya turned away.

'And you – you told us her ID was real,' Ian said to Pavel.

Pavel looked hollowed out. 'You know I get things wrong...'

'Not now, you two,' Emma said.

The officer tried again. 'Like I was saying, do you recognize this boy?'

Raya flushed. 'Yes, sir. That's Jake. We were both living at Angie's.'

'When was the last time you saw him?' the officer said.

Raya shrugged. 'I don't know. Whenever I left Angie's, I guess.'

'You guess?' the officer said.

'Rachel, are you hiding this boy here – upstairs or something?' Ian said.

'No! Of course not,' she said, and looked at her feet.

Bryony stepped next to Raya. 'Then why are you acting so guilty?'

Raya stared beyond them for a moment before she could speak. 'I think maybe he got the idea to run away to London from me.'

There was a moment of heavy quiet.

'Why do you say that?' Bryony said softly.

'He was talking about going to some museum here…'

The officer flipped pages in a small notebook. 'We'd appreciate anything you might know. We haven't got the most recent texts yet – waiting on those.'

'It was some engineering museum. Some famous guy. Something about tunnels under the Thames.'

'Must be the Brunel Museum,' Pavel said.

'That fits – he loves science, engineering,' Bryony said.

'I'll need your phone, miss,' the officer said and held out his hand. She gave it to him.

The police officer walked out of the cafe, punching buttons on his phone.

The sounds of passing traffic and a siren slid in when the officer went out. 'OK,' Bryony said, 'from what we can figure out, it looks like Jake had planned to come back to Angie's. There was some finished homework due later this week, sitting on his desk. His SIM card was in his drawer, but we couldn't find his phone. Seems he got a new one for his little jaunt–'

'Probably learned that off me, too' Raya said. She looked glum.

'It's not exactly rocket science,' Bryony said, then looked surprised at her own sharp tone. 'Sorry, I'm a bit frazzled.'

'No worries,' Raya said. *I didn't tell him to come, did I?* she thought.

Ian gave her a buddy squeeze around the shoulders.

Bryony continued. 'The CCTV footage they have so far shows Jake getting on the train at South Nutfield, with my, I mean his cat. The two of them got off at Victoria Station, but then the trail falls off.'

The bell on the door jingled and the officer walked back in. 'Someone's going over to the Brunel Museum now, see if he's anywhere around there – it's closed now, of course.'

'We've called all the hospitals, but no kids of his description. So that's where we are with it,' Bryony said.

'Not very far,' the officer said.

Bryony heaved a sigh, dug a folder out of her bag. 'Now, Raya, we'll have to place you in emergency care for tonight, then get you back to South Nutfield tomorrow.'

She felt like her stomach dropped three floors without her. Her heart raced and she felt hot. 'Why can't Emma and Ian be my foster carers?'

There was a moment of quiet except for the city sounds outside.

'How about I get everyone a cuppa?' Emma said overly cheerfully. They all gave their orders, Ian helped Emma with the drinks and snacks. They settled back into the large booth.

Emma nodded towards Ian. 'You know, it would be fine by us, if Beatrice, I mean Rachel, stayed. We've become a family of sorts,' Ian said. 'We'll fill out any paperwork, and Pavel here – you know he used to be a detective with the Metropolitan Po–'

'Oh, no need to bring all that up,' Pavel protested.

'You ex-Met?' the young officer said.

'A long time ago.'

The officer extended a hand. 'You know what they say, "once a police, always a police".' Pavel offered his hand as though it was dead.

'Pavel was with the Integrative Intelligence Unit in Whitechapel,' Emma said.

'Oh, yeah? That's a spooky lot,' the officer said.

'Oh, it was no big deal,' Pavel said.

'Well, that's all very interesting, but harbouring a minor is not exactly high on the list of criteria for foster carers,' Bryony said.

Pavel shook his head. 'That's my fault – I thought her ID was real – that she really was a few months off seventeen. And I should be able to tell–'

The officer interjected, 'The fake IDs are really good now…' It sounded like he held back adding 'old man'. '…so don't be too hard on yourself.'

Pavel flinched.

The officer looked like he was sorry and continued to Pavel in particular, 'And if you really thought she was sixteen, well, we all know we can't legally force them back home then – they vote with their feet.'

Bryony excavated her phone from her bag. 'Sure, we can start the process of either one of you applying as carer tomorrow, but in the meantime she'll have to go elsewhere at least for tonight. I'll make some calls.' She stepped away scrolling through her phone.

Raya's panic was replaced by a growing anger. She was angry at Bryony for finding her… and for NOT finding her sooner. *Wasn't she looking for me too? Well, I guess she loses lots of things; cats, kids…*

Bryony glanced around as though she'd been stung by a rubber band.

'Oh crap. Is she listening in on my thoughts? Aren't I locking them down properly? Raya tried to think in great detail about various food items she served, anything not personal.

Cumin, garlic, and, oh right – coriander. Raya tried to remember recipes she'd picked up from Ian.

Bryony returned to the booth. She looked tired – older than Raya remembered. 'You, young lady must have changed your clothes when you came to London. Not to mention your hair,' Bryony said and nodded toward Raya's new boring hairstyle.

'What? Oh, right. Maybe,' Raya said hearing how stupid and teen-agy she sounded before she could stop herself.

Bryony took in a long breath like she was about to go under water. 'After you boarded the train in Redhill the CCTV footage went cold– nothing, zip. We never stopped looking. Believe me,' Bryony said.

Tears suddenly threatened to give Raya away, a funny mixture of hurt and relief. Pressing her nails into her other palm, helped, too.

Bryony turned back to her paperwork. 'Anyway, I've found a placement for you tonight at least. It's not far from here. The foster carer will bring you back here in the morning. Then we'll look into the possibility of your staying here for the summer, but you'll have to stay in Ian or Emma's home, providing we can arrange that. Now Raya, don't set your heart on this; it's all a big if. And you'll most likely have to return to South Nutfield once school starts again in the autumn.'

Raya couldn't help but fall into intense hope, as though that alone could make it all come true.

Chapter 9
Getting It Wrong

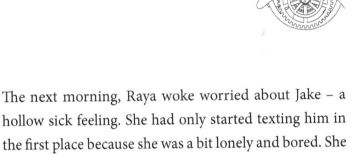

The next morning, Raya woke worried about Jake – a hollow sick feeling. She had only started texting him in the first place because she was a bit lonely and bored. She couldn't face the cereal floating in milk. She thought she might throw up.

'All these changes must be tough,' the foster lady said, and cleared the table.

The sky was a perfect grey, like a big piece of cardboard stuck behind the buildings. Raya trudged along with the foster carer. They left her unremarkable flat where she lived with her perfectly ordinary family and passed forgettable buildings. People rushed to work, traffic was thick. Foster Lady chatted away.

'We certainly hope you were comfortable with us.

Tonight's pizza night in our family, and usually we watch a film. You know – in case you come back.'

Raya shuddered. She did her best to nod and smile at the right places. She couldn't remember wanting to be any place for a really long time, and now she wanted to stay with Ian, Emma, and Pavel. It looked like life was about to prove, once again, she shouldn't let herself get attached.

She snugged her grey hoodie around her. The closer she got to the Cosmic, the better she felt. When she glimpsed Pavel through the window, she broke into a trot. Everyone turned as the door banged shut.

'Sorry,' Raya said. Breakfast smelled wonderful. Foster Lady followed her in and spoke with Ian and Emma. Raya bounded over to the booth where Pavel and Bryony sat, papers, mobiles, a laptop, and empty mugs in front of them. It took them a second to stop talking and look up at her.

'Hiya,' Raya said.

Pavel grinned and offered his fist for a friendly bump.

'Do I get to stay? Is it all settled?' Raya said. It felt like her heart and her stomach had switched places. She was afraid to ask about Jake, afraid of bad news or worse, none.

Bryony flashed a work smile. 'Oh, Raya, it's not going to happen that fast, I'm afraid. Most likely you'll stay at the emergency placement for another night or two.' She scrambled around in that shoulder bag of hers and came up with

Raya's phone – held it out like a peace offering. 'Here, the police got what they needed,' Bryony said and put her head back into the papers. Raya pocketed her phone.

'Why don't you go help out – like normal?' Pavel said, nodding towards Ian and Emma.

'Oh. OK.' Raya started to walk off, then stopped. 'Would you like more tea or coffee?'

The two looked up again. 'Sure. That would be nice,' Bryony offered with a sigh.

Raya tossed her overnight bag onto the booth next to Pavel and took the empty mugs behind the counter.

Foster Lady reached over, tapped her on the shoulder. 'Bye, Raya. Looks like you'll be coming to ours for another night or two.' She smiled.

'Oh, thanks. That's lovely.' Raya forced a smile in return.

Foster Lady left and Raya finished making the drinks. 'You never know. A lot could happen between now and then. Right?' Raya said to Ian.

'I don't know, don't get your hopes up, little sister,' he said while cooking. The nickname warmed and tugged at her.

Emma served a customer then turned to Raya. 'Hey, I made some of your favourites, almond-raspberry croissants. Help yourself, and get some for Bryony and Pavel, if you like.'

Raya returned to the booth with three steaming mugs and warm croissants. She scooted in next to Pavel. He'd shaved and was wearing an old but clean corduroy sports jacket.

'Hey, you clean up all right. So, what are we doing?' Raya said, taking a croissant for herself.

Bryony exhaled and shut a folder. 'I'm sorry, Raya. We're in the middle of an awful lot right now.'

'Can't I help?' Raya said, pushing the croissant away. Bryony looked at her as though she was reading her thoughts again.

'Would you stop that? Please,' Raya said.

'What?' Bryony said.

'I'm not able to lock-down my thoughts yet – you know, for privacy. And it's creeping me out, you reading my mind all the time,' Raya said.

'Sorry, Raya,' Bryony said. 'It's not on purpose. It can be pretty automatic, once you get the hang of it – like reading someone's facial expression.'

'Right.' Raya hunkered down in the booth.

'But well done!' Bryony said overly cheerfully. 'Pavel's told me how quickly you're coming along with your integrator skills.'

Raya was stunned – *So Bryony knew I was a witch too? Why didn't she say something? If I knew I hadn't been*

*losing my mind, but becoming a witch, for real, maybe I
wouldn't have run away to begin with. Then maybe none
of this would have happened to Jake. Doesn't she do anything right?*

Pavel looked quickly back and forth between the two
of them, and then at his watch. 'We've got to concentrate
on finding Jake, you two.'

An incoming email chimed on Bryony's laptop. She
bore into the screen like her eyes were guns. 'Nothing.'
They all deflated.

Pavel stood up. 'How about this? Raya, why don't
you come upstairs and help me set up some equipment?
Then, Bryony, you join us when you're done with your
paperwork.'

'Good idea,' Bryony said. She closed her laptop, and
handed it to Pavel.

'What equipment?' Raya said.

* * *

Upstairs in the room where Raya usually slept, Pavel
unfolded a table from behind the headboard. He unlocked
a cupboard in the wall above the wardrobe that Raya
hadn't noticed. At Pavel's request, Raya fetched some
chairs. When she returned, he was hooking up Bryony's
laptop to a dusty metal box with dials. He stood on a chair

and dug into the back of the cupboard. He handed her another metal box and what looked like a swimming cap with wires coming off it.

'What's all this?'

'Ah, welcome to the world of brain waves.'

Pavel connected wires, turned dials, and wiped dust off as he explained things. 'At Integrative Intelligence at the Met they had ways to enhance and verify what people call "psychic information".' He checked connections, studied the screen, adjusted dials.

'You know, like the information you've been picking up?'

Raya nodded.

He seemed a different person than the kind but lost, down-and-out. There were footsteps on the stairs.

'Are we ready?' Bryony asked, standing in the doorway.

'Almost,' Pavel said as he continued to tune dials and watch the screen.

'So what happens now?' Raya said.

'Bryony's been receiving messages, we think from Oscar, that cat that used to live with her. But they've been fuzzy. This should help,' Pavel said.

'I don't get it. I mean why don't you just use your powers to find Jake?' Raya said. She plonked down on one of the chairs, fiddled with the cord on her hoodie.

'It doesn't work like that,' Bryony said, then turned away to work the cap with wires onto her head.

'Why not?'

'It's another set of skills, but it doesn't mean they're all-powerful, or that you can always do what you want with them,' Pavel said.

Bryony sat staring at the screen, the wired cap was snug on her head. 'Getting anything?' Pavel asked Bryony.

'Not yet.' She took long, slow breaths and closed her eyes.

'Bryony was the last good witch Oscar worked with, so it makes sense he'd try to transmit to her when he needed help,' Pavel said.

'Last good witch?' Raya asked.

'Shh, later. If you two don't mind,' Bryony said.

After a few moments the static on the screen started to take form as Bryony explained what she saw. 'This looks like the same place I started picking up yesterday. Someone with a white coat just came in,' Bryony said. The midsection of a person in a white work smock appeared on the screen. They got closer, a wire door swung open, and an arm came in, placed a bowl in the cage.

'It looks like he's in some sort of animal facility, a pet store, or a lab,' Pavel said.

'Or a butchers,' Raya said and smirked.

'Quiet,' Bryony said. Then after a moment of her staring at the screen she said, 'Oscar, is that you? What? Yes. OK. Calm down. I'm sorry, but I don't think you can blame me for… Look, let's talk about that later. Just tell me where Jake is. Slower.… Are you sure?' Bryony blanched. 'Oh my God!'

'What?' Raya asked. She felt Bryony's fear – whether it was through being a witch, or just being a person, she wasn't sure.

Bryony took her phone out and motioned for Pavel to do the same. 'We've got to call round again. Someone must have got it wrong – he is in hospital. Jake was hit by a lorry.'

Chapter 10

Great Ormond Street Hospital

The black taxi jolted through traffic. The three of them stared out the windows. Raya didn't know what the others were thinking but she'd never felt so bad, so responsible for something so terrible. And to such a sweet kid. He really was pretty funny. She chewed on her bottom lip, then on her already short nails. Then she remembered something Bryony had said about that cat. She was relieved for the reprieve from thinking about Jake.

'So what did you mean back there – that you were the last good witch Oscar knew?' Raya asked.

Bryony turned her attention back to them, like she was coming out of a dream. 'What? Oh, that. Oscar had become really ill from being with a bad witch; his black fur even turned white. It can be fatal. Anyway, he was recovering with me, but he'd had enough of being a service animal by then. He wanted to go back to being a stray in London – where he started,' Bryony said.

'Prefers his freedom, eh?' Pavel chortled.

'It was more that he was sick of witches. And there were fishermen who fed the strays there on the Thames. Wasn't a bad life, the way he tells it.'

The taxi stopped in traffic. A double-decker bus chugged by.

'You don't know how many calls I'd had from the train people. Oscar kept sneaking on the train at South Nutfield, but he never got very far – no unaccompanied animals allowed, of course,' Bryony said.

'You don't think he encouraged Jake to come to London, do you? So he could hitch a ride?' Pavel suggested.

Bryony sighed, stared out the window again. 'You never know.'

The taxi slammed to a stop. A cyclist veered out of the way.

'In any event, the minute they got into Victoria Station Oscar took off, heading back to his stray life. Jake darted after him, but didn't look.'

They were all quiet. Raya knew how Oscar must feel. It sounded like they were both responsible. She wondered if the others blamed her too – tried to tune into their thoughts. Then she thought better of it – wasn't sure she wanted to know.

Bryony stopped gazing out the window. 'There is one funny part. Oscar said he fought like hell to go with Jake in the ambulance. They got tired of peeling him off the paramedics and didn't have the time to wait for the RSPCA to come get him, so they gave up and let him ride in the cab.'

* * *

After speaking to a few staff at the hospital, they confirmed a boy who had been mistakenly entered on the computer as a Jane Doe was admitted a couple of days ago. Nothing like ticking the wrong box. They hurried along the maze of pastel-tiled hallways, filled with the smells of disinfectant and stale anxiety.

What have we done? Me and that stupid cat. They reached the ward and Pavel pressed the button outside the locked doors.

After what seemed like ages, a nurse let them in. He listened to Pavel's explanation of who they were then led them to what he called the 'day room'. They waited there until the nurse returned with a folder. He smiled in a way that said, 'I'm sorry for you.'

'Who's the boy's parent or legal guardian?' he said.

'I'm his social worker,' Bryony said, and held up her ID.

'Come with me please, to identify the boy.' He turned and walked out with Bryony.

Raya sat on her hands and looked at her feet. Pavel leaned against the large windows and looked out at the light-dotted city. He seemed particularly uncomfortable in the hospital. After a few minutes, Bryony and the nurse returned. Bryony was ashen.

'The boy…' The nurse looked at his chart. '…Jake Smithson was brought in by ambulance two days ago in a coma after he was hit by the lorry.'

A helicopter flew over the hospital.

'The lorry driver felt terrible as you can imagine. Said he never saw the boy, only heard the thud. He came in to see him.' The nurse turned pages. 'Jake has a broken collarbone and arm, but the real problem is his head injury.'

Head injury – oh my God. And he enjoys his head so much. Raya felt numb. Now it was at least three of them responsible for Jake's state. But that didn't make her feel any better – just more confused. Pavel looked out the window again, miles away.

Raya tried to take in the rest of what the nurse said.

'The coiling wasn't working, so the next step is a craniotomy – brain surgery. They're getting Jake ready now,' the nurse said.

'Now? He goes in now?' Pavel was back in the room.

'Yes, with bleeds in the brain – he'll have the best chance the sooner we can plug him up.'

'Chance?' Bryony said.

The nurse looked at each of them. 'I'm sorry, I mean the best chance for the fullest recovery. Let me ask the paediatric neurosurgeon if she can pop in before she goes into theatre. She's one of the best in the country.' The nurse left.

A few minutes later, the surgeon breezed in and introduced herself. 'I've done this repair many times – it's my speciality. But you have to keep in mind that if he makes it, we won't know how well he'll recover for some time.'

'What do you mean "if he makes it"? And he might not recover… completely?' Raya said.

The surgeon looked at her kindly. 'I'm sorry, there's always a risk with surgery.' She paused, looked at them. 'A small chance they don't survive, and I am obliged to tell you that it is riskier when you're operating on the brain. But once we get him through the op – and we have every reason to think we will – we won't know immediately whether or not he'll have any permanent brain damage.

Although young people always do better in this regard,' she finished. A turgid silence filled the room.

The surgeon glanced at her watch. 'It's time for me to scrub up. I suggest you all go home, try to get some rest, and come back tomorrow. Before you go, could you please leave your contact details at the nurses' station?'

The three walked like zombies to the nurses' area. Bryony gave her contact details.

A nurse said, 'Oh that's right – there's that cat. Can any of you take him? They're still holding him downstairs; otherwise, the RSPCA will collect him in the morning.'

'Yes, of course. I can take him,' Bryony said.

Another nurse led the three out of the ward. When they reached the lobby, Pavel said, 'I'll let you two sort the cat. I've got a blistering headache,' and left.

The nurse led Bryony and Raya to the basement. Their footsteps echoed in the dim, empty corridor.

The nurse unlocked the door and flicked the light on. There was a wall of cages, with only one inhabitant, Oscar.

The nurse lifted a cat carrier from a shelf, opened it, then the cage. Bryony reached in, but Oscar dug his claws into the bedding.

'I'm not leaving Jake,' he said and gave a heart-breaking yowl.

'Oh, Oscar, we'll come back tomorrow. There's nothing any of us can do for him right now.'

'Oh, dear,' the nurse said. 'I'll let you three get on with it. Please close the door behind you when you leave. You remember your way out?' Bryony nodded again and the nurse left. They were silent until they could no longer hear her footsteps echoing down the empty hall.

'Oscar, this is Raya. You've met before.'

Oscar looked Raya over. *'Oh yeah. I remember you. The one who freaked out when I was complaining about the service at Angie's. Touchy, ain't ya?'* Oscar yawned while doing a yoga stretch, then moved out of the cage.

Raya laughed. 'It wasn't that – I was hearing your thoughts. That's what freaked me out.'

'Ah, that's what sent you bolting out of Angie's that morning? Your powers coming on? With your mother's history, you must have been scared out of your wits,' Bryony said.

'I was! Why didn't you say something?' Anger swelled.

Bryony took Oscar onto her lap, looked embarrassed. 'Sorry. I was going to. I only realised you are an integrator the evening before, when I'd popped over looking for Oscar. When you still didn't believe in witches – remember?'

Raya flushed. 'So you got all that in one go – that I AM one but that I didn't believe in them... I mean us?

But you're the social worker, the grown-up. You should have done something!' She buried her head in her hands. 'And maybe none of this would have happened… and Jake would still be OK.'

Raya broke into sobs.

'Oh Raya, you're the one who ran away, remember? I didn't have half a chance with you.' Bryony tried to smooth her hair, but Raya swatted her away. She grabbed the cat from Bryony's lap and hugged him like a teddy. Raya hadn't felt anything like this since she was little and she thought she'd failed to protect her mum from evil and aliens, and that's why she didn't get better. Where was a red Formica table when you needed one? *I'm useless. Worse than useless. I don't even deserve to live.*

Bryony looked startled and reached for Raya's hand. But it was as though Bryony was moving farther and farther away.

Oscar tried to free himself from the girl. *'Hey, I'm not doing this. Get me off her, Bryony – now!'* Oscar said. But the girl clamped down like the cat was a life ring.

'What's happening?' Raya said, but no sound came out of her mouth. Blue, grey, and black swirled around her. Cold gusts of wind jabbed at her. A high-pitched ringing hurt her ears. It was getting harder to see the room or Bryony. The sounds of the wind grew louder, the ringing became a deafening soulless screech. Raya clutched the cat within an inch of his furry life and everything went black.

Chapter 11

Not Even a Bicycle

Raya had that dream again. She was walking on top of the old city wall, but this time she was with Oscar the cat, not Alfie the dog. She peeped through one of the small holes in the outer wall rising up from the walkway. The world on the outside was nothing but countryside now. Dirt roads like chocolate ribbons disappeared into woods or green fields in the distance.

She walked on, tugging her hoodie against the wind. The sky was covered in low thick clouds like the underside of a giant animal. Oscar looked at the town inside the wall below them. Raya looked, too. It was the same oldy-worldy town as before. But this time, she saw more people bustling about, all in dreary clothes. Horses clopped along pulling carts. People's voices, but not their words, reached them. The smell of wood fires was a cosy contrast to the bleak day.

'Come on, Oscar,' she said. But he didn't respond. *That's weird. It's my dream, everyone should do what I want. This must be one of these lucid dreams Pavel told me about – when you know you're dreaming.*

'*This ain't no dream, baby,*' Oscar said.

'*What do you mean?*'

'*I'm pretty sure we've time travelled, shweetheart.*'

'*Shweetheart?*' Raya mimicked. '*So where'd you get THAT accent?*'

She marched forward towards the turn in the wall just like she saw in her dream before. Oscar ran to keep pace. Their breath made small puffs ahead of them.

'*Some people say I sound a bit like De Niro.*' Oscar looked pleased with himself. '*But anyway, I just want to say goodbye. I wish you all the best – I'm out of here. You got here, I'm sure you can get yourself back.*'

Raya gave him a look, '*What are you talking about?*'

'Stop! Who goes there?' came a man's voice from behind them.

The man was in short trousers, what looked like tights, a jacket that flared out over the hips and a metal helmet. He was holding a long spear.

'Now, why on earth would I invent you? Go away. Get out of my dream. Pavel will love hearing about all this.' She waved a hand in his face.

Oscar dodged behind her legs. *I don't want to get involved here, but I wouldn't do that if I were you–'*

'Shh, Cat. Not now.'

She stepped up to the man and knocked on his helmet three times. It made a satisfying ringing sound. 'Ouch.' She blew on her knuckles. 'Wow, this all seems so real–'

The man grabbed Raya around her upper arm. Ugh, did he pong.

'Aye, you cannot walk on the walls, lad. From where do you hail?'

This was losing its charm.

'I'm from Barking, originally, sir,' Raya tried playing along.

The man looked hard at Raya, sniffed her. 'Tain't never heard of no "Barking",' he growled. 'You work on the docks? Come in with a ship?'

'No, sir, I don't work around here. I–'

'Aye – a bloody foreigner AND looking for work?'

Raya wondered if this dream was trying to teach her to be more tolerant, less 'xenophobic' as Jake called it. *Uh oh, don't think about Jake, don't think about–*

The man called over his shoulder, 'Gavan, another one for the workhouse.'

Another man, larger and younger, but dressed like the first started towards them with a threatening grin. 'Aye, let us get rid of this vermin.'

'Run, Raya!' Oscar head-screamed.

She grunted. *'I'm trying!'* The first guy was gripping her arm so tight it was going numb. 'Let me go, you animal!' She flailed uselessly.

Gavan reached for her.

With a cat war cry, Oscar leapt up onto the first man's face and dug his claws into his chubby cheeks and oily scalp.

He screamed and batted at the cat. Raya ran, saw a stone stairwell ahead, and glanced back. The man jumped around in pain, unable to free himself of his cat blind-fold; Gavan tried to get around him, but couldn't. For a second they looked like they were dancing at a bizarre festival. Gavan finally wrenched Oscar free, leaving the man moaning against the wall and holding his bloodied face. When Gavan was about to fling Oscar over the wall, Raya saw red – she didn't want anyone else hurt because of her, even if it was a cranky cat.

'Noo!!' She was on them quicker than she thought possible and did the only thing she knew would work for sure – kicked him in the groin.

'Run!' she screamed out loud. Oscar went hell-bent for leather towards the stairwell, Raya at his tail. The two men, crumpled against the wall, groaning and swearing.

'You are not of God's creatures!' the first man bellowed at their backs.

The cat and girl hurtled themselves down the damp stone steps. They rolled out onto the belt of green between the wall and the town. Raya scrambled to her feet, grabbed the cat and dodged through a thick clot of sheep towards a large tree at the far edge of the green. Across the dirt road was a row of cottages where the town started in earnest. Women in old-fashioned bland clothing washed laundry in tubs, carried buckets, and other hard work. Kids either helped or larked about. Some turned to look beyond her as she panted against the tree. Raya peered around and saw Gavan at the bottom of the stairs, searching the scene in front of him.

'Shit,' Raya said. She spied a passageway splitting the row of cottages with glimpses of a crowded town beyond. 'Hold on,' Raya said, still clinging to the cat before darting across the road, nearly colliding with a horse-drawn cart laden with goods, and into the passageway. When she reached the end she allowed herself to glimpse back. Two women from the cottages were talking to Gavan. One pointed in the wrong direction. She held a basket against her hip with one hand, and her bonnet on her head with the other. *A bonnet?* The woman glanced her way and gave the slightest nod, before returning to her conversation. Raya turned the corner, into the town's centre, when she finally put the cat down. There were rows of two or three-storey buildings. Some were stone, others were rendered with wooden strips running across them in different directions. Most had thatched roofs. She fingered her phone in her pocket, but something told her not to use it.

'*What the hell is going on? This ISN'T a dream, is it?*' Raya said in head-speak.

'Gardyloo,' someone called overhead. Oscar yelled, '*MOVE!*' and Raya did just before an arm came out of a window and tipped a bowl, barely missing the girl-cat duo.

Raya gagged at the smell of human excrement. She looked up and waved her fist.

'That's disgusting! I hope someone poos on your life!' Raya shook her head, then realised people were staring at her. There were streams of them, all wore dreary clothes, the women in long dresses, the men in mostly short trousers. Some clucked and whispered when they saw her, they all steered clear. There wasn't a car in sight, not even a bicycle, but plenty of horse- and donkey-drawn carts. There were no electric signs, no telephone wires anywhere. The snippets of conversation she overheard didn't sound like the English she was used to.

'But time travel? How is that even possible?' she asked the cat.

'It must have been you. Familiars don't have that sort of power, not that it wouldn't have come in handy at times....' he trailed off.

'What are you talking about?'

'Forget it.' Oscar scurried into the thick of the market. *'Probably best to keep moving.'*

'Right. Sorry.' She stopped again. *'But hang on, I thought you said you were "out of here". Don't stay for me. I don't want your charity – even though I just saved your furry bum.'* She glowered at the large, now mostly black cat.

He twitched his tail and scowled back at her for a moment. *'OK, don't get your tail in a knot. I just saved you too, if your goldfish brain can remember.'*

'That's wrong – thinking goldfish have bad memories you know. Jake was telling me...' She was immediately sorry she brought up his name. She didn't even know if he got through the surgery. Oscar looked equally worried, slinked up next to her.

'OK – I take it back. Looks like we need each other to survive this time and place. I'll stick around a bit longer, all right?' the cat offered generously.

'Appreciate it.' How weird had her life become that she was looking to a cat for help?

There were more small buildings with thatched roofs. Both sides of the road were lined with market stalls brimming with pots and pans, shoes, hand tools, cheese, fish, and meat. The aroma of warm bread was welcome amidst the earthy human and animal smells. A thick crowd of adults and children pulsed throughout.

'How could I even DO this?'

Oscar stopped at a corner, looked in all directions and sighed. *'I can't teach you everything in five minutes.'*

'Well excuse me for asking, Mr Cat.' Raya marched off down a smaller, quieter road lined with a few shops and more cottages. Oscar trotted to catch up.

'Calm down,' Oscar said.

A cart clattered by, laden with rolls of cloth. The driver nodded 'hello'.

Somebody jumped off the back – Gavan.

Chapter 12

Menagerie Act

'Let me go! Put me down!' Raya shrieked as Gavan jumped back on the cart holding her like she was a sack of onions. He stuffed her in between the large bolts of cloth and held her there – her screams muffled. Oscar jumped on while the man's back was turned and burrowed in as the cart lurched forward. Gavan bent over her, his face inches from hers. His breath reeked of stale ale and bad teeth. His eyes were angry coals.

'You have had your fun me with – now it is my turn!' He kept her pinned down and muffled her every time she tried to scream or say anything by shoving a wodge of cloth into her mouth, gagging her. This made him laugh.

'Oscar, are you here?'

'Yeah – I'm under a bunch of cloth.'

She made a whimpering sound in the back of her throat. Gavan leaned his arm against her face. It hurt.

The metal cart wheels were noisy against the cobbled road, the vibrations went through her bones. It seemed like an hour before they rattled to a stop, but it was probably only minutes.

'I will hold him here whilst you fetch the lads,' Gavan snarled to the driver. Raya could feel the driver jump off of the cart and heard the bridle clinking as he tied up the horse.

'We're in front of some inn,' Oscar said. *'I'm jumping off while I have the chance.'*

'Don't go – please. I'm so scared. I may not be around much longer, anyway.'

'I said I'd stick around. No need to be a drama llama,' Oscar said.

Raya gave a choked whimper.

The driver returned with a young man. They stood at the back of the cart. Gavan flung Raya to a standing position, still on the cart and held her arms so tight he left bruises.

'This is him. An odd lad at that. Scrawny, with a girl's voice. But strong and scrappy.'

'They think I'm a BOY?'

'Go with it. The only women with short hair had it cut off as punishment – if we are when I think we are.'

'How do you know all this stuff?'

'Tell you later.'

The lad staring up at her wasn't much older than she was. He looked kind enough, with a shock of dark hair that could use a cut, not to mention a wash. He cocked his head looking at her.

'Does he speak English? Looks foreign,' the lad asked Gavan.

'English of a sort. Could be a Dutch accent,' Gavan said.

'What a numpty, I'm not–' Raya said to Oscar.

'Shh, you'll need an explanation for sounding different and there's loads of Dutch here in these times,' the cat interjected.

'Guess he'll do. We are in dire need of help since we lost Edward to the ague,' the lad said. He reached up and gave Gavan a coin who quickly pocketed it. He spun Raya around to face him. Spit flew as he spoke.

'I get half your wages for six months. If you fail to pay me, even once, then off to the workhouse with you. Understand?' He shoved her off the cart. She stumbled onto her knees. She glimpsed Oscar under a bush.

'What's "ague"?' Raya asked.

'Malaria.'

'Oh great.'

'Hey, you want plague? They got that, too.'

Raya ignored the cat.

'So when is this? How do you know?' Raya asked, but the cat didn't have time to answer.

'I'm Samuel,' the young man said, smiling awkwardly. 'Sorry about all that.' He gestured towards the cart as it left. 'I didn't realise this arrangement was a surprise to you. Working here is better than the workhouse, from what I hear anyways.'

Another lad, taller and leaner with ginger hair, handed the reins of a horse to a waiting customer, then turned towards them. 'And what with the war on, we have trouble finding help. I'm Nehemiah, by the way.'

'The Civil War?' Raya asked her cat companion.

'I think so.'

They were in front of a sizeable inn on a wider road. Raya was shaking with relief, but tried to hide it. She thought she was going to be killed and likely beat savagely beforehand, but there was no time to recover or contemplate, thrown into this next scenario. Her life as a foster kid with an unwell bio-mum looked like a day in the park from here.

A sign hung over the large wooden door, 'The Bull'. A

horse-drawn carriage stopped. People got out and workers crawled over it collecting trunks and heavy sacks. The carriage horses huffed and shuddered, hoofed the ground. Sweat steamed off their backs.

Suddenly, the empty carriage bolted forward. They were hit with the warmth and odour of the hard-worked animals. Sam leapt onto the side of the team, his feet dragging on the ground. The ginger Nehemiah charged to the front and grabbed the reins. Another customer rode up on a single horse as the boys brought the errant team back.

'You take that mare, mate – didn't get your name,' Sam called over his shoulder as the lads led the team through the archway at the side of the inn.

'Rach... Ralph,' she said, lowering her voice. Raya took the reins from the customer. She looked around for Oscar.

'You coming?'

He poked his head out of a bush. *'I'm not keen on horses.'*

'Oh for goodness' sake. Horses are the least of our problems.' She scooped him up with her free hand and carried on through the arch.

It opened up to a large courtyard, another world behind the road. Raya stopped with the horse. The two lads were unharnessing the team.

Oscar scrabbled against her, ears back, eyes slits. He climbed onto her shoulder.

'Ow – cut it out – you're digging into me.'

He jumped onto the horse, then clung on spread-eagled.

'Now who's the drama llama?'

'Shut up.'

A man sitting at a rough wooden table raised his tankard and called out, 'Aye, a menagerie act!' Others around the table started clambering for the act to begin.

'Could you give us a hand?' Oscar still looked frightened. *'I'll be nicer.'*

'And you'll help me get back home?'

'Yup.'

Raya took a slight bow, and lifted Oscar off the saddle. He unfurled his ears and opened his eyes. 'Thank you, kind gentleman, but I am afraid my cat has retired from menagerie work due to an injury and will not–'

'Oy, stop wasting time. You're not working in a menagerie now,' Nehemiah said as he walked one of the horses from the carriage team into the barn.

Raya nodded to the customers and made her way to the barn. A couple of old dogs wandered around. There was a patch of green behind the barn. A woman carried a basket of potatoes and onions into the back of the inn. Another dumped rubbish onto a heap. The aroma of roasting meat wafted over Raya. Her stomach growled.

Inside the barn smelled like sweet hay, leather and horse manure. Sam appeared from behind a horse in an open stall. He gestured towards the next box. Raya walked her horse in.

'Where are you?' Raya said aloud.

Sam stopped working, looked at Raya, 'I'm right here. Don't fret, I'll show you what needs doing.'

'I'm sorry. I'm looking for my cat,' Raya said. 'Don't know where he's got to.'

Sam laughed, 'Don't worry. He'll find you. You'll get food and blankets for sleeping…' he nodded towards a ladder to the loft, '…and ten shillings a week if you stay on.'

Nehemiah came out of another stall. 'Well, five for you and five for Gavan. I wouldn't try to cheat him.'

Raya got a shiver remembering him. *Maybe I should just think of Gavan like a one man employment agency.* She giggled to herself – she did that sometimes when she was nervous. Sam and Nehemiah both gave her funny looks.

'Watch it. You're a bloke, remember?'

Raya snapped out of her reverie. *'Right. Sorry. Where ARE you?'*

'Meow,' Oscar said from his perch on top of a beam. Raya jumped. She wasn't used to him making regular cat sounds.

Sam took a saddle off for cleaning. 'If he doesn't frighten the horses, he can earn his keep by mousing. Plenty around, and the rats look healthier than most people.'

'*Lucky me,*' Oscar said.

* * *

Samuel showed Raya what to do. She took the saddle off the mare, rubbed the sweat off her with a rough blanket, then brushed her before leading her out to the small green behind the barn. She beat blankets, cleaned saddles and tack, pretty much whatever Samuel pointed to. The hardest part was bringing water from the well. After she spilled the heavy buckets she was supposed to balance on a pole across her shoulders a couple of times, Samuel got fed up and did it for her, if she mucked out the stalls. Oscar had disappeared again – she figured for a nap. The sun started to set.

Nehemiah brought fresh straw up the ladder and told Raya to follow him.

'That's where I sleep, and that's Samuel's spot. You can choose anywhere else. After you bring in that last mare, get some food. Just go to the back door of the kitchen and ask the cook. She's knows there's a new stable hand,' Nehemiah said, then went down the ladder.

Oscar did one of those spine-bending cat stretches on a rafter in the loft.

'*Oh, there you are,*' Raya said.

'*Hey, can you bring me something from the kitchen while you're at it? Can't stand hunting – would be a vegetarian if I didn't like meat so much.*'

'*Sure.*'

Raya climbed down the ladder and went to fetch the horse. Halfway there, she realised she'd forgotten the bridle and returned to the barn. As she got close, she heard the two guys talking about her, so she stopped outside and listened.

'Don't know why Gavan was so rough on him, such a skinny boy,' Nehemiah said.

'Yeah, not much muscle to him, not much good with the heavy work,' Sam said.

'Well, he's better than nothing, seems all right with the horses. And we really need the help.'

'Odd English – Gavan said he was foreign, right?' Sam said. 'And from the looks of him, he's had a rough time of it, what with the bruises.'

Raya stepped noisily as she entered the barn to retrieve the bridle. After she got the mare into her stall, she went to the back door of the inn. A few customers sat at the outdoor tables. Lanterns glowed through windows, the pub was full and noisy. The old dogs were curled up by the kitchen door.

She leaned in the bottom half of the open split door, arms folded across her chest to hide any hint of womanhood. Warmth and delicious aromas came from the kitchen. It made her miss the Cosmic Cafe. A stout woman caught sight of her, wiped her hands on her apron, and came to the half-open door. The smaller dog struggled to stand up, its milky eyes aimed at the cook.

'Don't mind Shaggy, always begging. Afraid I don't help matters, him being my favourite, spoil him when I can,' the cook said.

Raya bent down, gave the dog a stroke. 'Oh, don't worry. I like dogs.'

'You must be the new stable boy,' the cook said. She looked Raya up and down. 'Not much of you,' she said then put a chunk of bread and cheese in a bowl and spooned a bit of meat stew on top. The woman looked over her shoulder before continuing.

'Do us a favour, pet, and don't tell anyone I gave you this,' she said, nodding towards the meat. The woman turned towards the tankards on the windowsill. 'I'll get you some ale to wash that down.'

'Oh, no thanks. But if you wouldn't mind, I could kill for a cup of tea.'

The cook turned on her heels. 'You could do WHAT?'

The cook looked scared and angry. Raya had no idea what she'd done wrong. 'Don't worry, I'll just have some water,' Raya said.

The cook threw her head back and cackled. 'You won't last long then, drinking the water.' She shook her head and leaned out of the top half of the door. 'I wouldn't go round threatening people's lives, lad, especially not over getting some odd foreign drink.'

Raya thought she might cry. It wasn't so much the cook telling her off – getting told off was nothing new in her career as a foster kid; it was one more stress at the end of the weirdest day in her life. The scruffy old dog looked up at Raya and whined. She bent down and gave him a good scratch behind the ears. 'You're not mad at me, are you?' she said.

A shadow came over her, blocking the moonlight, the cook leaning out of the door.

'Leave my dog alone!' the cook barked. Raya grabbed her bowl of food and ran back to the barn.

Chapter 13

Be Careful What You Feel

Raya, shaken from her interaction with the cook, was glad to have some time alone with Oscar.

She joined the cat in the loft, where they sat on the two rough blankets the lads had given her, and they ate their dinner. The guys had gone to the inn for a drink, and from what Oscar overheard, they would be there a while. Oscar was famished and wasn't very good at hiding it; he meowed, and rubbed his head against Raya. Raya tried the stew, made a face.

'It's all yours.'

'You sure? Mutton's lovely.' But he didn't wait for an answer.

Raya started on the chewy bread and sharp cheese. *'So you think we're sometime during the English Civil War?'*

Oscar took a minute to come up for air. *'Yeah, I'd say so. I've been trying to contact IHQ – to confirm,'* Oscar said.

'What's IHQ? What – like on a special mobile? This is all so bizarre. And anyway, how do you know all this stuff?'

The last of the sun beamed through the small window at the end of the loft. Oscar took his time washing his face, collecting the last drops of gravy.

'That's easy, at least. I went through familiar training – takes about eighteen months. You learn a human language, speaking and reading, two or three special skills and at least one topic in history.'

'You're joking, right?'

Oscar blinked at her. *'Do you want my help or not?'*

'God, you're touchy.'

They heard sounds of people at the tables behind the inn, and evening birds. Oscar suddenly looked away as though he was focusing on something Raya couldn't see. He put a paw up as if to say 'be quiet'. Then he jumped on her lap and turned to face forward. *'Here, they want to talk to you. Put your hands out.'*

'What?'

'Just DO it!'

She put her hands out and he put his paws in her open palms. She didn't know cats' paws could sweat.

Then she saw it – like TV without a TV. She was looking at some sort of command centre. People working on computers, talking to each other, big screens on one wall, piles of papers, mugs of forgotten tea. A woman came 'on screen'. She was older, maybe fifties, slender and smartly dressed, like a BBC newsreader. She gave a business-like smile.

'Oscar, great to see you. Glad your microchip is still working. Thanks for all your good works out there – we have noticed.'

He gave a gaping yawn. *'Ms Watts, you know I didn't sign up for this mission and I expect–'*

'Yes, you will be properly compensated when you get home. But right now we need to concentrate on getting you two home.' She gave that official smile again.

Raya gulped. Ms Watts continued. *'I take it that's Miss Rachel Hollingsworth with you?'*

'Hi, Miss. Yes, I'm Raya… um Rachel.'

'Nice to meet you, although of course I'm sorry it's under these difficult circumstances. I'm Sonya Watts, your social worker, Bryony Braxton's supervisor. I'm one of the directors here at IHQ – Integrator Headquarters in London. We're overseeing your case of mistaken time travel. These can be

quite tricky, but nothing we haven't seen before.' Someone asked her something off screen. She signed some papers, then returned to Raya and Oscar. *'We will be your team working on getting you home. But first, I have someone here who wants to say hello.'*

Pavel appeared on the screen.

'Omigod, Pavel! You don't know how good it is to see you! How's Jake? Is he OK?' Raya fought tears.

'He made it through the surgery – not quite himself yet, but getting there,' Pavel said.

A sob escaped her. *'Thank goodness! Will he be OK? And how're Emma and Ian? And how did I get here – back in time? How is this even possible? Do you know exactly when we are? Some horrible things have happened, and it's SO much to get my head around and–'*

'OK there, little sister. Slow down.'

She had a rush of relief, yearning and a fear of never returning home.

Pavel took a sip from a mug. *'Our time travel techies have been working on quadrangulating your position – you know, three dimensions plus time?'* But he didn't wait for a response. *'Anyway, we think you're in Colchester, Essex, mid-July 1645 – do you know what was going on then?'* He looked away.

'Well, the Civil War, right? People have mentioned it.'

Pavel looked uncomfortable. Raya wondered if she had done something wrong – besides time travel and bringing someone else's cat with her.

'If it's about the cat–'

'I'm right here,' Oscar said.

'Right, sorry. Look, I'm sorry if I did something wrong by bringing Oscar. That was just as much an accident as–'

Pavel smiled, but still looked troubled. 'I'll let Ms Watts explain it to you.' He bowed out of view.

Ms Official returned. 'You've landed a few days before some of the worst witch trials – if you can even call them trials – in British history.'

She thought a minute. 'Oh, shit! Sorry. Omigod, the Essex Witch Trials were now, weren't they?' A cold shiver rolled down her spine. Oscar pressed his sweaty paws into hers.

Ms Watts took her glasses off and looked across time into Raya's eyes. 'Yes. We think your feeling so awful about Jake, your feeling so terribly guilty and responsible is what got you back there.'

'I'm sorry. I don't understand.'

'Remember – you, Bryony and Oscar in the hospital basement?'

She did remember feeling so awful and responsible for Jake getting hit by a… she couldn't finish the thought. She remembered the swirling colours and cold, Bryony seeming so far away, and… her fleeting thoughts that she didn't even deserve to continue to live if this was what she'd done.

'Omigod – I've sent myself back to the worst punishment a witch could go through. Haven't I?'

'Looks like it.'

Chapter 14

Puss in Boots

'Oy. Get a move on – we have a lot to do.' Samuel's voice woke Raya. She moaned and Oscar emerged.

'Get up, you lazy adle pate.' Nehemiah prodded her with his boot. 'No skin off my nose. More grub for me.' His voice trailed off as he went down the ladder to the stables. She could hear him talking to Samuel.

'I tell you, this Ralph is a Roberta, if you know what I mean?' Nehemiah said. They laughed.

Raya heard the gentle clink of the various bits of horse equipment. Raya poked her head out of the blankets. She saw Oscar washing himself in a shaft of early sunshine. It couldn't have been later than six a.m.

Samuel's head appeared up the ladder. 'We need to get started. Three horses to ready, then we eat before we muck out.' He nodded and went back down to the stable.

'Coming.' Raya started down the ladder.

Raya tried hard to be helpful in the stable, ripe with the night's dirty straw. She handed the lads the wrong, and sometimes the right things. Then she put a saddle on backwards.

'Oh, that's it.' Nehemiah stood and shook his head. 'Samuel, this one is useless.'

Raya stood next to the horse with the backward saddle crimson-faced.

'Probably put off by the equipment, eh?' Nehemiah grinned while gesturing towards the stallion with the backward saddle.

Samuel shook his head and sorted the saddle. 'Come on now, even a filly knows the front from the back.'

Oh, no. They've made me for sure – know I'm a girl.

Nehemiah stood too close. His breath reeked. He gave a goofy grin and reached both hands towards her chest. 'Let's inspect you, eh?' Raya slapped his hands away and kicked him in the shin.

'Ow. Can't you take a joke?' Nehemiah rubbed his shin. Raya smirked. Samuel returned with the bridle.

'So, even if "Ralph" here is a lass, he or she can take care of the likes of you,' Samuel said, then turned to Raya. 'He's nothing but mouth, don't worry about him.'

Raya was relieved. One less piece of acting to carry off while learning all this other stuff. She was grateful for their kindness or indifference.

'You've had your share of bad luck, as best as I can see. No use us adding to it, right Nehemiah?' Nehemiah shrugged. Samuel handed Raya the reins of the horse they'd prepared and nodded towards the barn door. 'Take this horse round the front. The customer's waiting.'

Raya took the horse out of the barn and led it through the arch towards the front of the tavern, she turned her face upward soaking in the sun – you never knew how long it would last.

'*Raya. Can you hear me?*' Oscar broke through, '*A warning's come through from IHQ.*'

'*Give me a minute, I have to deliver this horse.*'

Raya spied a man waiting. She made that little *tchk, tchk* she heard others give horses to move them along. She handed the horse over to the customer after confirming it was his.

People passed on the road in front of the inn. Carts stopped and delivered food. Kitchen staff carried the goods to the back. A carriage and a man on a horse rode up. They seemed to be together. The carriage driver stopped his two horses and called down to Raya, 'Hey, lad, should I bring the carriage and team round the back?'

'No, sir. One of our stable hands will do that for you,' she said as she glanced over her shoulder and saw Nehemiah coming. He spoke to the driver and took the carriage.

Raya approached the man on horseback, not very old and dressed fancier than the others. His hat was bigger with feathers sticking up from the brim. His hair went down to his oversized crisp white collar, but his beard was very short. He wore a long cape that draped behind him onto the horse, and mirror-shiny knee-high boots with spurs. She would have been impressed except he looked like a jerk. She couldn't wait to hear what Oscar thought about this guy.

'Oscar, you should see this clown who just pulled up. Looks like Puss in Boots.'

'Don't you recognize him?' Oscar said. There was the sound like a deflating balloon and the transmission cut out.

Puss in Boots cleared his throat. He was still on his horse. 'Good morning, sir. May I take your horse?' she said.

The man scowled, exhaled through flared nostrils, but said nothing.

Raya stood extra tall with her hands behind her back. 'I assure you we take excellent care of the horses,' she said, then looked away. She figured he must be something to do with the war, he looked official, but he seemed like a right idiot; she was afraid she'd burst out laughing.

'No one unknown to me touches my horse, and I do not know you,' he added with an emphatic nod then looked around to see if anyone was watching. He flounced his cape. 'Where is the other lad, the one with the dark hair?'

Raya knew the type. She gave a deep bow. 'That would be Samuel, sir. I assure you he remains in charge of the stable. I'm new here–'

'I can see that,' Puss in Boots said, flicking something off his cape.

'Why don't I lead you and your fine horse back to the stables?' Raya offered.

Puss in Boots nodded the slimmest of approvals. Raya guided the horse by the bridle. The three walked through the momentary shadow of the arch in silence except for the soft hoof falls. Raya squinted into the bright sun in the garden as she made out Samuel leading another horse towards the arch. He gave her a quick look to say he would tell her about this guy later, then turned towards the guest and bowed.

'Good morning, General Hopkins. So nice to have your honourable self with us again.'

Chapter 15
Worst Witch

The General dismounted and handed Samuel the reins. 'Thank you, young man,' he said, even though he was not much older. 'They should have brought my things in from the carriage by now.' He nodded with a slight tip of his extravagant hat and turned towards the inn.

'Well, go on, now. Standing like a statue won't help. Go get the special stall ready for the General's horse. Nehemiah knows which one it is,' Samuel said to Raya, who reanimated. She ran towards the barn as Samuel led the horse to the green beyond it.

In the barn, she found Nehemiah mucking out a stall.

'A general's arrived and we have to look after his horse,' Raya said' skidding to a stop. Nehemiah continued working without saying anything. 'Didn't you hear me? A general.'

Nehemiah tossed one more shovelful of dirty straw into the wheelbarrow, spat on the floor. 'Tain't no general. Just calls himself one, is all.' He saddled up a horse, tugging extra hard at the straps.

'What do you mean?' Raya said.

'That man don't know nothing 'bout real war. Not like my brother who's in the thick of it.'

Raya nodded sympathetically, but by then the penny dropped and her blood had turned to Freon. *Of course, 'General' Matthew Hopkins, that was what Oscar was trying to tell her.*

Nehemiah continued, 'This idiot Hopkins fancies himself "the Witchfinder General". Rounds up women by the score and puts them in jail. Tain't a real man, forget about a real general.' He spat again. 'By the way, your cat's been acting peculiar, running around the horses.' Nehemiah shook his head and shovelled more dirty straw. 'Can't have it scaring them.'

Raya tried to get in touch with Oscar, but got no response. She peered up the ladder. 'I'll keep an eye on him, I promise,' Raya said. But Nehemiah wasn't listening any more. She changed the subject.

'Samuel said we should get the "special" stall ready for the General's horse.'

'You start, then.' He nodded towards the one next to

where he was working. 'The General insists his horse stay in this box here. He makes a big show of seeing that his horse is looked after properly. Has his share of enemies,' then under his breath, 'comes as no surprise.'

She used the slowed breathing Pavel had taught her. Here she was a real witch and talking to Matthew Hopkins. What could go more wrong? *It doesn't mean anything will happen to me – no one's died, no crops have failed like I read about people getting blamed for*, she coached herself. She still hadn't found Oscar when Sam called her over to help.

Raya, Samuel and Nehemiah worked hard over the next hours, with no time for breakfast in the end. They took a break for lunch, which was like porridge with a bit of fish and vegetables. If she hadn't been starving, she wouldn't have touched it. She saved some for Oscar and filled a tin cup with fresh water that had been boiled, before excusing herself. The lads said they were going to take a break in the sun.

She climbed the ladder to see if he was taking a nap. In the hayloft, the blankets she'd rolled up looked jumbled. She tugged at the top one and a large white cat, dead asleep, or plain dead, spilled out.

'Oscar?' She remembered Bryony saying something about familiars getting ill and losing their colour if they're around bad witches. She gathered up the woozy cat. 'It's

me, Raya. Come on, wake up.' He was all white except for
a slim black stripe along his spine. She clutched the large
limp cat against her, burying her face in his warm fur.

'*What's happened? You can't leave me, I need you, you
cranky fur ball.*'

Oscar cracked open his eyes, '*That was weak. You
could do better.*' He tried to smile.

'*Don't die on me, I couldn't take that.*'

'*Sorry, mate. This one, this Witch Gone Bad's hit me
like a ton of bricks.*'

'*Who? This Hopkins plonker?*'

'*The one and only.*'

'Ralph,' Samuel called from the stables below, 'You
need to come down here. We're about to have... an
inspection.'

Raya peered down. Some other people were in the
stables besides the two lads.

'Inspection?' she said.

Nehemiah looked up the ladder. 'Yes, the Honourable
Mr Hopkins,' he said with deadpan sarcasm, 'has requested
an inspection of his horse's quarters. One can never be too
careful.'

'Yes, of course. I'll be right there.' Even though it was
hot in the loft, Raya made a bed out of the blankets for
Oscar. She remembered her nan bundling her up when

she was ill. She buried her face in his neck and whispered.
'Hang in there, fur-buddy – please.'

She leapt down the ladder.

Chapter 16
A Few Days

Mr Hopkins, Samuel and Nehemiah stood in front of the empty stall prepared for Mr Hopkins's horse. There was a woman standing with them. It took Raya a moment to recognize her – the cook. There was an awkward silence.

'At your service, sir,' Raya said, not knowing what else to do. 'Good afternoon, madam,' she added.

The cook pointed at Raya. 'That's the one. That's him!' The cook looked very upset.

'Come on, Mrs Jennings, that dog was ancient. You even said yourself he wasn't looking good earlier this week, remember?' Nehemiah said. Raya looked from one person to the other.

Samuel put his hand on Raya's shoulder. 'Ralph, Mrs Jennings here says–'

The General broke in. 'Do not touch him. You are not educated in such matters. You could be NEXT.'

'Next? What are you–' Raya protested but stopped when Hopkins grabbed her by the arm. When he touched her, she saw nothing but mud, smelled rotting things and tasted metal.

'You killed this good woman's dog!' His eyes bore into Raya. She averted hers, instinctively. 'All because she denied you your favourite witches' brew!' He swished his cape for emphasis.

Raya gasped. 'What are you talking about? I would never do such a thing. I stroked it.' Raya looked at the cook, trying to gain empathy.

The cook gasped and dodged behind Nehemiah, who looked annoyed and stepped aside. The cook collected herself, then took one step forward as though this was the bravest thing she'd ever done.

'This lad came to me for his supper, but that was not good enough. No, he wanted "T" and said he would kill for it. I don't know what this "T" is. Some drink of the Devil, I'm sure! And he kept his promise. By the time I finished up and left for home, there was Shaggy, stone-cold dead and stiff already, right outside the kitchen door.'

Raya felt her blood drain. 'I'm ever so sorry. Where I come from, we drink something called "tea", spelled t-e–'

Nehemiah stepped forward. 'You see, sir, Ralph is from the Netherlands, then worked on a travelling menagerie with his special cat, but the cat got injured. They joined us yesterday.'

'A special cat?' Hopkins arched an eyebrow.

'Yes, sir. Ralph is a menagerie performer. He's no witch, I assure you. He's hardworking and has been mistreated himself,' Samuel said and nodded towards the bruises on Raya's arms. Samuel stepped in front of Raya, but Hopkins was having none of it.

He inflated his cape and expelled a chortle.

'Ah, I don't expect the likes of you to understand what is at stake here. We are fighting the evil that flows through the Royalists and papists, Laudians, and all the misled wretches who are waging war to steal not only our country but our very souls,' Hopkins intoned as though he was in a pulpit.

Raya looked at the two stable hands for an explanation. Nehemiah gave the slightest eye roll. Samuel shot them a quick look. Hopkins caught their silent communication and delighted at their insolence. He thrust his shoulders back and spoke in a whisper that sounded like the hiss of a snake.

'Yes, the very battle between good and evil, played out even in the lowliest of lives like yours. Witches killing dogs because they did not get their favourite drink.'

The cook gasped in a combination of horror and delight.

Something tumbled out of the loft. They all turned towards the sound, like a sack of flour hitting the floor. There was Oscar, a white lump at the bottom of the ladder. Raya rushed to him.

'Oh, Oscar.'

Hopkins strode up to the girl cradling her cat. 'Ah, so your familiar has already shown itself. Excellent,' Hopkins sneered.

Nehemiah spat on the floor. 'Mr Hopkins, you may be an important man with much education, but that is a cat, nothing more, nothing less.' He stepped towards the trio, but Samuel grabbed him by the upper arm.

'Don't go with... him...' Oscar's head talking was a weak whisper. The single black stripe on his back had broken into dashes. Raya shot Hopkins a look then turned back to Oscar.

'You will come with me now for Watching,' Hopkins said. The lads looked horrified. The cook looked relieved and pleased.

'Watching what? I'm not going anywhere with you.' Raya recoiled and clung to the cat. Hopkins stepped closer, his breath hot, cloying.

'Let me see that beast.' Hopkins tried to prize Raya's arms open. 'Let me inspect that thing!'

Raya shrieked and backed away. Hopkins grabbed at Raya's arms, snarled and growled, like an animal himself. Raya kicked at Hopkins and tried to bite him, getting only a mouthful of cape.

'Samuel, Nehemiah, help me!'

The lads struggled to reach her but were stuck in place – frozen by some unseen force, their limbs flailing uselessly like a bad cartoon.

'Behold, you evil creature. I'm more powerful than the likes of any of you,' Hopkins roared. Wind whipped up straw. The tack clinked on the walls. Nehemiah and Samuel continued to fight their paralysis, but in vain.

'Good will prevail over evil. Don't try to stop this. I can see who you truly are – a lass and a witch as well!' Hopkins boomed.

The wind shrieked.

Hopkins looked through the doorway. 'Get in here, now!' he said. Two large men came in. 'Take her to the house for Watching. You know the place.'

* * *

The cart bumped along the cobbled roads. They turned away from the city and its walls. Raya tried to jump off a few times, but the human watchdog held her back. Then he bound her feet and tied a rope around her with Oscar tucked in her arms. She sang him songs, a lullaby she hadn't known she remembered. After about ten minutes, the cart was on dirt roads.

'Where are we going?' she asked the watchdog. He opened an eye, but didn't answer. He went back to sleeping, or pretending.

'Oscar, what do we do now?' Raya said, even though she'd had no response from him since they were put on the cart. She looked at the fields and occasional houses. Sometimes a horse, some cows or sheep looked up as they passed. She held him in her lap, his paws in her hands. Maybe she could get some help from IHQ.

She received a quick image of Pavel that disappeared again.

'Pavel? Can you hear me?' She tried to be receptive, slowed her breathing and relaxed as he had taught her. She got more flashes of Pavel at IHQ with other people around him. The images quickened, like an old-timey film. Pavel looked worried. Then the transmission came in full bore. She sat up, rustled against the wooden cart, stirring the sleeping watchdog. She faked sleep and he left her alone.

Behind Pavel's worried, kind face stood Ms Sonya Watts. Other people she didn't know rushed around, barked out questions, pushed themselves along on wheeled office chairs, at the command centre. She stroked Oscar's sweaty front paws. She welled up.

'*Are they taking me to, you know, to kill me?*' She remembered reading about them 'swimming witches' – if they drowned they were innocent, if they didn't they were guilty so they killed them some other way. She felt numb.

'*This guy didn't work that way. We should still have a few days.*'

'A FEW DAYS?!'

Pavel blanched – as though he forgot who he was talking to. '*Look, we're getting ready to send Bryony back. We've been working on it day and night. It's just a bit tricky to transport someone to an exact time – anything too far off and you won't see each other.*'

'*Bryony? I mean, she seems nice and everything, but isn't there anyone else? She's always in a bit in a muddle.*'

Ms Watts leaned over Pavel's desk and stuck her head in front of the 'camera'. '*Rachel?*' she said.

Raya nodded.

'*Just hold on. Bryony IS the best person for this mission. We wouldn't send her if she wasn't. She should be with you soon. So don't be surprised and play along with whatever story she concocts to fit in.*'

Raya nodded again.

'I'm afraid we have to sign out – get back to work to give you the best chance at coming home as soon as possible.' And with that, Ms Watts, Pavel and any shadow of the command centre were gone. She didn't even have time to ask if there was anything she could do to save Oscar.

Chapter 17
The Watching

The sunset bled into the edges of the village. Smoke curled out of the cottage chimney like a crooked finger. A woman stood at the door, arms folded. She wore a long skirt, a white blouse with a bodice on top and a hat. Raya wondered if these hats helped hide dirty hair. But her musings on the horrors of seventeenth century fashion and hygiene were cut short when the watchdog jumped off the back of the cart and carried her into the house, still tied up.

He plopped her down on a wooden chair. It was in the middle of the main room of the cottage. There were a couple more chairs, a jug, cups, and some candles. Another younger, solid woman stared at Raya. She thought these might be the two she saw arrive in the carriage that came with Hopkins. Hard to tell, with them all dressing the same.

The two women spoke to the man who then left. Raya listened to the cart pull away until the sound of beating hooves and rattling wheels faded to nothing. She started to feel a little less nervous. The younger woman was old enough to be her mother, and the older one, her grandmother. Surely they would show her some kindness.

'I'm so sorry. This is a mistake. I didn't hurt anyone, not even that dog. I'm only fourteen.'

The older woman tugged at the young woman's sleeve. 'Don't let the Devil trick you. He takes all forms.'

The younger woman blushed, averted her gaze. 'Yes, Hester. Thank you.' Hester straightened with her authority and whispered to the younger one, loud enough for Raya to hear.

'We might as well get started,' the older woman said, stepping behind Raya and holding her shoulders firmly. 'Grace, untie her.'

It felt good to have the ropes removed, but she didn't want to let go of Oscar. She thought the dashes of black along his back had become a little bigger.

'Be careful, Grace. Don't touch that thing,' Hester said, pointing to Oscar. 'It could burn you.'

'Stand up,' Hester commanded. Raya stood, holding Oscar in her arms.

'Put that thing down. Now. So we can search you,' Hester said.

Raya curled him up on the wooden chair. Hester tugged at Raya's clothing, starting to take it off, grunting and making faces of disgust.

'Get off me! What the heck do you think you're doing?' Raya said. She pulled her clothes back on as they tried to take them off. Raya screeched, wrestled, and kicked, but she was no match for Grace, who restrained her while Hester undressed her.

'Why is she dressed like a boy?' Grace asked Hester.

'Don't ask me, probably in hiding like the criminal she is,' Hester suggested.

'I didn't DO anything!' Raya said, but the women acted like they didn't hear her.

Hester grunted as she wrested Raya's hoodie off.

'My word, what odd clothing,' Hester said. She snapped the elastic on Raya's crop top. 'Oy. Watch yourself, Grace. The Devil is as old as time, and much smarter than either of us.'

'You're right. I should be more careful,' Grace said. Hester shook her head.

'Take those off,' Hester said, indicating Raya's crop top and underpants.

'Forget it!' Raya said.

Hester grabbed Raya by the shoulders. 'Grace, get these off this wretch, will you?' she said.

'Stop it, you pervs! You can see I don't have any weapons!' The three of them struggled and tussled. Raya had never been so humiliated, angry and embarrassed at once. Grace pulled her crop top off, Hester ripped off her panties. *God almighty!* She started to cry and hated herself for it. She had thought having to go for a bra fitting with a rubbish foster carer – the one before Angie – was the most awful experience. That didn't touch this. Raya stood before them naked and shivering trying to cover herself with her hands.

Grace blushed.

'Keep a lookout for any odd moles, extra teats, anything at all unusual – these are the marks of the Devil, you know,' Hester instructed and Grace nodded.

'Extra teats? OK, you two have REALLY gone too far. I have two – like everyone else!' Raya thrashed against Grace, who only clamped down harder.

Hester looked at Grace, satisfied. 'See. What did I tell thou? She must be hiding something. Bring her over here, so I can get a better look,' Hester said.

Grace dragged Raya to the wall and pinned her there. Raya grunted and strained. Hester grabbed a lit candle from the mantel.

Raya gave a small shriek, whimpered, and clamped her eyes shut. 'Don't burn me. Please,' she said.

Raya could feel the older woman's warmth on her goose-bumped skin. 'Ah, the fires of hell will get you soon enough,' Hester cackled. She inspected Raya's back in great detail, touching, poking, and scratching at places as though she was trying to loosen old paint.

The two women conferred and clucked but were not satisfied with anything they saw. At Hester's command, Grace turned Raya around like a rag doll. Hester continued to poke her. Raya could have killed them, and not by witchcraft.

Grace gasped. 'Hester. There it is.' She nodded towards Raya's waist. There was a mole that had been rubbed raw by the waistband on her trousers. Grace seemed delighted and disgusted in equal measure.

The two women quickly finished searching Raya for any other incriminating marks, then Grace shoved Raya towards her clothes. She stumbled and fell to the cold floor. The two women spoke in hushed tones by the fireplace. Dirty clothes never felt so good.

She remained crouched down next to the chair with Oscar on it, stroking the warm but still unresponsive cat, trying to buy a few moments. The black on his back had joined up again into a thicker stripe. She slipped Oscar's paw into her hand and tried to transmit to IHQ.

'Anybody there? Pavel? Ms Watts? Anyone know when Bryony's coming? I don't know how much more I can take.' She cried as quietly as she could.

'Pavel? Please? I need your help.' The briefest static-y flash of Ms Watts at the screen came through.

'Please come back.' She didn't realise she was talking out loud. Another brief flash of IHQ came across. 'Please, I'm scared. Ms Watts?'

Raya realised the two women had become quiet. Raya turned and rose from her squatting position to see Hester and Grace huddled together. Grace clutched Hester's arm. The fire flickered across Grace's frightened and Hester's smug faces.

Hester's eyes narrowed and her voice was low and steady. 'Calling more of your familiars, are you? A wee thing like you and one familiar is not enough?' She turned towards Grace. 'Master Hopkins will be well pleased with this.' She turned back to Raya. 'Stand up, you evil creature.'

'Now walk!' Hester commanded.

'Walk? Walk where?' Raya said.

Hester waved her arm across the room. 'Across the room, around the room, back and forth, however we say. Now move!' Hester snarled.

Raya walked and walked. 'Can't I sit down for a minute, please?' she asked from time to time, which only got her shoved, kicked, or prodded to keep her moving. She was exhausted, frightened and parched. Hunger came in waves. Her stomach growled, tied itself in empty knots.

'Did you lay down with the Devil? What form did he take? A handsome lad? A goat? What other witches do you know?' Hester peppered her with questions.

As much as she tried not to, there were moments when Raya whimpered, cried or pleaded. 'Please, miss, can I have something to eat? A bit of bread?'

Grace slapped her on the cheek, 'Stop your begging, you're making this hard on us,' Grace said. They did allow her the occasional sip of water.

After a while, Hester and Grace's chatter and insults blurred into white noise. Another feeling brewed – anger.

She was angry at Matthew Hopkins. *What an arrogant hypocrite – a witch gone monumentally bad himself.* Angry at these ridiculous women Watchers. *How could they believe all this rubbish?* There was another, larger feeling growing in her like a snowball rolling into an avalanche – sadness. She missed Pavel, Emma and Ian, the aromas of the cafe, the jingle of the bell on the door. She laughed as she remembered some of her joking around with Jake. She felt wistful remembering working with Bryony and Pavel trying to find Jake.

'*Rachel, Rachel Hollingsworth. Do you hear me?*' It was Ms Watts. She snapped into focus in Raya's head. She was surprised at getting a transmission without even touching Oscar's paws.

'*Oh, I'm sorry, Ms Watts. Were you trying to reach me?*' Raya blinked out of her melancholy musings.

'*Don't worry. We know what you're going through. You've been transmitting quite well. Your skills are coming along. You don't even need contact with the microchipped cat any more. Well done.*' Ms Watts smiled – a real one, then went back to her game face.

'Ms Watts, I'm frightened.' Raya didn't realise she was talking out loud.

'*Anyone would be. Hang tight. We're about to send Bryony back to you.*'

'Thank you, thank you all so much,' Raya said, but the transmission broke. Tears rolled down her cheeks.

'Who is she talking to?' Grace said to Hester, she sounded genuinely scared.

'She sounds desperate,' Hester said as she spat on the floor. 'Good, she should be. We got her now.' Hester poked Raya in the leg with the toe of her shoe. 'Keep moving, you disgusting creature, no rest for the wicked.'

* * *

The dawn broke with a mocking glare through the bare windows. Raya squinted and tried to shield her eyes with her arm, but Hester slapped it away then pointed to the middle of the floor.

'Ha. I knew more familiars would come,' Hester said then stepped away from Raya and stared at a spot on the floor. Raya and Grace joined her to see what it was – a spider.

'Oh for goodness' sake, it is just a spider,' Raya said.

Hester got close to Raya's face. Her breath was vile. 'I'm no fool. That is *not* a natural spider; it's a minion of Satan! Is this the one you call "Ms Watts"?'

Grace kept a safe distance and said, 'It must be. I saw it come in under the door when this witch–'

'My name is Rachel,' Raya snapped. 'And don't be ridiculous. What the heck does a spider have to do with anything?' Raya said and stomped on it. 'There, no more spider – satisfied?'

The two women shrieked. 'You killed your own familiar! What sort of demon are you?' Hester rubbed her hands together. 'Oh, Master Hopkins will be well pleased. Grace, pick up that poor dead creature and put it in an empty glass. I will delight in watching you hang!'

Chapter 18
Girls' Night In

Two sharp raps at the door were followed by Matthew Hopkins striding in before anyone answered. He had on the same getup as before – ridiculous cape, feathered hat, and shiny boots – but this time he was also holding a staff and had a greyhound at his side. Oscar gave a low growl.

'My good Watcher Women, what did you find?' he sang out. Hester minced up to Hopkins, batted her eyes.

'Oh, Master Hopkins, you will be well pleased. We proved this wretch a witch through and through,' Hester said.

Grace flounced up to them. 'We found an extra teat where she suckles that familiar she calls Oscar.'

'And we heard her calling other familiars – three of them, Ms Watts, Pavel and Bryony,' Hester said.

'Yes, and one of these imps came. The one she called "Ms Watts" – a spider, but like no spider I've ever seen before,' Hester said in hushed, reverent tones.

Raya gathered Oscar in her arms and edged towards the door.

'Its eyes were like a human's. Grace and I could feel it staring at us,' Hester added.

'Yes, sir. This is God's truth. This was not a natural spider. And what's more, she killed it without a moment's hesitation,' Grace said.

Hester nodded sagely. 'Yes, that's the truth. Killed her very own familiar!'

Raya took a few more steps towards the door.

Hopkins's arm came up like the barrier at a tollbooth. 'Don't think you can outsmart me, you wretch.' Raya tried to push past him, but that human watchdog, the one who had brought her in, appeared. He snatched her up while Hopkins's greyhound went wild, jumping towards Oscar. The brute carried her to the cart waiting in front of the cottage.

'You scum!' Raya screamed. She loathed Hopkins as she'd never hated anyone before. He was despicable.

He stood akimbo in the doorway, Grace and Hester by his sides. His cape fluttered, he tossed back his hair. A sneer crawled across his lips. *How can this egotistical, complete idiot have so much power?* She strained and twisted to get free. She thought if she did, she'd go back and literally scratch his eyes out.

* * *

'Hey. Hey! Where are we going?' she said as they bumped back over the country road away from the cottage. But Watchdog Man looked away without answering. She crouched with Oscar still in her arms. The chill of the morning lifted to a bright, warm July day. Farmers drove carts of goods, others led sheep to graze. It was a bucolic scene that belied the rot underneath.

Oscar started purring. She looked down to see that the lone black stripe down his back had shrunk to a faint line of dots. Then she remembered someone once told her that cats don't only purr when they're content and happy. Sometimes they purr when they're very, very ill.

'Oh, Oscar.' She buried her face in his fur. It seemed like everything she did lately hurt those around her.

Soon there were more houses and shops and the streets became cobbled. She recognized things they'd passed on their way out. The driver pulled up the horse and cart at the east gate of the Colchester city wall, the same one she'd tumbled down a few days ago. He waited until there was a sufficient break in what Raya had already come to think of as normal traffic – people, horses with and without carts, and strings of sheep. The driver gave a cluck of his tongue and shake of the reins and the cart jolted forward. People stared and pointed.

Raya felt ashamed even though she knew she hadn't done anything wrong. Some people threw things or spat at her. Watchdog Man told them off and brushed them away. The cart continued until they reached another wall she hadn't seen before. Watchdog Man spoke to a man at the gate then drove through.

Beyond the gate was a cluster of small buildings in front of a massive, rundown stone castle. There was a canal between the village and castle with a wooden bridge connecting the two. People bustled to and fro, carrying bread, sacks of grain or flour, and pails of water. The wooden slats on the bridge clacked in rhythm as the cart crossed. The moat stank like a fetid swamp and open sewer. At the end of the bridge was a huge stone archway, like the gaping, toothless mouth of an ailing monster. The hairs on her neck stood up. Oscar stopped purring.

The driver pulled up at the arch. Watchdog jumped out and walked into the darkness. He returned and untied the rope around Raya's torso, but left her ankles tied together. He carried her into the arch, holding her in his arms like a child. Oscar burrowed his head into her.

Once her eyes adjusted to the dim light, she saw a large, rough man. He looked worse than Watchdog Man – he looked mean.

'Mr Hoy, this is the prisoner.'

'Aye, that Mr Hopkins ridding the world of evil, eh?' Hoy arched an eyebrow at Watchdog. 'Well I am not going to carry the witch like you are. Put her down – let her walk,' Hoy said.

Watchdog put Raya down and cut the rope. Hoy grabbed her upper arm and dragged her.

'I can walk,' Raya snapped.

Hoy looked at Watchdog. 'Another troublemaker, eh?'

Watchdog looked uncomfortable. 'A mere child is all. Says she's Dutch, but she doesn't sound like it to me. I don't know why she's done this to herself. I'm told she cut her own hair off.' He shook his head. 'And hiding as a boy in those odd clothes.'

Watchdog glanced behind him across the bridge before turning back to Hoy and Raya. 'My job is done,' he said and hurried off.

Hoy held Raya until Watchdog and the cart pulled away. Then he slapped her hard in the face with the back of his hand.

'That will be the last time you speak to me unless I speak to you first. Got it?' Hoy crouched down at

Raya's feet. Before she realised what was happening, he was clamping leg irons around her ankles. Raya was gobsmacked.

'What the hell's going on here?' came out of her mouth, which earned her another slap. He shoved her forward. She struggled to keep Oscar hidden.

'Oy, what have you got there?' Hoy said and prized open her arms. Oscar batted his eyes up at Hoy, then meowed.

'Ach. A miserable cat. Well, he'll have plenty to eat here.' Hoy's laughter echoed down the stone passageway. He knocked Oscar out of her arms and clamped irons on her wrists as well.

Raya stared beyond Hoy into the cavernous dark ahead. Oscar made his way along, staying in the shadows.

Hoy grabbed a lantern from a niche in the wall and hurried Raya forward with regular prods and shoves. It was hard to walk in the shackles.

'Aye, that scurrying sound? Rats.' Hoy guffawed.

Raya tripped and fell twice, once onto the cold stone floor, and once onto an ancient mosaic. The lantern swung in Hoy's hand, making shadows dance on the dank stone walls. Hoy's large ring of keys jangled with each step. They went through a maze of halls until they reached stone stairs going down. She struggled with the steps. Hoy shoved her, making her slide down the last of them on her bottom. The stench of human waste slapped her as hard as Hoy had. They took another two turns until they reached a large wooden door. There was an iron grate in the top half of the door.

Hoy fumbled with the keys then opened it. Inside was a small room. Filthy straw lined the floor. The stench made her eyes water. She retched, her empty stomach bringing up nothing but bile. Oscar slid in behind her. Raya heard faint murmurings. She strained to see in this even dimmer light. There were two wooden doors on adjoining walls. Hoy grabbed her by the shoulder of her hoodie, pulling her close to him. He held the lantern up, illuminating their faces. She stared back.

'Welcome to Colchester Castle Keep. You'll have no problem paying for your stay – the Dutch are rich.' Hoy laughed as though he was telling a story at a pub. He fetched another key and opened one of the wooden doors. He laughed again as he shoved Raya into this next room. Oscar slunk in. Hoy slammed the door.

The key turned.

Murmurings grew more audible; women's voices. She heard footsteps and clinking shackles. She bent down and extended her hand into the dark. Oscar butted his head against it. She scooped him up.

'Who are you?' a voice said. It was so close, Raya jumped and dropped Oscar. Her eyes hadn't adjusted yet.

'Look what we have here – a boy,' the voice said.

'My name is Rachel. I'm a girl.'

'What happened to your hair?' another voice said.

'How old are you?' a younger voice said.

'Fourteen,' Raya answered.

'Me too,' said the voice. Raya gasped. Her eyes had adjusted, she could see better now. 'Don't be afraid. We won't hurt you,' said the fourteen-year-old, blinking large, innocent eyes at Raya. 'I'm Rebecca. Can I hold your cat?'

A smack rang out in the small room. 'Ow! Mother, what did I do?'

'We have troubles of our own. Don't bring more on us, you foolish girl,' the mother said as she stole a glance at Raya. 'This girl, boy, whatever it is, was put here for a reason, like us, and that's her familiar.'

A cackle came from the edge of the room. What looked like a heap of rags came to life, a worn, old woman. She raised herself up with a stick. She only had one leg.

The others fell quiet. The woman hopped up to Raya. Rebecca picked up Oscar behind her mother's back and gave him a cuddle.

'Helen, help me, dear,' the old woman said, nodding towards the woman who had asked about Raya's hair.

Helen stepped forward and supported the old woman. 'Yes, Mother Clarke, of course.'

The old woman inspected Raya, lifted her short hair with an encrusted, crooked finger, sniffed at the nape of her neck, and touched her clothing. Meanwhile, Raya sized up the room and the situation. There was the one heavy wooden door she'd come through, and a barred window that looked out to the ante room. They both looked pretty impenetrable. There was a wooden cupboard door high off the ground, but no ladder in sight.

Raya quickly tried to scan the thoughts of her cellmates to see if there were any fellow witches. Not a single one. There were six women, well, five women and Rebecca, who seemed young for her age. Mother Clarke ran her hand down Raya's chest. Raya jumped back, alarmed.

'Aye, this one is a lass after all,' Mother Clarke said.

'What did you do? Kill a child? A cow, maybe?' Helen said.

Other voices asked questions all at once. The six of them circled Raya.

She spun a story from the parts already in place; being Dutch, said she was an orphan who had worked in a travelling menagerie.

'But why were you brought here?' Helen said.

'Oh, right,' Raya said. She told them she'd disguised herself as a lad in order to get work at a stable. She then told the story of the cook accusing her of killing her dog. This made sense to them. Raya then asked them why they were all here, grateful to turn the spotlight away from herself.

The six women told their stories of what they did and how they came to be here, in the Colchester Castle Keep, awaiting trial. What astounded Raya the most were not the bizarre things they were all accused of – killing children, feeding spirit animals, making a horse ill, killing a pig – all by sorcery and witchcraft, but that they believed they were guilty. All of these women lived on their own, or with their children. It sounded like they were all pretty poor.

Raya was about to try to explain that losing your temper, even momentarily wishing bad luck on someone, did not make any of these things happen.

'Don't even go there, Raya,' Oscar said. He was curled up on her lap now. The black dots on Oscar's back had become a solid line once again and had grown wider. He was regaining his strength, maybe she could do good.

'But this is so sad. These women admitting to crimes that weren't even possible.'

Raya and Oscar had chatted into what was likely the night. It was impossible to tell with no natural light filtering this far into the bowels of the castle. It turned out Raya had been lucky. The others, even the young Rebecca, all endured much longer Watching. Three days was typical. One had been 'swum' – tied to a chair and held under water, and because she didn't drown – well, that made her guilty.

'What about your lawyers? Don't you get one?' Raya asked. This resulted in a shower of guffaws, snorts, and questions. Luckily, she had the excuse of being a foreigner to explain all her odd ideas. The others settled into their spots on the floor and, to Raya's surprise, fell asleep. But she couldn't. She lay awake, cold and hungry.

Was Bryony ever coming?

Chapter 19

Conjure Me Home

Raya must have dozed off because she was startled awake by Hoy running a metal cup along the window grate. The sound of a key in the heavy wooden door was followed by Hoy coming in with a pot of pottage and a bunch of metal cups, although not enough for everyone. No one even said anything, used to taking turns. The food was gruesome, like thin, lukewarm porridge with a slight fishy taste, but hunger won. Hoy let them relieve themselves in the straw in the ante room, although not everyone had been able to wait. After a few minutes Hoy left them with the pottage and locked them back in.

About an hour later Hoy returned, calling out, 'Hello, ladies. I have a surprise for you.'

He unlocked the door and shoved another shackled woman inside. She fell to her knees. She wore a tattered version of the usual sombre getup, including one of those stupid bonnets. She tripped on her long skirt trying to get up. Helen helped her.

'Thank you. I don't mean to be any trouble,' the new woman said. Her voice was familiar – Bryony! Something between a gasp and sob came out of Raya.

Bryony put her arm around her. 'Rachel, my dear niece, so it is true – you are in here!' Bryony said. *Don't worry. Just play along,* she said telepathically.

Raya nodded while she caught her breath. 'Oh, Auntie Bryony…' but saying that made her cry harder.

The other women looked on; kind faces of different ages blurred through Raya's tears.

'Shh, it's OK, let it out. You've been through a terrible time,' Bryony said.

'Haven't we all,' Helen said.

Rebecca stepped up to Raya and Bryony, her eyes wide. 'You know each other?' she said.

'Are you daft or just deaf, girl? That's the girl's aunt,' her mother said.

'Come on, Anne, we're all on our last nerves in here

– the girl didn't mean anything,' Mother Clarke said.

Anne West smoothed her daughter's hair. 'You're right. I'm sorry, Rebecca,' Anne said, then she stiffened, looked Bryony up and down as much as the dim light would allow. 'So just how did you manage to get in here, the same place where your niece is? That sounds like some powerful witchcraft if you ask me.'

The women backed away from Bryony.

'Come now. Who in their right mind would try to get in here on purpose? Even if you wanted to save one of us, you certainly couldn't do it from in here,' Mother Clarke said.

The women murmured amongst themselves.

'You're right,' Bryony's voice cut through the buzz of gossip. 'I had been looking for Rachel, for a long time, and that led me here. But not how you think,' Bryony said. Oscar wound around Bryony's legs. She reached down and stroked him.

Rebecca sat down in front of Bryony as though she was about to hear a good campfire story. The others looked at her expectantly.

'Rachel's my brother's daughter. He moved…'

I've told them I'm Dutch, Raya interjected.

Bryony didn't miss a beat, '…to the Netherlands, worked in the docks in Amsterdam, married a woman there, and they had Rachel. He died of pneumonia when Rachel was about…' Bryony said telepathically to Raya, *'Come on, chime in every so often, like people do.'*

'I… I was ten when my dad died,' Raya said and felt a wave of sadness about losing her grandfather when she was much younger.

Bryony continued, 'Then a few years later, Rachel's mum came down with the plague. She only had a few days, but had a letter sent saying she'd arranged for Rachel to come back to England, to stay with me. She would get passage to Colchester.'

'But when I arrived at Colchester, I couldn't find my auntie. I waited around the port for a couple of days, but that was all the money I had for lodging, so I had no choice but to look for work,' Raya added.

'What happened, Auntie Bryony? Why weren't you there?' Rebecca said.

She's not YOUR Auntie, you little twerp, Raya thought, surprised at her stab of jealousy.

'My auntie tried, but something happened, she couldn't get there in time,' Raya said.

Bryony gave Raya a little squeeze around the shoulders. 'Yes, that's right. There were no carriages going that way for a while; everyone's horses kept getting taken for the war effort.'

'Where were you coming from?' Rebecca said.

Bryony looked at each woman in turn. 'Devon, I was coming from west Devon, not far from Cornwall,' Bryony said.

'That explains your accent,' Helen said.

'I never met anyone from Devon before,' Mother Clarke said.

Raya was impressed – maybe Bryony wasn't completely incompetent.

Bryony shook her head, looked woeful. 'By the time I finally got to Colchester, Rachel was gone and I had no way to find her. I left word at the dock, at inns, and with anyone else I could think of, but eventually I had to go home,' Bryony said.

'So how did you find me now?' Raya said.

'I got lucky. It must have been when you returned to Colchester after your stint with the menagerie, someone thought you fit the description and sent me a letter. That was about a month ago. I came as fast as I could,' Bryony said.

'But how'd you land in *here*?' Anne asked.

'Oh, that was by accident,' Bryony said. The women were rapt.

'I was rushing across the road and didn't see a rider on a horse. I don't know how I could have missed him, quite a sight in a cape with a wide-brimmed hat–' Bryony said.

'No, not the General!' Rebecca said.

'The one and only. His horse reared up, then hurt his leg when he came down. The caped man blew up like a cannon. He was sure I had bewitched his horse, because his horse shouldn't have hurt himself by simply rearing up.'

When Bryony finished her story, the women went back to their usual routine; sitting quietly, chatting, sleeping, and praying. After all the practice Raya had head-chatting with Oscar, she was able to do this with Bryony, too. Oscar lay on Bryony's lap, his colour returning.

Raya dragged her filthy sleeve across her eyes. *'We CAN get out of here – you can do this, right?'*

'Don't worry. I've done it before.'

This was nerve-wracking – her only hope of getting home was up to someone Raya had little faith in. She changed the subject, *'How is everybody back home? How's Pavel, Emma, Ian?'* She swallowed. *'Is Jake getting better?'*

'Everyone's fine. Jake's coming along, getting better all the time,' Bryony said.

Raya let out a huge sigh. She was about to ask some more questions about Jake – like if he could talk and read all right, if he was paralysed in any way – but thought better of it, wasn't sure she wanted to know.

'Raya, I don't mean to be harsh, but we've got to get down to work. It's not going to be easy, and well–'

'*I know, I know… time's running out.*'

Bryony sighed, '*Right, only two days to get home.*'

Chapter 20

Dracula Dance

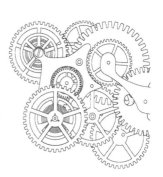

Hoy's metal cup raked across the window grate again the next morning. He lit the torches in the wall outside their cell. The women stretched and hobbled about in their leg irons, including Raya and Bryony.

They had tried to transport home all night. *'All transports are feeling-led. Get your head and heart there and your body follows. You flung yourself here accidentally, but it was still driven by your feeling like you deserved to be punished, and you realising you're a witch.'* Bryony paused, took a large breath which she regretted by the expression on her face, before continuing. *'So now, we imagine what it's like to be back home – let's try imagining being in the Cosmic, eh?'*

They had tried all night, leading each other in detailed

visualizations in an effort to help. They had finally dosed off while still trying.

'*Oh shit, we're still here,*' Raya said.

Bryony blinked, looked around. '*I don't understand why this isn't working.*'

'*We still have a couple of days, right?*' Raya, said unnerved by Bryony's tone.

'*Well, technically. But we'll be taken to the assizes this afternoon for the trial tomorrow, and the hang–*'

'*I get it, I get it,*' Raya said.

Bryony was distracted, thinking aloud, '*I need to contact IHQ – get help. Something's wrong.*'

'*What? Was I doing something wrong?*' Raya said, but Bryony had stepped away.

Hoy had come in and was handing out the usual slop. Raya had been hungry for days, the rations were so meagre. She forced a couple of gulps of the disgusting pottage then put the cup in Bryony's hand. Bryony, trying hard to transmit to IHQ, failed to grip it. Raya managed to catch it before it hit the floor. Hoy saw this and gave Raya another one of his backhands for almost wasting valuable food.

'There'll be none for you next time, since you see fit to throw it around,' Hoy said, then laughed as though this was an inside joke.

'Today, you wretches are off to Chelmsford. Each of

you will get a bill for your stay, to be paid if you live or not,' he said, and laughed again.

The women were quiet. Rebecca cried to her mother. No one asked anything about Bryony huddled in a corner, even when she started muttering. The others must have assumed she was praying for her soul as they prayed for theirs. Through the murmurings, Raya heard pleas for forgiveness, and begging to be spared the fires of hell.

Rebecca, bored with praying, tried to play with Oscar. She wiggled a bit of straw in front of his face.

'*Oh, how humiliating,*' Oscar groaned.

'*Come on. Be nice to the poor girl. She doesn't have long…*' Raya choked on the words. '*…like the rest of us.*' A sob blurted out of her, there was no holding it back now. It looked like she was right – that Bryony wasn't up to the task. She knew it was her own doing, her being here, but was it her fault? All that stuff people explained about new witches having power surges, like stomping on the accelerator, blah, blah. *Oh, who cares about all that – I just want to live. I mean I haven't done anything yet. Haven't had a real boyfriend. Never driven a car. I'll never get to have my own flat.* Her sobs were free and unfettered. *And now I'll have my last days in this disgusting stink-hole.*

* * *

Faint footsteps got louder. There were two sets, and two voices. The key clanked in the lock on the outer door, and then in the cell door. There was a collective gasp at the silhouette of Matthew Hopkins, the Witchfinder General.

Raya snatched Oscar from the floor. The black colour ebbed and flowed as she clutched him to her.

'Bryony,' Raya called out in head talk. The grown-up witch followed Raya's gaze towards the cat in her arms.

She startled at seeing Matthew Hopkins, then her jaw set, and even though her eyes were open, you could tell her mind was elsewhere, probably trying to get them out of there.

Hopkins strolled into the cell as though he was walking onto a stage. Hoy, much larger than Hopkins, was a funny sight, simpering, holding a lantern above Hopkins with every step. At least Hopkins didn't have that dumb dog with him. He nodded to the huddled, filthy group. Some continued to murmur prayers, others whimpered or pleaded. Rebecca held onto her mother, rocking back and forth on her feet.

Raya stepped closer to Bryony, who placed a hand on the cat. The black stripe down his back repeatedly got thicker then thinner. It looked like Hopkins and Bryony were evenly matched.

The young witch turned away and closed her arms around Oscar. He gave a small squeak.

'Sorry,' Raya said aloud.

'Silence,' Hopkins bellowed. He twirled on his heels making an arc with his idiotic cape. He stopped when he saw Raya.

'Aye, I remember you, you arrogant little witch.' He stepped close to Raya and jabbed a finger at her without touching her. 'There is another charge against you now.'

'Whatever,' Raya said.

Hopkins licked his finger and paged through the sheaf of papers he'd held under his arm. He stopped and cleared his throat.

'Rachel Hollingsworth, approximate age fourteen, of unknown history is hereby accused of: killing the Good Wife Robertson's dog when denied a cup of her favourite witch's brew, and…' Hopkins paused for dramatic effect, '…of cursing the Good Mother Atkinson when she emptied her chamber pot, and thereby ruining her ale, robbing her of one week's earnings.'

Raya burst out laughing. 'You're all nuts, you know that?'

Rebecca clapped her hands and laughed, too.

Bryony and Anne West scrambled to quiet the girls. Hopkins acted as though he didn't hear a thing. He turned to the first page of papers, cleared his throat then proclaimed: 'I hereby summon the following persons to be tried tomorrow on the seventeenth of July this twenty-first year of His Royal Highness, King Charles's reign, at the Chelmsford Assizes.' Hopkins then read out the name of each woman and the accusations against them – injuring or killing people or animals, thievery or ruining goods – all by 'sorcery and witchcraft'. The praying and crying got louder.

Rebecca said over and over, 'You're all nuts, you're all nuts,' clapping, giggling and spinning in circles. Anyone could see Rebecca was losing it.

'Stop!' Hopkins said. Hoy's lantern swung above him. Dracula shadows danced on the walls. But Rebecca was in her own world now, singing, talking to herself, telling herself everything was going to be all right. Her mother stepped between Hopkins and Rebecca and put her arms around the frantic child.

'That's quite enough!' Hopkins bellowed to Hoy. Hoy kicked Anne West's feet out from under her and dragged the shackled and flailing Rebecca out of the cell. Anne threw herself at Hopkins.

'Take me instead. I BEG you. She's just a girl, she doesn't know what she does.' Hoy kicked Anne, launching her away from Hopkins, who turned with another flourish and left.

Raya's fear mushroomed, became focused and sharp. This was no game, no TV show. On top of all that, she felt responsible, at least partially, for starting Rebecca off. Bryony went straight back into trying to conjure them home. The other women prayed incessantly, their voices blending into one mournful undulation. Raya hugged Oscar.

* * *

The keys clinked in the outer and inner doors again and Hoy appeared with another prison guard, but no sign of Hopkins or Rebecca.

'Where's my daughter, you monster?' Anne West was almost spitting. But Hoy paid her no mind. Instead, he worked with the other guard unshackling the women's leg irons. Hoy stood and glared at Anne.

'Master Hopkins got the truth out of that girl – it is you who is the witch, not that simple lass. Your daughter will not be tried now, but will testify against you,' Hoy said to Anne, and spat onto the already sodden straw.

Chapter 21
Town Fete

Hoy and the other guard immediately herded the women out of the cell. Some limped, others rubbed their sore and bloody ankles. Anne West sobbed openly. Bryony nudged Raya lost in thought, clutching Oscar. Her heart beat like a drum, she was in a cold sweat; faced with Rebecca having to testify against her mother, condemning her to death, in order to win her own freedom made her want to vomit. *Wait – I remember that now from school. Rebecca DOES testify, and Anne is…*

Was this really that much different than when she had to tell the social services about all the crazy stuff her mother did? It felt like such a betrayal – twice – once for telling them, and once for failing to keep her mother safe to begin with. All the adults kept reassuring her that it wasn't her job to keep her mother well, and that it was for both of their goods that she needed to tell people what had been going on. It sure didn't feel like it. And the treatment didn't really work, her mother could never stick with it, and Raya never lived with her mother properly again.

'Bryony?'

'Hmm?'

'You know, I had to testify against my mother–'

Bryony hugged the filthy girl around her shoulders. 'No, Raya. That WAS different. Listen to me – it really, really was.'

Big tears dropped to the stone floor as she walked on.

Hoy took up the rear of the group of sad women, taking joy in shoving them up the stone steps and through the cold hallways. The halls widened and the ceilings got higher. The stench of human waste weakened, replaced by a more general dankness. Raya recognized the route. They awkwardly spilled out of the huge archway, squinting, shading their eyes from the light, clattering onto the wooden bridge over the fetid moat. Even sunlight filtered through clouds on this overcast day blinded these poor souls, some of whom had not seen natural light for months.

They followed another group of prisoners, some of them men, across the bridge. Three open wooden wagons waited. Raya recognized the driver who had taken her to and from that weird ordeal – the Watching. She found it odd that she felt almost fond of this driver and tried to get onto his wagon. Recognition flashed across his face.

'Get along now. Onto the next wagon with you – this one is full,' he said.

Raya looked at the half-empty wagon and started to get on anyway, but Bryony pulled her away.

'Leave him, Raya. He can't bear to bring you where we're going. Don't you understand?'

Raya was shoved onto the second wagon and jammed against other prisoners. Oscar was a warm mass in her lap, his heart giving slow, weak beats. Bryony was wedged next to her. Hoy clambered in next to the driver of the first cart and they were off.

The ride was a bone-jarring, teeth-clattering three hours. Finally, the buildings became more frequent and the road became cobbled. In town, people shook their fists, spat, swore, and called them names. The wagons rode into the market square. The driver of the first one tied up his horses and spoke to the other drivers before marching off in the direction of a stone building at the end of the square. Throughout the town centre, people were setting up stalls, carting bottles, carrying boxes and baskets of freshly baked pies and other food. Raya's empty stomach lurched awake and hollered. Carpenters hammered away at a couple of wooden structures. She elbowed Bryony.

'What's all this?' Bryony started to answer but was interrupted by Rebecca's mother, Anne.

'Aye, this is for us,' Anne said, giving a rueful laugh that turned into a wheezing cough. 'Come now, surely this can't be your first hanging.' Anne gestured with her head towards the busy square. 'These people will make more money tomorrow than they have in the last three months. They will feed the hungry crowds, and slake their thirst, and sell them trinkets to remember the show...'

'Souvenirs?' Raya said. 'That's disgusting.'

Anne was consumed again by the terrible cough, but not so much so that it kept her from pointing to one of the wooden structures the men were building in the centre of the square.

Raya looked at Bryony.

'Gallows,' Bryony said.

* * *

The first driver returned and the prisoners were herded off the wagons into a dilapidated building. They were hustled into a cramped, dank room on the ground floor. The women took turns looking out the small grated window. The commotion and noise increased as day turned into night. People amassed in the square. Some even camped out.

Bryony stood with her eyes closed, speaking in hushed tones. Raya wanted to contact IHQ herself, if for no other reason than to say goodbye. She missed them. She wished more than anything to apologize to Jake.

The night dragged on inside the cell, but outside was a party. People talked and laughed, some drunk and noisy. Others worked on their stalls for the next day. Raya thought about her life – what she would have done differently, what she missed out on, like proper sex and even finishing school. But mostly it was the small things she thought about: tasting more of Emma's new muffins; learning cool stuff from Pavel; even hanging out with Jake. These were the moments she would miss the most. She even thought about Angie. She would do anything for one of her DVD nights. Part of her couldn't believe they might die and the other part of her tasted terror with no end.

She hadn't known how intense hunger could be. She quickly vowed to give food to every down-and-out she'd come across, should she ever get home, even if she thought they were really after money for drink or drugs.

'Oscar, I hereby solemnly swear to give food to every homeless person I see from here on – you are my witness,' she told the cat telepathically.

'*Nice one, kid.*' Oscar opened one eye, waking from another nap and looked at her.

Raya gasped and squeezed the cat. '*Are we going to get out of this?*'

'*Beats me. Where are we? Catch me up,*' Oscar said and sat up.

'*They brought us from the Colchester Castle Gaol to Chelmsford, to something called the assizes. That must be what they called the court back in those days,*' Raya told Oscar, but he seemed distracted. His nose and whiskers were going.

'*Hey. You listening, or what?*' Raya said.

'*What? No. I mean yes, I am listening. I just could have sworn I smelled kebab,*' Oscar said.

Chapter 22
Silent Puppets

A few hours after the cruelly early British summer sunrise, church bells rang and someone made long sounds on something that sounded like a trumpet. Raya pushed in with the women at the small window. Bryony remained in the corner, lost in her work.

Outside, there was a parade of sorts. In contrast to the usual sea of drab, there were men on horseback with metal armour on their chests and helmets. Others marched, carrying long spears. One of these guys carried a colourful flag, nothing Raya recognized. The crowd cheered their appreciation; what for, she didn't know. Then she saw two men behind the spear and flag men, also on horseback, one behind the other. It seemed the second was the important one as his outfit was fancier, and because of the way he nodded to people.

Mr Important had long hair and a moustache that swooped up, like a permanent smile above his mouth. He wore red knee-length trousers and a jacket, an extra-fancy metal armour chest thing, an amazing large brimmed black hat with feathers, and tall boots.

'*Let me see,*' Oscar urged. Raya held him up to the window.

'*Who is that guy?*' Raya asked.

'*Must be Robert Rich, the second Earl of Warwick.*' Oscar gestured with his head to Mr Important. '*He's here to preside over the trials.*'

Raya looked out the window with Oscar. The Earl of Warwick dismounted along with the second guy, clearly his helper. They walked into a church at the end of the square. The throng dispersed and went back to enjoying the fete.

The next hours were excruciating. They were given no food, only disgusting water that would likely kill them if they lasted long enough. Their fear formed a stupefying fog in the cell. Raya's stomach taunted again, bringing her thoughts back to kebab. She shook those away too and walked over to Bryony.

She squatted down next to the grown-up witch and touched her shoulder. Bryony startled, opened her eyes – pools of pure fear.

'*I'm trying, Raya. I don't understand, IHQ doesn't understand. I've time travelled plenty and...*' Bryony looked away. *'...all my Time Travel Retrievals have been successful.'*

'*So far,*' Raya added. She could see Bryony was doing her best – but a growing anger pulsed at her core. Yeah, she knew it was her fault she was here, but kids make mistakes, right? And adults are supposed to help sort them out. This would be yet one more grown-up who let her down, whose problems or weaknesses, or dying inconveniently, screwed up her life. And she was bloody sick of it.

Two men burst through the door. One held a document and read out a list of names including Raya, Bryony, Anne West, and the old woman with one leg, Elizabeth Clarke. They shuffled out of the cell and up the stairs, helping Mother Clarke. As they passed a window on the landing, the onlookers roared outside. You would have thought it was a football match. Her anger doubled. Up a few more steps and a couple of turns and an official sort of man in another funny outfit opened a large wooden door to the courtroom.

The women slunk in with Raya, who held Oscar. It wasn't like the courtrooms she'd seen on TV. There was a buzz of talk and laughter from the people in the rows at the back. Some had bread and cheese spread on cloths on their laps with bottles at their feet.

'Jeez, our lives are on the line, and they're having a fucking picnic? Like it's the best show they've seen all year!' Raya said to Oscar.

'All year? Try all decade,' he said.

The onlookers jeered and spat. The noise increased, and finally the Earl, who was sitting at a long table in the front, banged a wooden gavel and told the noisy crowd off, which worked briefly. At the Earl's side were six men, all in ornate outfits, although not as nice as the Earl's.

The guard led the prisoners to a pen. Raya looked over her shoulder at the audience. She caught a glimpse of Matthew Hopkins, Witchfinder Jerk General. She shuddered. She opened her arms slightly and saw the black stripe on Oscar's back narrow in front of her eyes.

'Oscar, hold on!' He didn't respond, only buried his head under her arm. Raya reached for Bryony's hand and placed it on Oscar. His black stripe thickened. *'Oscar, even if we don't make it, you can – just run for it after we're gone.'* The gavel sounded again and there was a brief silence.

One of the two men seated in front of the prisoners walked over to a stand near the Earl's table and called on each of the women prisoners to swear them in and read them their charges. One by one, they all pleaded 'not guilty'. Raya had to nudge Bryony quite hard to get her out of her mind work. She put up her right hand and swore to tell only the truth. The clerk read the charges. A hush went through the crowd.

'And how do you plead?' the court official asked Bryony.

'Not guilty, sir,' Bryony said. The crowd roared like their favourite team made a goal. They ate their picnic lunches, booed and hissed, drank their ale. The throng outside pressed at the windows, yelled, shook their fists, wishing them all swift trips to hell.

* * *

One of the two men seated in front of the prisoners called the witnesses against Anne West: Matthew Hopkins and Rebecca West, daughter of Anne. The crowd gasped. Raya twisted around to see. The girl looked like a zombie as she approached the bench, eyes glassy. The hair on Raya's neck stood on end and cold sweat trickled down her back. She cried for Rebecca, she cried for herself.

Rebecca answered the questions robotically, 'Yes, I saw my mother convening with other witches. Yes, I saw her lay with the Devil. Yes, I heard my mother swear allegiance to Satan, himself.'

The crowd whooped, cheered, booed and yelled, despite the Earl's repeated admonishments.

Anne hung her head. She recanted her prior confession, but it made no difference. Other witnesses testified, describing how Anne had caused the death of a boy and a pig (*a pig!*) by wishing it, after she argued with someone. Others testified about her familiars, which sounded like ordinary pets. Finally, the Earl asked the jury for their verdict.

'We of the jury of the Chelmsford Assizes,' the foreman declared, 'find Anne West *culpabilis* of Witchcraft and Sorcery, to be sentenced by suspension by the neck until dead.' The words hung for a moment before the cheers crescendoed to a roar. Rebecca crumpled to a heap, sobbing, screaming and wailing. Others tried to calm her, to no avail. Raya trembled. This was beyond anything she could have imagined.

Two more women were tried, then Bryony. Raya felt like she was watching something on television – it seemed unreal. Then the sounds became distorted, or she heard nothing at all, people's mouths moving like silent puppets.

Raya was next. She placed Oscar in Bryony's lap. Matthew Hopkins testified against her, of course, wagging his finger and screwing up his face. Hopkins ranted, although Raya couldn't hear a thing by that time; creepy cartoon music in her imagination drowned out all else. She read the lips of the jury foreman when he read out her sentence – 'suspension by the neck until dead.' The Earl smashed down the gavel.

* * *

As Raya walked through the courtroom towards the gallows, her numbness was chased out by exquisite awareness. She heard every strand of conversation, smelled the cheese and yeasty bread of the court watchers, felt the change in temperature as they left the courtroom for the cooler hallway. The dappled light through the window was beautiful. The onlookers outside sounded like a murder of crows.

The sweet sting of sun outside made her smile. Then she saw them – the first three condemned lurched and gagged as they swung from the gallows. Relatives begged for permission to tug on them to put them out of their misery, but witches were denied this last humanity. The sounds of the world blended into a buzz. Finally, the bodies hung limp and were removed. Raya couldn't feel her legs as she was marched up the gallows' steps. She wanted to let go of Oscar, but she couldn't – desperate to feel warmth and fur and friendship for as long as possible. *I'll let go of him soon enough.* They slipped the noose around Bryony, next to her; she, faced forward, eyes open but unreadable.

The noose was slipped around Raya. Then her empty stomach spoke up, demanded her attention. She smiled at her memory of meeting Pavel and watching him eat that kebab. She could hear the traffic, feel the cooling evening, and boy did that food smell wonderful. That would be one of the regrets of her short life, never getting one of those kebabs. Raya laughed. Laughed at the ordinariness of hunger – of life's persistence in spite of everything. The precious world was blotted out with swirling colours. They started to pulse to faint music. She strained to hear it – a weird old song her nan used to like. The hangman got his command. Everything went black.

Chapter 23
Giving Zakat

The kebab smelled amazing. A stout, bearded man in a long green coat and turban poked sizzling meat on a grill at a kiosk. It took all of Raya's strength not to grab the kebab and wolf it down. She must have been staring, because the kebab seller elbowed his friend and nodded towards her. The two men exchanged what seemed like banter although she couldn't understand the language.

'Raya? You OK?' Bryony said. Raya widened her gaze. They were on a cobbled pavement in front of an archway with a busy market beyond. People bustled about, all in long, colourful outfits. The women were veiled and most of them wore funky little hats that sat off centre, like cool new fascinators. *Have to look for one of those,* she thought. Then a tsunami of joy and relief crashed over her.

'Bryony, we made it! We're back in London!' Raya cheered. She put the woozy cat down and literally jumped for joy. 'You did it. You saved us!' The girl was as surprised as she was thrilled. She hugged the air out of Bryony, who looked less enthused.

'I'm not so sure we're...'

'I can't wait to have a shower and clean clothes. Won't that be heaven? But wow, doesn't that kebab smell great?' She laughed and dug in the pocket of her filthy jeans and extracted the pound coin the old man walking the dog had given her what seemed like ages ago. She'd been holding onto it for good luck.

'Excuse me, sir, and I know this is an odd thing to ask, but my auntie and I have had a bit of bad luck, and we lost our money, but I'd... we'd be ever so grateful if you might find it in your heart to give us whatever you could for this pound. I'll come back tomorrow and pay you the rest–'

The kebab man put his hand up to stop her and had a rapid conversation with the customer.

'Raya,' said Bryony. 'This definitely isn't–'

'I wish I knew what they were saying,' Raya said.

The men argued back and forth, gesturing towards the odd threesome. Oscar settled against the kiosk and started what would need to be a heroic tongue bath. Then,

Raya started understanding a few words here and there. The kebab seller elbowed the customer and said something about 'Come on, Musta. Why don't you give your…' Weird. Then weirder, more and more words became clear. They must have been speaking English all along.

Grateful to be back with regular people, Raya interrupted their ribbing each other. 'I really will bring more money tomorrow. Please! You have no idea how hungry we are.'

The men looked at her, each other, and shrugged. Funny. Maybe it was her accent. She stepped closer, offered the coin. The kebab seller examined it, shook his head, and returned it.

The customer, Musta, tore off a corner of his kebab and tossed it to Oscar, who gulped it down. A queue had formed.

'All right, all right.' The kebab seller sighed. 'I will do the right thing by these poor women.'

The kebab seller quickly made two kebabs and handed them to Raya.

'One for you and one for your auntie,' he said, nodding towards Bryony who was a few steps away, looking around.

The customers bantered with the seller. Raya burst into tears of happiness while thanking him profusely.

'That's OK,' the kebab seller said and he tossed Oscar a few more scraps. 'Let him eat, too. Your lovely cat is welcome at my kiosk any time – keep away the rats,' the seller said then turned back to his customers.

Raya and Bryony settled against the outer wall of the archway and sank into their food. Raya's stomach jumped at the sudden rich influx. Something told her this might not be such a good idea, gobbling down a luscious kebab in one go after starving for over a week, but she couldn't stop herself. After they finished they sat in silence and watched the passing parade of people mostly going in or out of the market, some carrying things, others pushing carts, some leading animals, all wearing a variety of long, colourful clothing. Oscar sauntered over, licking his lips. The stripe on his back was thicker again. Maybe all this back and forth for the poor cat would be over for good. Raya crouched down and stroked him.

'Raya?' Bryony interrupted the girl-cat moment. 'Can you understand what people are saying?'

'I didn't at first, but it kind of came on. Not every word. Must have got used to their accents, I guess. Why, can't you?' Raya said.

Bryony looked right at Raya, in a way that made her nervous.

'What's the matter?' she said.

Bryony didn't answer but asked another question. 'Raya, tell me what you were thinking, what was going on in your head, right before we landed here.'

Raya laughed. 'He started it. That cat put the idea of kebab in my head, thought he could smell it.'

'I'm right here, you know,' Oscar said. The women ignored him.

Bryony stood up and took a few deep breaths. She looked worn out, frustrated, maybe even mad.

'Come on – relax, already. We're home and alive!'

Bryony looked around carefully then spoke slowly, methodically, 'Raya, we're NOT home – look around. Does this look like the twenty-first century London to you?' she snapped.

Raya wiped her mouth with her filthy sleeve and stood up. 'Don't get mad at me. I didn't do anything wrong. You're the time travel expert, right?'

Bryony didn't answer, pursed her lips and studied their surroundings. A couple of camels laden with goods were led past and through the gate. The market beyond beckoned. 'I'll be right inside there, OK? Come get me when you're ready,' Raya said and wandered off.

Chapter 24

Coming Clean

Raya wove through the swarm in the market, more crowded than Oxford Street on Boxing Day – men, women and children, in billowing trousers, jewel-dotted dresses, embroidered coats, scarves laced with gold, and white turbaned heads like so many seabirds bobbing on the surface. Donkeys carrying goods wove their way behind their drivers.

Raya slowed down, almost to a stop, as though the sumptuous kaleidoscope of the market made the air itself thick. Stalls lined the cobbled street, stuffed with rows and piles of all sorts of glorious things: colourful fabric; strings of glass lanterns hung like oversized gems; rugs unfurled for display, others rolled in stacks; metal pots; carved jugs; some sort of pipe contraptions; clothing; jewellery;

knives; rifles; even watches. Shopkeepers sat in front of their stalls, either on low stools or plush cushions. Some sipped from small cups, some chatted with other sellers or customers, although none of them seemed fussed about selling things.

Customers, both men and women meandered in and out of the shops. Raya noticed some women had gorgeous, soft leather, yellow shoes. She wondered where they got those. A man wandered around with a fancy metal jug on a leather strap around his back and a tray of small cups around his neck. He stopped every so often and sold a cup of whatever it was. The market had a perfume of its own; a blend of wool, wood and spices. She inhaled deeply.

Bryony and Oscar caught up with her. 'I'm sorry I snapped,' Bryony offered. Raya didn't want a whole conversation right now. She walked on to the next stall, fingered the luxurious stack of folded dresses. She wanted to just be. Just be a teenage girl in this amazing mall. She didn't want to think about mind-bending things like time travel, being a witch, or how to escape death. She shuddered.

Bryony followed her, spoke to her back. 'Raya, you're right – I'm upset I couldn't save us…. More than upset. Mortified and well, stymied. But never mind about all that.' She took Raya by her slim shoulders and turned her around to face her. 'You saved us. I know it was you

because of the kebab connection, and with your understanding the language – that cinches it – it's called "time
traveller's advantage".'

'Whatever,' was all Raya gave her and returned to her
browsing.

Bryony grabbed her by the wrist. Raya wriggled to get
away, then gave in with a huff and a glare. 'What? What
do you want me to say?'

'*Oo, I like a good cat fight – especially when it doesn't
involve me,*' Oscar said.

'*Shut up!*' Bryony and Raya said simultaneously. A
hairline crack formed in the ice between them. Raya
wished she could pop her headphones in and listen to
her music good and loud, watch a bad film – anything
to blot out whatever complicated truth she could feel
coming. She was exhausted beyond comprehension. She
touched her neck where the noose had been less than an
hour ago and looked around wherever and whenever this
wonderful place was.

'We're in Istanbul – this is the Grand Bazaar. I know
because I've been here, but a few hundred years later, on
holiday,' Bryony interjected, a smile creasing lines around
her eyes Raya hadn't noticed before.

'Agh! Stop eavesdropping on my thoughts – I just need
some space!'

Oscar sat at their feet watching them, his tail twitching. People swarmed by, taking no notice. *'OK you two. It's been great. Well actually, it hasn't, but I've done my bit. And from what I've seen with that nice kebab man, the Turkish are really nice to animals. So, bye you guys.'* He trotted away from the woman and girl. *'Have a nice life,'* he called out over his shoulder as he wove amongst the sea of legs, and was gone.

Bryony looked panicked. 'We've GOT to go get him. Come on.' She darted after him.

'Does it really matter?' Raya said to Bryony's back as she disappeared into the crowd. Maybe they should let Oscar have his own life – it's what he wanted all along, and being with them certainly hadn't done him any good.

She sauntered along the market, keeping her eye out for those luscious yellow shoes, and those cheeky fascinators when she saw Bryony stopped ahead. As Raya walked towards her, she started to feel heavy, tired. Maybe Oscar was right. Maybe they should all go their separate ways now. After all, if it was she who saved them and not Bryony, then maybe Bryony would only hold them back, or even hurt their chances of anything good.

Raya caught up to Bryony at an intersection with a square stone fountain in the centre. People collected water in jugs, washed their hands and feet. Bryony was holding

Oscar in a tight grip – he looked less than thrilled. She was gesturing and pantomiming to three shopkeepers who seemed to be upset or concerned on her behalf. She looked haggard.

Another messed up grown-up in my life, Raya was careful to lock-down her thoughts this time. She didn't hate her, didn't want to hurt her feelings, but didn't want the responsibility of trying to help her as well. Maybe it was time to strike out on her own again. That had been her plan all along, too.

'I am sorry. I'll get proper clothing as soon as I can,' Bryony said to the shopkeepers, even though they couldn't understand her – such was the human inclination to try to communicate. They looked a combination of nosey, curious, and concerned, but not menacing. They wore long coats, white baggy trousers, and turbans. One stroked his beard. They obviously didn't understand Bryony. They gestured and spoke over each other. Raya figured it wouldn't hurt to help with translation.

'They're worried you're not wearing a veil and that your head is uncovered. One of them says you're likely Christian and maybe even foreign, and should be excused, at least for now,' Raya continued summarizing for Bryony although it was hard to tease apart who said what because the men talked at the same time. One of them argued that Bryony

needed to cover her 'private parts', which made the other two laugh. Another retorted that this may explain the first guy's lack of luck with women. Then the first man said, 'What could be more private than a person's face – giving away her emotions at all times?' This made the other two stroke their beards and look thoughtful.

A fourth man walked up to the little group and joined them. It was Musta from the kebab stand. Raya smiled. He nodded to Bryony and Raya. The three men already knew him, which made for cacophonous greetings. Like water around rocks, people streamed around them as though this sort of interaction, noisy and involving foreigners, was nothing unusual.

'Don't listen to these gibbering fools,' Musta said to Bryony and Raya.

Oscar had wriggled out of Bryony's grasp and was weaving figures of eight around Musta's legs. Musta reached down and stroked the cat while continuing to debate with his friends. After another few minutes of enthusiastic discussion about philosophy, religion, politics, and coffee (coffee?), they agreed on a plan. Musta would take the two women to another friend's shop where they sold women's clothing. Surely that friend could give his zakat, which Raya now understood meant charity. After they got their new clean clothing (but before they put it on), Musta would bring them to the hammam, the baths, because one thing they could all agree on was these two stank. Bryony laughed when Raya translated that part. Raya decided to stick around a little longer – the baths and new clothes sounded all right.

Musta strode down one of the crossroads away from the fountain. Raya, Bryony, and Oscar followed him – he seemed to really like this Musta. Raya rubbernecked as they turned through more, crowded market streets, each street lined with mostly one sort of good.

After a few more turns, they stopped in front of a stall overflowing with women's clothing. An older man with a grey beard sat on a wooden stool in front of the shop. He wore a long mustard-coloured cloak with embroidered lapels, a leather belt gathered under his generous belly, and leather shoes embossed with gold. His white turban had a black cord running through it.

'Well hello, my good friend,' he said as he leveraged himself up with a carved walking stick inlaid with mother of pearl and silver. He nodded towards the women, 'I can see you brought me two customers. They look like they have a lot of money to spend,' he said and winked.

'*Wow these people are really kind,*' Raya said.

'*Nice for a change, isn't it,*' Bryony replied. Raya could see Bryony was relieved that she was sticking around.

Maybe she hadn't locked down her thoughts so well after all – or maybe it had been all over her face.

'These women barely escaped with their lives – look at them, Tahir,' Musta told his friend the shopkeeper.

As Tahir looked at the two women, great sadness washed across his face. Raya thought he might cry. 'Who would do this? And this young one, not much more than a child – chopping off her hair like that?'

Oscar jumped on a pile of folded scarves and started to settle in for a nap.

'I thought you were striking out on your own, mate?' Raya intoned.

'Just checking out my options.'

Bryony swooped him up of the clean clothing and held him.

'Don't worry. I don't mind, but Melek might,' Tahir said. Then, what had looked like a poorly folded, fluffy white scarf at the end of the table came alive – a cat. She stretched and meandered up to Tahir, rubbing her head against his hand. The Turkish certainly did seem to like their pets.

'Please, let them choose anything they like,' Tahir said to Musta as he bustled about the shop, agile for a man of his size.

Tahir held up different long dresses for Bryony and Raya. They were somewhere between a coat and a dress.

Raya startled, opened her mouth at his generosity but didn't say anything, remembering she couldn't speak the language. Tahir seemed to take this as disapproval of his initial offerings and looked a little hurt.

Bryony tried pantomiming an apology.

Tahir shrugged and pulled out more dresses for them to consider. Bryony agreed to a dark cranberry one and pantomimed a big thank you. Tahir held out a deep teal one and an orange one.

Raya smiled and pointed to the teal-blue dress. Tahir was pleased, then shuffled sideways between the crowded table and shelves to another part of the shop where he gathered some other things. He bundled everything together, tied it in string and handed it to Musta.

'The jinn should be pleased with me tonight, maybe even for the rest of the week,' Tahir said to Musta. Sweat glistened on his brow.

'Gin?' What is he talking about?' Raya said.

'No, jinn, with a 'j' – they're a type of spirit being in the Islamic world. People leave food for them at night, to appease them, so these jinn don't make any trouble,' Bryony said.

Musta gestured for them follow him out of the shop. Bryony and then Raya pantomimed their thanks to Tahir, who smiled and told them to stop by anytime. Bryony nudged Raya and Oscar to follow Musta.

'*You know, I'd actually like a warm bath, too. Don't want to have to lick all this disgusting old English grime off me,*' Oscar said.

Raya raised an eyebrow, '*Really?*'

Bryony scooped the cat up and he climbed onto her shoulders. 'Good thinking, Oscar. Glad to have you along,' Bryony said and gave Raya a look to say they should encourage the cat to stick around.

Musta barrelled ahead as they retraced their steps through the market, back through the arch they'd first entered. The street was lined with wooden buildings, most no more than two storeys. They followed as he took a couple of turns.

They joined Musta across the street in front of a grand, domed, stone building. He was talking to a woman at the entrance. He gave the parcel of clothes to her while explaining Bryony and Raya's predicament and great need of a full going over. Women brushed by, going in and out, some alone, others in small groups. Some had attendants who carried boxes and bundles. Warmth, steam and perfume rolled out from inside. The woman who had been speaking to Musta gestured for Bryony and Raya to enter. Bryony pointed to Oscar and made a questioning expression on her face.

'Of course, pets are welcome. Everyone knows that,' the woman said.

'*What did I tell ya?*' Oscar said.

Raya was so drawn into this place she had already stepped inside. '*Definitely worth sticking around for, this.*' It was a huge room. The high ceiling had intricate designs. There were women everywhere, all wrapped in plain cloth, chatting as they poured water on themselves from fountains. It was warm, humid and misty. Some women had the water poured over them by other, topless women. Raya automatically put her arm across her own chest.

The woman who brought them in took her veil off. Another one of these topless women joined her. *Don't look, don't look*, Raya tried to act nonchalant and relaxed. The two women and Bryony laughed. Bryony was stepping out of her clothes. *Oh no. Naked with your social worker – maybe even weirder than time travel!*

The two women workers tugged at Raya's filthy clothes until she gave in. The topless one made a face at the state of them before walking off with the garments. The first woman gave them each one of the thin cloth wraps and a pair of odd wooden slippers. Some sort of clog with two rectangles of wood on the bottoms. Maybe these were their idea of platform shoes.

The first woman realised only Raya understood them, so told her that she and Bryony should rinse themselves thoroughly, stressing the thoroughly part, with the hot and cold running water from the fountains. She was already walking away when Raya called after her, 'What about our clothes?' but the woman had no idea Raya was talking to her.

'I wish they could understand me,' Raya said to Bryony as they found a place at a fountain and started splashing themselves.

'That should happen, too. Usually takes a little longer. Oh, that feels so good. I am so tired of being filthy,' Bryony said.

'Yeah, me too.'

'Oo, this marble is heated,' Oscar said as he jumped up on top of one of the fountains, closing his eyes in the warm spray misting over him. Raya made a face at the oddly water loving cat.

'We need him,' Bryony whispered, covered by the sounds of water and women's voices bouncing against polished stone.

Women of all ages, shapes, and sizes splashed themselves with water and chatted. A few young ones paraded around as though they were showing off.

'The cat? What for?' Raya asked as she let hot water from a fountain pummelled her shoulders.

Bryony leaned against the fountain and closed her eyes. 'With his microchip, he helps us transmit back to headquarters – like a Wi-Fi booster. And we'll need their help to get back.'

Just then, the topless woman who had taken their horrid clothes came over and told them it was time to go to the next room.

Chapter 25

Embarrassment Red

Raya and Bryony clomped on their wooden clogs through the archway into the second room, a vast octagon. Beams of light, like gentle blue-tinged spotlights, shined from a circle of skylights in the domed ceiling high above their heads. Steam made the whole thing look soft. Women were lying on a large stone platform in the centre of the room, right under the shafts of light. Attendants and servants worked on the women, scrubbing, kneading, flipping them over and doing it all over again, like so many blobs of dough.

Oscar had followed them in. He hunched by their feet, ears flat against his head.

'Maybe this is too much moisture for me after all.' His tail twitched and he eyed the door.

Bryony sat on the edge of the stone platform and patted the space beside her. *'Come on, I've seen you take a warm bath at home.'*

'That's true.' He could hardly keep his eyes open, he looked so tired, but managed to jump up. There was a familiarity between them Raya hadn't noticed before. Bryony scratched him under his chin.

Raya looked around for an empty spot on the marble slab. Bryony lay face down on hers. Children played and larked about nearby. There was a collective hum from the conversations, punctuated by laughter that ricocheted against the marble surfaces.

Some of the attendants appeared to be private servants. Women were getting waxed and plucked, their hair dyed. This was civilized. One of the attendants started working on Bryony, soaping her up all over her back.

An attendant not much older than Raya encouraged her onto a space as a woman vacated it. The young woman started soaping Raya's back when Oscar jumped up next to her. The attendant asked Raya if she wanted them to wash the cat for her. He was filthy, matted and reeked. *'Oh, why not?'* Oscar told Raya. She nodded to the attendant, then another young woman wrapped him in a cloth and took him away. Raya sank into the experience. It was wonderful. After soaping her up, the attendant put on a rough mitt and started rubbing. It felt like something between a loofa and sandpaper. Her slight gasps just made the attendant giggle without letting up. Raya soon got used to it. She certainly could use it after her adventures in filth.

* * *

'Look at the poor thing. I bet she's worried about that son of hers,' a pretty woman said. She was in her late thirties with long dark hair, like most of the women. She was talking to a younger version of herself, probably her daughter, who looked not much older than Raya.

'Go on, give her some hope,' the mum said and nodded towards an older woman who was having her hair coloured.

The daughter smirked, waved away her servant and hopped off the slab. She strutted, absolutely starkers in front of the older woman, who didn't look particularly worried about anything. Meanwhile, the mother got off the slab and walked behind her daughter with two servants in tow. The mum made a show of being surprised to come across the older woman.

'Well, hello there, Macide. How lovely to bump into you here,' the mother said. The mother and Macide went on to talk about whether Macide might consider the young woman a suitable match for her son. Macide dismissed the idea, but the mother persisted. Raya could see the daughter talking with her friends. She knew the type: people who thought their good luck was their doing, and that people with bad luck deserved it.

Raya suddenly felt a pang in her guts. The kebab had caught up with her. She needed a toilet. Now. Raya dashed out of the main room, down a short hall, to what appeared to be a bathroom. Inside, there was a marble bench with a series of holes. Water flowed below. Much better than what 1645 England had to offer.

On her return, she passed Strutting Girl gossiping to her friends.

'Like we'd ever consider that horrible son of hers for marriage. I mean puh-lease.' The girl did an imitation of a man limping. All three girls collapsed with laughter. Raya returned to her spot on the warm marble platform, her attendant waiting. She finished the scrub then gave Raya a sarong-like cloth to wrap herself in and guided her through another archway into a third room.

And what a room it was. Here the women seemed to be relaxing after all that other relaxing and being washed. The posh ones with servants were obvious now. They lay back on cushioned couches, wrapped in warm robes while they were served treats. Attendants sprayed perfume, offered scented oils, and make-up. Wow – this was the life.

Raya was led to a couch and attendants came around offering little drinks in small metal cups on big metal trays, sweets she didn't recognize but was certainly willing to try, and then the best, coffee.

'Not bad, eh?' Bryony plonked down next to her on the couch. 'I've been trying to get in touch with IHQ, but nothing yet.'

Raya sipped the strong coffee from a little porcelain cup and saucer. Even better than the best coffee back home.

An attendant walked up to them with a folded cloth with a cat's head sticking out. She placed Oscar on the couch between Raya and Bryony. He had a bow around his neck. The attendant left.

'*It's not funny. Take it off,*' Oscar said.

Raya was about to say something smart, but Bryony caught her eye, reminding her they needed the cat, so she shut her mouth and undid the bow.

'May I read your coffee cup?' a fully dressed woman asked.

'Umm, no thanks,' Bryony answered forgetting they wouldn't understand her. She shook her head and the woman moved off.

'Read mine, please.' It was Strutting Girl. She and her mother were sitting on a couch behind theirs. The coffee reader went to her, inspected the cup, returned it to the girl with the saucer on top, and told her to make a wish. The girl murmured something then turned the cup round a few times before turning it upside down. The coffee reader nodded her approval and said she would return in a few minutes when the cup was ready.

'Oh, I can't wait to find out about my future. I wonder if I'll become rich and famous,' she said.

'More like you'll be a mean old cow, just like your mum. You've got a good start,' Raya said under her breath.

The room erupted in laughter, the women all looked at Raya, many with approval.

'Didn't I say that in English? What's going on?' Raya head-talked to Bryony.

'Nope. Not English. Your ability to speak must have come on.'

'Well, a little warning would have been nice!' Raya fumed.

The mum summoned one of the attendants and insisted Bryony and Raya and their horrid pet be removed at once. It seemed this mother-daughter duo were not well-liked, but for whatever reason people didn't seem to think they could stand up to them. The attendant was doing her best imitation of looking 'dreadfully sorry', and promised to 'take care of the problem at once'.

'Nice – a few hours in a new place and you've got us our first ban – from the baths no less. Good work, Raya,' Oscar added in.

'We've got bigger problems, Oscar – like where to stay and how to survive. Don't you think?' Bryony retorted.

Raya thought it was sweet Bryony was defending her against a cat. But any warm and fuzzy feelings ebbed away with the reality Bryony's words underscored – once again she had nowhere to go, and no way to get food – none of them did.

Chapter 26

Han, Sweet Home

Raya accepted the neatly tied bundle of clothes from the attendant and dressed as quickly as she could given all the items these outfits entailed. The young attendant briefly met Raya's gaze. It said, 'I'm ever so sorry, but my hands are tied.'

The mother and daughter she'd insulted glared at them. The rest of the bathers and attendants had fallen into an uncomfortable silence, moving around like guilty ghosts.

'Where're we going?' Raya said.

'I don't know.' She fussed over the girl and straightened her veil. 'I'm a witch, not a fortune teller.'

Raya looked sullen.

'Relax – it's a joke. Come on, we're alive, that's the best surprise.'

Raya fought sudden tears, her anger giving away to fear. 'I'm scared, Bryony. What if I… we can't ever get home?'

Bryony looked right into Raya's eyes, put her hands on her shoulders.

'Raya, you've got terrific natural talent. I know you can learn to control your powers. I'll teach you – I promise.' That scared her even more, that their getting back home might depend on Bryony's skills in any form. She turned away and locked down her thoughts.

'Come on you two, time to make a move,' Oscar said.

All eyes were on them as they were escorted out of this wonderful place. Raya wondered if Oscar was right and they were now banned – she certainly hoped not.

Macide stood next to the door. Raya blushed with fresh embarrassment. Then, wham – Raya was sprawled on the floor. She must have tripped. *Darn these long dresses.* Macide helped her up and whispered, 'Follow the road to the Grand Bazaar and I'll catch up with you.'

Raya stumbled out with Bryony, and Oscar at their sides. They retraced their steps towards the market.

A hundred or so yards down the road, Macide reappeared and led them onto a larger road then disappeared into an archway into what looked like some kind of compound. It was surrounded by a pink masonry wall.

Beyond the wall were balconied buildings in more of the pink stucco. Macide turned and gave them the briefest look and nod, before disappearing again.

Raya stopped before she entered the archway. 'You sure this is OK?' Raya asked the adult witch, despite her misgivings about Bryony's abilities.

'Oh, right. Sorry. My reading of it says she's absolutely fine, but go on – have a go yourself. And two minds are always better than one.'

'What?' Raya said.

'You know – like Pavel had been teaching you.'

'Oh,' Raya said, a bit surprised not having realised those skills could be applied here. She relaxed and thought of Macide, and at the same time did her slowed breathing, emptied her mind of random thoughts – or more realistically, didn't pay attention to them. She saw Macide in the baths in her mind's eye and replayed what she remembered. Then she felt cosy and smelled Ian's wonderful vegetarian chilli, heard the bell jingle above the door. Raya relaxed and smiled. 'I'm getting associations with being at the Cosmic Cafe – I saw Ian, he was making a big pot of his veggie chilli. I could even smell it – gave me a warm, safe feeling with it. So that tells me Macide and her offer are OK?' She felt a little funny asking Bryony for reassurance.

Bryony smiled, 'Yes, exactly. Come on, let's not keep her waiting.'

They entered the archway, but didn't get very far. A man stood at the other end and halted the trio.

'I'm sorry, but we don't accommodate women. Try the Sufi centre down the road. They might have some ideas.'

Macide bustled up to the guard. 'I'm ever so sorry. I had to get a few things ready, didn't have time to tell you. These are our cousins, on my beloved husband's side of the family, may he rest in peace. They'll be staying in our personal family quarters.'

The guard bowed to Bryony and Raya. 'I do apologise, I hadn't been informed.' He arched an eyebrow at Macide.

Raya barely heard any of this as she walked out into the large courtyard. It was green and luscious with a tree in the middle, shading another one of those fancy cube-shaped stone fountains. These people sure liked their flowing water. A man was collecting some in a leather bucket. She heard a faint whinny. A horse stood in a stable on the ground floor, looking out at the man getting the water. Other animals stood in the stalls, including a few camels.

The balconies ran along all sides of the building above the stables, overlooking the courtyard. Men in various long robes and turbans sat on their balconies, presumably in front of their rooms. Some smoked, others sipped from small cups. One snored in a chair.

Bryony and Macide were talking, or rather, pantomiming. Macide acted out eating, then sleeping, then working – washing dishes, shaking and folding cloth – doing laundry. Raya looked on and voiced the last part. Macide laughed.

'Of course, you speak Turkish, I momentarily forgot. I gather you are from another land. I know what that's like. Especially as a woman without family here. We'd be happy to provide you accommodation in trade for some help.'

'If you're sure?' Raya said. She was still taken aback by all this kindness towards strangers – it made her a little wary.

Bryony watched the conversation; she seemed to be reading body language and likely any thoughts she could pick up. Raya and Bryony followed Macide who moved rather quickly for being so old, Raya thought. They went up one of two sets of stairs at the back of the courtyard, then along one length of the balcony towards the front of the building to the door third from the end. It looked like an old-fashioned hotel room, except that the furnishings were much nicer and more interesting. There were two wooden stools and a small table, a couple of brightly coloured oil lamps, like she'd seen hanging in the bazaar, and equally colourful bedding on two beds with loads of pillows. Macide needlessly adjusted things then unlocked an interior door that led into what looked like quite a large flat.

'In good time, we will show you your role here. But tonight, you are our guests. After you settle in, please join me and my son Abbas for something to eat,' Macide said. 'And don't worry, your cat will eat well, too, with all the cat dinner ladies around here.'

'Pardon me?' Raya said.

'Twice a day, women come out with freshly cooked food and feed all the cats,' Macide said.

'Really?' Raya said.

'Well hello, mister, and how do you do!' Oscar said.

'See, something in it for you too – sticking around,' Bryony said.

'It's one way to give zakat, to do charitable works – one of the things required by Islam,' Macide said.

'I'm converting,' Oscar said.

'Macide started towards her flat. She paused before disappearing. 'Come right in through this door, no need to knock.'

* * *

Raya took her veil off and flopped down on the bed.

Bryony checked to make sure the door between their room and Macide's apartment was closed.

Oscar settled next to Raya on the bed. Bryony sat down, stood up, opened the shutters then closed them halfway.

'You OK?' Raya asked. She obviously wasn't.

'Just a lot on my mind,' Bryony said. Her smile was not reassuring. 'Tell you what, why don't you and Oscar have a little wander around our new neighbourhood?' Bryony said. 'I want to try transmitting to IHQ.'

'Don't you need the cat?'

I'm right here, you know.

'As long as he's within about half a mile, his microchip boosts the signal.'

'We won't go far. Will they send someone to get us back home?' Raya's question was innocent – genuine, but the adult witch bristled.

'No, I just need some info, that's all. So we know what we're working with.'

Raya shrugged, tied her veil back on and left with Oscar. Girl and cat squinted in the dazzle of the sinking sun. The warmth was welcome after her stint in cold, old England. They walked the length of the balcony, down the stairs and across the green courtyard. Two men worked in the garden, trimming things and sweeping the paths. They nodded to Raya. Oscar found a discreet spot under a bush to relieve himself and reappeared as the calls of the cat feeders started: '*Kedi et, kedi et* – cat food.'

'Good evening, sir. My cat and I would like to take a walk. We'll be back shortly,' Raya said.

The gatekeeper furrowed his eyebrows, cocked his head. 'You're not from Istanbul, are you? Young women don't usually go out unaccompanied here. Does Miss Macide approve?' he said.

'Yes, of course. My cat was hoping to find a meal.'

'In that case, take a left out of gate, go to the first break in the wall and turn left again. You'll come across lots back there,' he said and gestured towards the exit.

Raya and Oscar quickly found themselves in a system of alleyways behind the buildings. Women, mostly old, called again and again, '*Kedi et, kedi et*', and ladled food from pots. Cats ran from all directions.

'*Well, you better get in there if you want anything,*' Raya said. Lamb stew wafted their way and he was off.

'*You know your way back? I'm going back to lie down before dinner,*' Raya called out. Oscar nodded and Raya started back towards the *han*. She heard a couple of cat yowls and glanced over her shoulder. A double-wide cat was not pleased with Oscar's arrival – nothing he couldn't handle. A woman in a long black dress and veil ladled food into a number of bowls, admonishing the cats to share.

* * *

Raya walked back to the inn. The gatekeeper nodded. She now felt how very tired she was. She trudged up the steps and back to their room and was about to knock before she picked up Bryony's transmission to headquarters.

'*I know,*' Bryony said. '*So we've got about two weeks at best…*'

There was a moment of quiet. Raya thought she heard someone sigh. '*I'm afraid so–*' it was Ms Watts.

'*Hold that thought, Sonya. I need to secure the line,*' Bryony said, and the transmission cut out.

Raya tiptoed about halfway back down the balcony, then returned to the room with her normal clunking steps and knocked on the door.

'Come on in, it's your room too,' Bryony sang out.

Raya nodded, fiddled with the bedspread. 'I thought I'd take a nap, if that's OK.'

Bryony checked herself in the small mirror on the wooden table. 'Actually, we don't have time. It's time to go to Macide's for dinner.'

Chapter 27

Luck and Luxuries

A little hesitantly, Raya knocked on the door.

'Come in, come in, no need to knock,' Macide said. In the far part of the living area three pretty couches surrounded a coffee table. Closer to the door was a table laid for dinner with a dish of rice, some flat breads, and three jugs in the centre.

'What would you ladies like to drink? Wine? Sherbet? Water?' Macide asked.

Raya translated. Bryony chose wine. Raya asked Macide what sherbet was – a fruit juice concoction without alcohol. She picked that. Bryony and Raya were invited to take their seats when a man walked in through another door a bit awkwardly carrying a steaming terrine. He placed it on the table and beamed at the two women.

'This is my son, Abbas,' Macide said. 'Here are Bryony and Rachel, the two I told you about.' Abbas was younger and fitter than Raya expected given the way Strutting Girl went on. He was wiry with broad shoulders, thick dark hair and beard and sparkling, playful eyes below the edge of his snow white turban. Raya liked him immediately and tried to ask Bryony what she thought through head talk, but she wasn't answering.

Dinner was delicious, something like a lamb curry, and rice with bits of veg and herbs. Her body still craved food in a way it never had before her stint in old England. They laughed and ate and joked with Raya translating for Bryony, except that she seemed rather distracted and worried.

After dinner they relaxed on the couches. Macide and Abbas were curious about how Bryony and Raya came to Istanbul. Bryony fed Raya material through head chat, spinning a story about escaping cruel treatment in England and embarking to Istanbul where they'd heard women were treated decently, could even own businesses, and certainly weren't killed for having a few skills. But Bryony had a question. *It sounds like they're saying 'Istanbul'. I thought the name was Constantinople at this time.* Raya asked their hosts. They chuckled.

'Ah, yes. All you Western Europeans call it "Constantinople" but no one uses that name here. Not really, except on some official documents and things. "Istanbul", my dear!' Abbas paused and grinned, waiting for her to get it. Then the penny dropped and she heard the *meaning* of the word, not just the familiar sound of the name.

'Oh, "The City", like there's only one!' Raya said. Abbas and Macide laughed.

'So how did you come to learn Turkish, my dear?' Macide asked. She sounded grandmotherly, or at least auntie-like.

Raya retold the tale in her newly acquired Ottoman Turkish. This was fun. The words danced across her tongue and made her lips do new tricks. She was smiling and laughing at the joy of it. Macide and Abbas were charmed, elbowing each other and remarking on her Turkish.

There was a scratching at the door. Abbas opened it and crouched down to stroke Oscar. He pulled out a handkerchief and dabbed at spots of bright blood on his fingers. 'Looks like your friend's been in a few scrapes. Probably with the other cats that get fed, nothing serious.'

'*You should see the other guy,*' Oscar said to the two witches then sauntered to a warm corner and curled up.

217

'Raya, ask about them – what brought them here. Macide mentioned she's from someplace else,' Bryony said.

'Now? I'm so tired,' Raya answered.

'Yes, now. It's polite to show interest in other people… and if we're stuck here for a while, we'll need to know how foreigners get by.'

The idea was like a bucket of cold water. She realised she'd been carried along by their good luck over the last hours, a welcome break. Yes, being alive was great, but now she had to face being a teenager in the wrong place and time with no clue how to get home. And the supposed expert sent in for the job – seemingly useless. She knew she had a bad feeling about them sending Bryony to save her from the witch trials. She inhaled and held it a second before asking the adult witch, *'So, YOU can't get us home from here, either? Not even worth trying?'* A not unobvious ember of resentment glowed at her centre.

Bryony looked reproachful, and clamped her thoughts down – a metal security gate clanged shut. *'Just ask them, please?'*

Raya translated the question to Macide and Abbas but only partially paid attention to what they said. A steam train of emotions was pulling in.

Macide's story played out on her face as she retold it. She was from the Balkans and the Ottomans took her brother from the family when he was ten. Apparently this was a thing they did, to train up workers as they wanted. Her brother was clever and rose up in the ranks of the Palace and eventually sent for his sister, Macide. But that was once they were adults, and Macide's first husband and two kids had died of the plague. *Boy, a lot of that going around.* So she came here and lived in the Palace along with her brother. That got Raya's attention – sounded pretty cool.

Macide pushed herself up from the couch and sighed. 'Let me get us coffee and sweets,' she said and bustled away.

Abbas lowered his voice. 'But then my uncle fell out of favour with the Sultan and was beheaded,' he said.

This brought Raya's attention fully back to the room. Everyone was quiet for a moment, the only sounds were Macide's clinking china at a distance.

'So who is the Sultan now? I'm afraid we're ignorant of such things in much of Europe,' Bryony asked, and Raya translated. She knew Bryony was trying to pinpoint their exact time.

'Oh,' Abbas sighed, 'it's Crazy Ibrahim.' He shook his head, as Macide returned with the coffee and a plate of sweets.

'He's a real piece of work this Sultan and we've had our share of oddballs,' Macide said as she arranged the things on the table. Bryony reached for a piece of Turkish delight.

Macide and Abbas told the rest of their story – how Macide met his father, a janissary, a special sort of soldier, but retired at the time, and how Macide's brother organised them getting this *han* to run.

'When my father died about ten years ago, the *han* went to my mother and myself,' Abbas added.

'And then, of course, Abbas has run the place fulltime since he was injured fighting the Venetians,' Macide said, her mood darkened.

'Come on, Mother. Let's not go into all that,' Abbas said.

Macide dabbed at her eyes and gave a taut smile. 'Right then, let's tell Abbas how we met – there's a good story.'

Macide retold how Strutting Girl and her mother cruelly teased her, including some pretty funny imitations. 'That woman in the baths,' she told Bryony and Raya, 'her uncle is a top advisor to the Sultan, and he's in charge of a lot of public funding, including for this *han*.'

Abbas swirled the dredges in his coffee cup. 'So, do you two know how to read coffee grounds?' Abbas said.

Bryony sat forward. 'I used to know – a Turkish friend in England taught me,' Raya translated. Abbas smiled and put the saucer on top of his cup, then turned it this way and that, flipped it over, and handed it to Bryony. She took the saucer off and studied the muddy smudges. She frowned and looked some more. 'I'm afraid I'm not seeing anything at the moment.'

Raya reached for the cup from Bryony.

There was a firm knock at Macide's door. It was one of the groundsmen. He wanted food for offerings to the jinn – those spirits people fed here, like at the dress sellers at the market.

'The situation has become quite dire, two more have moved into the courtyard. They're teasing the camels and other livestock something terrible,' the guard said.

Abbas got up and hobbled to the where the dinner dishes were. 'We can't have that,' he said and heaped leftovers onto two plates. The guard left, relieved. Raya tried to ask Bryony through head chat if these jinn were real, but she either didn't hear, or still wasn't talking to her. Raya sighed inwardly and looked at the coffee cup she'd been holding. At first it just looked like the mess you'd expect, then things started to take form. She concentrated, could see a man. It was Abbas, then another. Then the scene started to move, like a miniature black and white film. She was afraid if she looked away, it would all stop – afraid to blink.

'It was your good friend, wasn't it?' Raya said. You were trying to protect him when you were injured. Then he stayed behind – didn't come home with the rest of the soldiers. He married someone there,' Raya said.

Abbas and Macide stared at Raya.

'He's sorry. Your friend is truly sorry,' Raya added.

Abbas and Macide crowded around Raya, peered into the coffee cup and asked her how she'd seen all that.

Raya stretched with a yawn worthy of a cat. 'I don't know. A little scene just appeared in the coffee cup.'

'Praise be to God. This girl is gifted,' Abbas exclaimed.

Chapter 28

Unwanted Truth

A thick, opaque silence filled the room as the woman and girl readied for bed. They took their long dresses off to sleep in the light cotton undergarments. Oscar jumped onto Bryony's bed, turned a few circles and settled down.

'I don't know why you're so mad at me. I mean I'M the one who saved us!' Raya folded her headscarf with a vengeance.

Bryony turned around from sorting her bed. Started to say something a couple of times then didn't. Finally she said, 'I think you're the one who's mad at me.'

Like a pin in a balloon, Raya let fly. 'Wouldn't YOU be? I thought you were supposed to "save" us – fat lot of good that did. I KNEW you couldn't do it – had a feeling. I mean you lose everything – your cat, other people's kids – why would anyone think you could have fixed this?'

Bryony flushed and fussed with the pillows. 'You're right, Raya.' Her voice was small. 'I failed – we all know that. And I don't understand why.'

Raya felt guilty about being so harsh, but it was all true, and she'd been holding it all back for a while.

Bryony took a huge breath and plunked down on the bed. 'Thank God you saved us.' She shook her head. 'I can't tell you how grateful I am.' She was quiet for a moment. 'And I'm so sorry I failed you – us.' She leaned forward and took the girl's hands across the space between their beds. Raya wrenched away.

'Raya, I've got to talk to you about something else – about our situation now.'

'*This should be good,*' Oscar sat up and opened his eyes as though he was about to watch a show. The two witches ignored him.

'Raya, we may not be able to get home. We have to face this possibility.'

'Stop saying that! Why do you keep saying that?'

'*Because it's true?*' Oscar said.

Bryony shooed the cat off her bed and opened their door to the balcony. 'Why don't you go take a walk?'

She encouraged the cat out with a gentle foot under his midsection.

'I can take a hint.' Oscar sauntered out.

Bryony waited a beat, seemed to be gathering her thoughts which she had kept locked down since dinner. 'I contacted IHQ while you were out with Oscar...' she angled an eyebrow, '...as you know. And we've got our work cut out for us.'

'So we CAN get home? Make up your mind!'

'Possibly.' The word hung in the air, like fate itself, inscrutable, it taunted with hope.

'Headquarters confirmed it definitely was you who got us here. And they put us in the time frame that matches with the Sultan Abbas mentioned – Ibrahim Deli, they call him. "Deli" means crazy. We most likely slid over to a different place, but in the same time, a common transport error.' Bryony paused. 'And a life-saving one.' She smiled gratitude, but she looked as exhausted as Raya felt.

Raya started to say something, but Bryony put her hand up. 'Let me tell you everything before you ask questions, OK?' The young witch nodded.

'We've got about two weeks to get home. After that it's very unlikely, or...' Bryony stifled a sigh 'Or impossible. And Rachel, it has to be you who does the transport.' Bryony looked at her, as though she was waiting for this to sink in.

The fear train pulled all the way into the station. 'Why only two weeks? What do you mean I have to do it? That's not fair!' It came out whiny, like a little kid when they don't get an ice cream. But she didn't mean it like that. She meant it in the infinite order of the universe sort of way, or lack thereof as Jake would point out. *Don't think about him – it'll only make things worse,* she told herself.

Bryony heaved a sigh. 'Of course it's not fair, Raya. It's nothing to do with "fair". It has to do with the natural laws of time travel. Whoever drives the bus in has to drive it back out. We both had transported to old England – so either, or both, of us could have transported us out.'

A chill ran through her. 'Driving the bus' – just like she had told Jake. In control of her own life was what she had wanted. And now she was responsible, not only for the fine mess she found herself in, but for someone else's situation, too. Didn't feel as good as she'd anticipated. There were soft sounds of animals shifting in their stalls outside.

'But if we don't know what went wrong, how can we fix it?' Raya asked.

'Headquarters is looking into it as fast as they can – they've brought extra people in. Meanwhile, the best thing we can do is get you trained up in transporting as quickly as possible. That means practising every day. Around here at first – no time travel. We'll start tomorrow.'

They stopped talking – nothing left to say, but sleep wouldn't take her. Tendrils of moonlight through the shutters' slats graced the plaster ceiling. She could tell Bryony wasn't sleeping either.

'Did you hear anything about Jake?' Raya asked.

There was a beat before Bryony answered. 'I'm afraid he's had a setback. Another emergency surgery – I think for his leg, this time. We should know more tomorrow.'

Chapter 29

Bad Elves

'Help! They're after me! Let me in!' It was Oscar.

Raya stumbled to semi-wakefulness, not long after she'd finally fallen asleep and opened the shuttered window. Oscar jumped in.

'Who's after you?' Bryony blinked awake.

He crouched on the floor and kept glancing up at the window, his ears flattened against his head, his tail twitching like it had a life of its own. *'I don't know – never saw anything or anyone like them.'*

There was a whoosh and a gentle thud, like something landing on Bryony's bed, but Raya couldn't see anything. She opened the shutters further to let more moonlight in, but it didn't help. Oscar hissed and growled, in full Hallowe'en cat mode.

'There you are, Cat – you're mine!' a raspy male voice snarled. Raya stared at the foot of Bryony's bed where the voice seemed to come from, but she still couldn't see anyone.

'Can't you see him?' Bryony asked. She reached towards the foot of her bed, and poked her finger slowly back and forth, as though she was touching something.

'Where?' Raya said.

'On the end of my bed. He's short, fat and bald, with a tartan loin cloth, and what looks like a spout on the top of his head,' Bryony said.

'You flatter me,' came the snide male voice. *'But it's a valve.'*

'He's talking? That ugly piece of work has been chasing me around the courtyard,' Oscar said. *'What's he saying?'*

'Nothing important,' Raya said.

'Your cat might disagree. We're going to barbeque him!' The being guffawed, and made a hideous screech. Raya looked at Bryony who seemed to be able to hear AND see him.

'He's pressing that valve on top of his head and making that sound with his mouth – like he has a trumpet built in,' Bryony explained. She stopped when another whooshing sound came through the window, followed by two thuds on the floor.

'Two more have joined us,' Bryony continued her narration. 'One's a very tall, thin woman, like a circus performer on stilts, but without stilts.'

'*How do you do?*' came in an ultra-high female voice – like a cartoon character.

'Yes, nice to meet you, too,' Bryony replied. Raya was speechless. Oscar not being able to hear them was spared their ridiculous chatter. Bryony went on to describe the third one, 'This last one looks like a male model, unbelievably fit and handsome, but with purple and orange striped skin. Actually, that's all he's wearing, so to speak.'

'*Well hello there, pretty little lady.*' It must have been the striped one. He'd said it right into Raya's ear. She shrieked and jumped clear off her bed.

Bryony poked a finger in the air above the foot of her bed again. 'Are you jinn?'

'*Next stupid question, please. Now, Cat, you ate our offerings. That's punishable by death.*' That was the first voice, the raspy one. Raya checked with Oscar, '*Did you hear that?*' Oscar shook his head. This was really weird.

Bryony stood up, gave the slightest bow. *What was she doing?*

'I am honoured to meet you. I am from another land, and have only read about jinn in books. I'm most delighted to have this opportunity.'

'*Hm, you can see AND hear us? You're no fun,*' the raspy one said to Bryony. '*Whatever. We'll just take your cat and go.*'

Bryony opened the door to the balcony. 'Why don't we go outside. Let my human friend here sleep, we've had a very long journey, and I'd like to ask you a few questions. I understand jinn are very knowledgeable and wise.' Raya thought Bryony was either a good actress, or had lost her mind. Bryony, Oscar, and the three jinn left the room for the remainder of the moon-lit night.

* * *

Raya woke up with the hot sun slashing through the shutters. It must have been after ten in the morning. The door to Macide's was left ajar. She threw on her dress and went in.

'Morning, Miss Rachel,' Abbas said. 'We were just trying to explain to your auntie how grateful the groundsmen, all of us, are for her getting rid of the jinn! With Bryony's ability to see and hear them, she knows when they're gone. Not to mention, the animals staying with us are now a lot calmer.'

Macide handed Raya a plate. She chose from the array of hard boiled eggs, salad, cheese, olives and bread. It took her a second to remember what they were talking about. She'd been so tired, and there'd been so many weird and fantastic experiences since yesterday, she'd halfway wondered if those jinn things were from a dream. She was kind of hoping they were.

'Oh that's nice,' she said. *Glad she's good at something,* she thought.

Macide put a piece of baklava on Raya's plate, even though she didn't ask for any. Her face told her she thought she was too thin. Raya put it back onto the serving plate, despite Macide's frown – she could only eat so much.

'Word's already got around – about your auntie's way with jinn. This is a wonderful skill. So many people have jinn problems.' Abbas shook his head.

'Rachel, dear, ask your auntie if she'd be willing to help other people get rid of their jinn,' Macide said. 'This would be much more important work than helping around here. You could stay here and help us – with cooking and laundry, if you don't mind.'

Oh, great. I get stuck with the crap jobs – figures. Raya put her plate down and related all this to Bryony.

'One of our groundsmen can take her to the jobs in our carriage, and we can provide a dragoman – a translator,' Abbas added.

Bryony looked a bit nervous. *'Raya, we need to stay together, so I can help you practise. I know I haven't been a lot of help so far. But at least I can teach you what I do know. We might as well use everything we've got, eh? Tell them you can translate for me.'*

Raya hated it when people acted all 'poor me', especially when it was adults who were supposed to be in charge. It made her skin crawl. *'Sure, I'll explain it to them.'*

After some discussion, they agreed Raya would accompany Bryony on her jinn riddance work and translate. They would start tomorrow. They spent the rest of the day sleeping and eating, still carrying deficits in both of these areas.

Whenever they were awake, Bryony had Raya practise the most simple transports – so simple the girl witch rolled her eyes, but Bryony didn't bite. Raya merely transported from one side of their room to the other. The room was small enough that it wasn't much more than a few steps. She'd stare at the part of the room she intended to move to until she had it memorised. Then closed her eyes and imagined it as fully as possible and slowed her breathing to a counted rhythm – all as Bryony had instructed her. When it worked – pop – she was there. She had a number of awkward misfires where she didn't move at all, or landed on the bed, or on her bum in the middle of the floor. But pretty soon she was doing it reliably and smoothly.

'I think I'm ready for the next step,' Raya said.

Bryony was staring straight ahead, with Oscar on her lap, his front paws in her palms. 'Join me, I'm trying to transmit to IHQ, I'm not able to get a good signal.'

Why am I not surprised? Raya thought after locking hers down. Raya sat next to Bryony and slipped one of Oscar's back paws into her hand.

A choppy view of IHQ came in, like a broken mosaic.

'Hi Bryony. How's it going?'

'Hi Pavel. We're OK, actually. These people are very nice and it's a good place to stay, in trade for a bit of work – thanks to Raya.'

Raya flushed from embarrassment about her mouthing off at the baths, although thinking about it that way – maybe it was a good thing. Pavel's face chopped into squares and jittered like a weak digital TV signal.

'Before I forget. Tell us, how's Jake? Any news? How did the surgery go?' Bryony said.

Pavel turned away for a moment to answer someone off screen then returned. *'Well, it looks like–'* The transmission went dead.

Bryony grabbed at Oscars paws, massaged them, put a hand on his back. 'Are you getting anything, Raya?'

Raya shook her head, patted Oscar in different places.

'Something's wrong,' Bryony patted the cat frantically. She looked like she might cry. 'I was getting a lot better transmission yesterday.'

Raya's shoulders slumped. She didn't know what else could go wrong. Hopelessness tasted sour and dry.

Bryony looked at her hand. Blood. There was a gash in Oscar's skin on the back of his neck.

'Oo, that's good. A little to the left, if you don't mind.'

'Oh, Oscar. I asked you to avoid fights,' Bryony said.

'Hey, I have just as much right to the cat dinners as any of the others,' Oscar explained.

Bryony gently pressed all along the back of Oscar's neck, going in neat rows back and forth, careful not to pull at the bright red gash. She shook her head. 'It's gone – no more microchip. Well, that's the end of that.'

Both woman and girl sat staring past the cat. Oscar washed behind his ears. Raya's stomach and heart traded places. Now it was really down to her and Bryony. Down to her.

'Hey, I bet we can transmit without Oscar's microchip,' Raya said.

'We can try,' Bryony said, but looked about as hopeful as a single man in a maternity ward. And she was right. No matter how they tried, the two humans, with the cat but without the microchip, couldn't connect to headquarters. Raya heard a loud popping sound in her mind, like a huge rubber band being snapped, like a glider plane released from a Piper Cub.

Chapter 30

Jinn Riddance

The next two days, their third and fourth in Istanbul, were a blur of work, transporting and beseeching eyes. All those eyes. Bryony's desperate, frightened and so sorry. Customers' worried and hopeful for a remedy to their jinn problems. And other eyes pulling at dreams, yearning for answers when Raya did more coffee cup readings. She did these for people in the houses and shops they went to for the jinn business – for a break from practising transporting. A break from the gnawing, sleep-stealing worries that were wearing a trench in her soul.

Bryony didn't need her at her side every minute, only at the start and finish of each job to talk to the customers for her. While Bryony inspected for jinn, they'd find an empty room, or better two, where Raya could practise her transporting, explaining to the family that they needed to be alone with doors closed for their jinn work. This allowed her to pop around without being noticed. She made a couple of mistakes, accidentally transporting to the kitchen where she'd smelled something delicious. 'Well, we know your stomach is a strong determinant,' Bryony had said. By the second day of their jinn work, she had this local transport thing down pat and could do it with no more thought than walking.

About half of the jinn jobs weren't jinn at all. Some of these were people who thought there were jinn, when there weren't any – their anguish was real, even if the cause wasn't. Then there were others who blamed jinn, used them as an excuse for their behaviour, whether that was having an affair, spending too much money, drinking too much, all the usual human stuff. Raya watched as Bryony handled each type and each person differently. Sometimes, when people were very anxious, but there were no jinn and no real reason for the person's upset, Bryony would pretend she'd found and got rid of them. Other times, when people were hiding behind the idea of jinn to excuse their behaviour, Bryony would talk to them privately about what she saw was going on, and encourage them to sort things out properly. Sometimes Bryony wouldn't accept any payment for the cases where there weren't any jinn, but other times she did. Raya questioned her on this. She explained that she took payment when she could see it would keep the jinn riddance real for the customer in a way that helped them or their relationships, until they could sort things out properly. 'But don't worry, I'm keeping that money separate – we'll give it as zakat.'

Bryony was OK – at least in some ways.

The groundsman drove them in the carriage, wooden with cloth seats and roof that helped cut the impact of the relentless sun, to their next assignment. The smell of hibiscus seemed to be everywhere. They arrived at another lovely house in the outskirts of Istanbul. White masonry on the ground floor, with a wooden storey above. More beautiful mosaic tiled floors and walls, more handsome wooden furniture and rich upholstery. The woman of the house greeted them and described their jinn problems. The grandmother sat at the table and listened. As Bryony went upstairs the older woman beckoned Raya.

'I heard you're quite the coffee cup reader.' Her eyes twinkled from her honey-coloured, lined face. A few strands of grey hair escaped her headscarf. She reached out for Raya's hand with her leathery, calloused one. Her touch was cool. 'Would you do mine?' She pushed her cup forward, the saucer already on top.

Raya glanced towards the stairs. Bryony was already out of sight, doing her jinn survey no doubt. She decide to give herself a break with the reading before going upstairs to find a place to practise popping, as she now thought of it.

'*You're all right. You don't need to be glued to old auntie iron-pants,*' a crackly voice said. She snapped her head around looking, but no one was there.

'Did you just say something?' she asked the grandmother.

'What? Oh no dear. That's probably one of these jinn. I can't hear or see them. But my daughter says there's a pesky one likes to hang around the kitchen. Do you want to go tell your auntie?'

'*Spoil-sport!*' the jinn said and literally buzzed off.

'No, I think it's gone now. I'll tell her later, if she doesn't find it herself.' Raya smiled and returned to the reading. She went through the ritual of turning the coffee cup, tapping it, asking the woman to make a wish and so on, waiting for the visualizations to start. And they did. She supressed a gasp, turned the cup some more and looked again. The same images replayed. The old woman was going to lose someone soon, her granddaughter – about Raya's age. She saw the girl's face – she was smart and funny. She had long, dark hair, a round face with almond-shaped eyes. Then Raya saw Rebecca West, the fourteen-year-old who only saved her own life by testifying against her mother, and then she saw her own face reflected in these girls – a swirl of chance, and life and sorrow. *How can I tell this sweet old lady her granddaughter's going to die? Should I?* Suddenly this 'gift' didn't seem so great.

She did her best to keep all this off her face, but from the look on the woman's face, she wasn't succeeding. Bryony had started to teach Raya how to handle bad news in her readings, but she couldn't remember any of it now. Her head started to spin. 'I'm sorry, I'm not feeling so well, could I use your–'

'Losing it, are you? Why don't we get out of here – you and me, baby!' It was the kitchen jinn again.

'Shut up, you'll be gone soon enough.' Raya swatted the air around her, wishing she could see the darned things.

'Oh dear – that jinn's bothering you again.' The grandmother got up from her chair. 'You do look a little faint, dear. Why don't you go splash some cool water on yourself? I'll show you the way.'

The walls looked skewed and the hallway looked impossibly long. How many more sad things would she have to tell people? What if she saw her own fate?

Bryony's? Was that possible? Was that why she was seeing her own face mixed up with the granddaughter's? Did it mean her life was ending soon too? Or just that she related to this girl, a bit too strongly?

'All good questions!' the kitchen jinn cackled. Raya quickly closed the door to the bathroom hoping she'd shut this jinn out, if that was possible – there was so much she didn't know yet. She was grateful for their marvellous running water. It soothed and cooled. The sound of splashing against the marble basin was a welcome salve. She heard the jinn laugh some more, then everything went black.

Chapter 31
A Nice Surprise

She blinked and looked around. It was warm and steamy and smelled of lavender. She was on her stomach being pummelled by a young woman in the second room at the baths. The baths – wow. But wait, this wasn't on purpose. Any relaxation was bulldozed out by panic. What if she'd transported someplace else entirely? And on her own? What would happen to Bryony? She didn't hate her that much – she would help her get home, if she could. Or had she wished herself here to the baths – subconsciously? Her thoughts were like one of those impossible drawings where a staircase simultaneously goes up and down. At least she seemed to have lost that annoying jinn. The women's chatter brought her out of her head. They sounded like a flock of happy birds.

When she entered the third room, she realised she only had the sarong wrap. She asked the staff if she might have her clothes, and an attendant brought a beautiful dress in emerald green, her favourite colour, with a matching veil. She could only assume her other dress, the one Tahir had given her, was heaped on the bathroom floor of the house she'd just left.

Women came around offering sweets and sherbet. She took some baklava and a cup of the fruity drink.

Two teenage girls approached her.

'That's her,' the first girl elbowed the other. 'They said she had light eyes. Go on, ask her.'

'Wasn't it you and your mother who got thrown out for upsetting the Karatays?' Second Girl said.

'It was my auntie, actually. And I AM sorry,' Raya said.

'Oh, don't be. Only wish I saw it!' First Girl said. The two of them looked at her expectantly, conspiratorially.

Raya knew this type of girl – they never liked her. Usually they'd make fun of her, behind her back, but loud enough for her to hear. She was too alternative, too poor and too cynical – the foster kid – to be of any interest to these social climbers. The 'runners up', as Raya thought of them. The kids who wished they were at the top of the pecking order with the über-kids, the ones whose nannies dropped them off in luxury four-by-fours – an oxymoron

243

if she ever heard one. To be fair, she didn't like either of these types of kid. Then why did the attention of these two feel kind of good?

She studied the two girls for a moment. Bryony's lessons about how to approach a reading and prepare for any possible sad information were coming back to her. She did her best to read them as she might before starting a coffee cup reading, so she wouldn't be caught off guard. The other thing Bryony taught her was to focus on what the person could do about any bad stuff, even if that was simply to work less and enjoy their time more, rather than talking directly about it. She didn't pick up anything sad or negative around these lucky two girls.

'Would you like me to read your coffee cups? I'm just learning – just for fun. I won't charge anything.' Raya wanted to try being normal, see what it felt like to fit in.

She'd hit exactly the right note. The girls quickly got themselves and Raya coffees. They gulped theirs down, impatient for their futures. These were straightforward, clear reads, with lots of life ahead. They still tried to pay her, but she refused, suggesting they give the money as their zakat, which only made them wrinkle their noses and put the coins back in their purses. Maybe they weren't her sort, after all.

Others came up and asked her for readings. People referred to her in whispers as the 'reader the Karatays discovered' even thought that wasn't exactly right, and the 'foreign girl with the light eyes'. She was more than fitting in, she was the cool new girl in town.

She agreed to three more readings, and let them pay. *Maybe this will be enough to get Bryony another dress, too. I know she'd love to have a change of clothes – wash the one she's been wearing.* She didn't know if she'd be in trouble – although she didn't have to worry about being grounded. This cracked her up. But to be fair, she couldn't imagine how Bryony would have explained her evaporation from the woman's bathroom – she figured she owed her one.

She left the sanctuary of the bathhouse, out into the hot, sun-bleached afternoon. With her coins in her pocket, she walked to the Grand Bazaar. She knew women, especially young ones, didn't usually go places by themselves, so she walked near clutches of other women without anyone noticing too much. As she reached the market entrance, the flow of people thickened. She saw the kebab seller from her first day and waited for him to finish serving a customer.

'What can I get for you, young lady?'

'Oh, no. Thank you, sir. I only wanted to say hello

and thank you, again, for the kebabs you gave me and my auntie. It was a few days ago. We were in quite a state.'

The kebab seller peered at her eyes above her veil, then broke into a broad smile. 'I didn't recognize you. When did you learn Turkish? That was quick! How is your auntie? Your splendid cat?'

The kebab seller offered her one. She wasn't hungry, forget about figuring out how to eat street food while wearing a veil, or if that was even polite, but she could see he would be offended if she didn't accept it. Luckily he wrapped it up for her.

'Thank you. These are truly the best in the world.' She smiled with her eyes and nodded goodbye.

She walked through the stone arch entrance. It was as magical as she remembered; the smells of wood, incense, and wool; the kaleidoscope of goods that trailed out as far as she could see. When she was able to push her enormous worries out of her head, this was all pretty amazing.

Once she arrived at Tahir's shop, it took him a second to recognize her, as well, as he'd only seen her without a veil before and, looking decidedly foreign, filthy and wearing trousers. But he was delighted once he did. She convinced him to accept the kebab to save her from carrying it around. It was so nice to not be starving any more. He promised not to tell his friend, the kebab seller. Everyone seemed to know each other.

'Yes, Istanbul – the village of a million people,' he said.

Tahir was gracious, but not at all pleased to see Raya in such a wonderful dress that was not from his shop.

'Actually, this dress is too fancy for me, but Macide the very kind woman who runs the *han* where we stay, lent it to me while the one from your shop is in the laundry. In fact, that was one reason I've stopped by today,' she said and pulled out her coins. 'I don't know if this is enough, but I'd like to buy my auntie another dress.'

'Ach, your money is no good here,' Tahir said, and summarily brushed that spoiled blob of a cat, Melek, off a pile of folded dresses. 'These are your auntie's size. Pick one, I insist.'

'Oh, I couldn't.' Raya stopped when she could see Tahir would be insulted if she didn't accept. *What is this with everyone getting insulted if you don't take their stuff for free? Just a TAD different than home.* She looked through the dresses and quickly settled on a deep-blue one with turquoise beads at the neck and wrists.

Tahir nodded approval. 'Yes, that will go nicely with her auburn hair,' he said. Then he bustled to another part of his shop and pulled out two small items and bundled them together with the dress. 'Don't forget the veil and headscarf,' he said.

'Thank you, they're lovely, and it's so kind of you – once again.' She picked up the bundle and readied to leave.

'I assume you'll go say hello to your friend, Musta, Mustafa bin Abdullah.' Tahir rocked back and forth on his heels in emphasis. 'I'm sure you don't want me to tell him you came all this way and didn't bother to see him?' Tahir crooked an eyebrow on his large kind face.

Raya got a flash of Pavel's face when she remembered this Musta – the most intriguing of everyone that day. She figured that was a good sign, the way she'd got images (and smells) of Ian cooking his vegetarian chilli when she thought about Macide. This Musta must offer similar things as Pavel – and was probably also someone she could trust.

* * *

Raya followed Tahir's directions passing a few other coffee houses by the time she reached Musta's favourite at the edge of a mosque complex. She stopped in the doorway, unsure if she was allowed in. There were only men inside, except for a woman doing something like a fully dressed belly dance on a small platform at the centre. It was another white masonry building, offering some protection from the heat and glare. It had high ceilings and large, arched windows. Otherwise, it was like stepping into a jewellery box – the walls and ceilings completely covered with painted geometric designs and tiles. The dancing girl just added to the effect – Raya wondered if she'd flop down, inanimate when the doors closed. The men sat at wooden tables with their small cups of coffee, and long pipes, or lounged on richly upholstered couches. Music played. The hip coffee shops in London didn't come close. She didn't see Musta. She fingered the coins in her pocket she'd earned at the bath house and had an idea.

She'd seen women coffee cup readers at work in a couple of the other coffee houses she'd passed, so she asked the waiter, a fit young man without a shirt, as he rushed by, a tray over his head.

'Is this the coffee house Mustafa frequents? He thought you might be able to use a coffee cup reader.'

The young man looked puzzled. 'Do you mean Mustafa bin Abdullah, the one they call Kâtip Çelebi, or Mustafa bin Ibra…?' he said.

'Yes, yes, the first one.' Raya cleared her throat, hoping she remembered correctly.

'Oh…' the young man said, looked around, '…well if he recommended you. He isn't here yet, although he usually is.'

This was easier than she'd expected. She figured, in for a penny, in for a pound as far as being in any trouble once she got home. And now that she was away from Bryony, she realised being around her amplified her stress and worries about their situation. It was nice to have a break.

The young man and an older man, who looked like he ran the coffee house, arranged a small table with two chairs next to the door.

The older man asked how she wanted to be addressed.

'Um, yes, please call me Rachel of London, uh… with the Light Eyes,' she threw in, recalling her recent experience at the baths.

The man made the announcement over the din of the coffee house. Raya sat at her table and waited.

Eventually a few men came forward to have their cups read.

'Whatever you believe is fair' became her standard response when they asked her fee. The coins were piling up. Certainly she would have enough for a pair of those wonderful yellow shoes she'd seen on her first day.

Time was going by and she knew that coming home too much later was not a good idea, so she said she could only do one more.

'Read mine, please, before you depart, Miss Rachel of London,' a sonorous voice said as an arm reached across the others and placed an overturned cup on her table. Only his turban and the top left quarter of his face were visible from behind another man.

'Kâtip, Kâtip Çelebi, don't torture the girl, show your-self,' another man said. Others agreed.

'In good time, my friends, in good time,' said the voice.

Raya didn't miss a beat. 'Sir, did you only drink from one side?'

'Yes I did,' said this Kâtip Çelebi.

'And after that, did you put the saucer on top, make a wish, and turn it anti-clockwise, holding it at chest level?' Raya realised she was showing off, but couldn't help it.

'Yes,' said the hidden man. 'I know how this works. Please, this is your payment.'

The coin was larger and heavier than any of the others she'd received. 'That is very generous, sir.' She turned the cup upright and went through the motions of looking at different quadrants of the cup and saucer until her visu-alizations began.

She saw a green field encircled by woods. In the centre was a small stone house with a thatched roof. Smoke puffed out of the chimney. All of a sudden she was right in front of the door to this cottage – it took up her whole visual field. A pair of small birds with bright blue breasts and yellow feathers on their heads swirled from behind her carrying a ribbon. They tied it on the door handle and then perched on the lintel and chirped. They were inviting her to open the door. But when she tried, the doorknob moved to another part of the door. She smiled. Kâtip shushed the nosey, noisy men. Her visualization continued.

In her imagination, she reached for the doorknob again and again, but every time it slid to another part of the door. The birds held their bellies with their wings, laughed, and flew off. The visualization stopped.

She handed the man in front of this Mr Kâtip Çelebi the hefty silver coin. 'Please tell your friend Mr Çelebi that I cannot take his money; I cannot "get a handle on him".' She smiled at the visual joke. Kâtip Çelebi stepped into view and looked at Raya sternly. Musta.

Chapter 32
Cherished

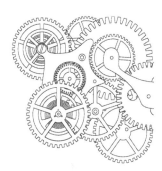

After studying the girl's eyes, a look of recognition softened Mustafa's, Kâtip Çelebi's expression.

'Hi, Musta. I had stopped by Tahir's shop and he said I should be sure to stop and say hello to you, too.' She felt shy, nervous and excited to be in his company. But she also felt immediately drawn and comfortable around him – the comparison her head, or was it her heart, had made with Pavel. She looked away, fought sudden tears. She missed Pavel and the gang. Had the briefest thought about Jake that she brushed away like a moth.

Musta had been watching her face, or more precisely her eyes. 'Yes my dear "niece".' This seemed a polite explanation for their relationship, Musta, or Kâtip, appeared to be the type that didn't like a lot of prying and the coffee house looked ripe for gossip and teasing. 'Why don't we take a walk?' he said as he ushered her out of the coffee house. Raya scooped up the nice little pile of coins as she left.

Raya spilled over in telling Musta about all she'd seen and done so far. She told him about Bryony's jinn riddance business, about her ability to read coffee cups, and about Macide and Abbas's generosity in letting them stay at their *han*.

'This Abbas, was he a janissary, injured fighting and walks with a limp?' Kâtip asked. She nodded as she prattled on, and he steered her in the direction of the *han*.

It turned out he was a professor or writer or something and the 'science of magic' was one of his specialities. *No wonder he reminds me of Pavel.*

When they reached the entrance to the *han*, Raya finally stopped talking and looked up at him.

'Why do they call you Kâtip Çelebi? I thought your name was Mustafa?'

'It's a nickname. But you can call me Musta,' he said, 'Uncle Musta is fine.'

The guard at the gate looked suspiciously at Kâtip just as Abbas strode over, grinning with his robe billowing out behind him.

'Mr Kâtip Çelebi. To what do we owe this honour? I certainly hope she hasn't caused any trouble. We've been worried,' Abbas said. He seemed nervous around Musta, like he was someone important.

'No, no trouble at all. We bumped into each other in the coffee shop. Actually, this was the second time we've met. I thought it best I walk this young lady home,' Musta said.

'Well, if it isn't Mr Kâtip Çelebi in the flesh!' Macide said, rushing up. 'Please come up to our flat and have some refreshments.' Macide turned to Raya. 'Rachel, please go to the kitchen and ask for a pilaf, some fresh böreks and whatever else looks nice.'

Raya rushed off to the kitchen. Relieved to avoid Bryony even a little longer. Musta was accompanied upstairs, despite his polite protests.

* * *

It was a heady evening, as cosy as a lock-in at the Cosmic Cafe but even more interesting. Musta knew about so many different things, and Abbas and Macide were right in there with him, as was Bryony who had started to understand some of the Ottoman Turkish. *'Understanding can come on for co-time travellers, too. It's like a cross between meditation and getting used to an accent. Although speaking is a different matter – a lot harder.'*

Raya nodded to indicate she understood then responded through head chat, *'Should I keep translating what you want to say to them, then?'*

'If you don't mind.'

They talked about politics, religion, art, even engineering. They ate delicious hot spinach and cheese böreks, pilaf, salad and fruit, and just when they all thought they'd burst, one of the kitchen staff came up with a tray of baklava fresh from the oven. It smelled amazing, like Emma's buttery croissants.

Bryony took a deep sigh, and Raya could tell, even without being a witch, that she couldn't avoid talking about what happened today any longer. It was as though Bryony had waited until everyone was at the coffee stage, had let them all have a nice evening together before bringing up the hard stuff. Or rather, asking Raya to say it for her. But she had no idea how much of all this, transporting, and what about time travel – she should talk about with Macide, Abbas and Musta. She looked at Bryony.

'It's OK – Abbas and Macide are both quite open to the idea of transporting. We talked about it before you got home. Or rather, I listened and they talked with the carriage driver after we returned. He'd rushed in to see what was wrong when he heard the grandmother screaming

after you disappeared, leaving a puddle of clothes on the floor. We'll see what this Kâtip Çelebi thinks about it – but he's clearly a real forward thinker,' Bryony reassured her. *'But I agree – let's not talk about the time travel. One thing at a time.'*

Raya balked. Bryony nodded encouragement, then said aloud in English, 'Go on, Rachel, tell them what happened today – how you managed to leave your clothes in a pile on the floor and vanish.' She was even smiling a little.

Raya retold the story, including her getting the sad visions about the granddaughter dying and how this set off a series of strong and complicated emotions she couldn't deal with. She included Rebecca West's story – remembering that they were supposedly from this same time in England, so it was OK. Musta leaned forward, interested. Abbas and Macide nodded, confirming they'd discussed much of this before.

'I thought the poor grandmother might have a heart attack – she was convinced the jinn took you. So I reassured her they'd surely have enough of you and bring you back home soon,' Bryony asked Raya to translate this for her. She did with a roll of her eyes. The adults laughed. *Very funny.*

The other three had been talking amongst themselves. Macide smiled the way she did when she complimented her on her Turkish. 'Rachel, you're so talented. This is amazing, what you can do!' She beamed.

Musta nodded sagely. 'I would be honoured if you would allow me to study this phenomenon. After all, we cannot merely stare at the world like cows,' he said between mouthfuls of baklava. 'This is a wonderful opportunity to learn more about the science of magic.'

'Yes, we thought you could practise this magic transportation of yours from the *han* to the Grand Bazaar, where you'd check in with Musta, of course,' Abbas was glowing with excitement.

'With your permission, once we know more about it, I'd like to write about this for other scholars,' Musta added.

Raya was speechless. She looked from Abbas, to Macide, to Musta – all of them with warm expectant faces. Bryony looked tired and worried – nothing new there.

'Don't look so shocked, Rachel,' Abbas said. 'We know amazing things can happen. After all, if a man can fly over the Bosphorus Strait on wings he made himself, who knows what's possible?'

'And that was twenty years ago,' Musta added. She could see him already writing up the first draft of his esteemed report, in his head.

But it wasn't their open-mindedness, their willingness to help, or even their possible over-keenness to be part of this 'discovery'. It was something else, something she hadn't felt for a long time. It felt like a strong, soft cloth that would catch her if she fell, and would also polish her to make her shine. Cherished. That's what it was. She felt an avalanche of old, unmet yearning. All the times she'd seen the 'real' kids in her foster placements get these looks, this sort of love, while she stood on the sidelines not knowing where to look or how to plug the jagged hole in her heart. Sometimes she wondered if having that early taste of it – from her grandparents and even her mum before she went whacko – made it worse. Every cell in her body knew what she was missing and screamed out for it, like a junkie needing a fix. But she was supposed to be leaving here, too, and returning to modern-day London. This was getting confusing, it was starting to feel awfully nice here, awfully quickly. But she'd only been here a few days. Bryony kept telling her this was the 'holiday effect' – that she needed to wait longer to know for sure. But long enough to know was likely longer than they had.

It was time for Musta to leave, and everyone was tired. They said their goodbyes and goodnights, with the promise that Raya would start this exciting scientific study with them tomorrow.

Back in their room Raya gave Bryony the blue dress with turquoise beads. She flushed. 'Thanks, Raya, that was really kind of you.' She beamed in a way that told Raya she didn't get a lot of presents. She didn't have the heart to tell her she got it for free.

Bryony put the dress on a shelf. 'Raya, we've got to talk about your transporting.'

'I SAID I was sorry – it wasn't on purpose,' she said defensively.

Bryony sat down on her bed and lifted the cat off the floor onto her lap. 'Raya, I'm not mad at you. Well, let me put it this way, it's not about you being "naughty". It's about you learning as quickly as possible how this skill works so you can get us home. We only have ten days left, and it's not a lot of time, especially if your transports are still so out of control.'

Raya's cheeks flushed with anger.

'Look, I'm really not telling you off. This rate of learning would be fine, excellent even if you were simply in witching academy.'

'There's such a thing?'

'What? Oh, yes, and you'd be a great candidate, but let's talk about that later – when we're home. Like I was saying, it will help if we really understand what transported you – so you can learn to harness it, that's all. We've got ten days left, Raya. It's not a lot of time.'

'Oh. OK.' The fight was out of her. She did understand.

'We've got to help you miss home, really yearn for it,' Bryony offered.

The girl witch nodded.

'Well, do you? Do you think about it, miss it at all?'

She shrugged. 'A little, I guess.'

Chapter 33
Yellow Shoes

The next morning, Bryony left for her jinn work after breakfast. It was their fifth day in old Istanbul. She looked small and alone as she made her way across the courtyard towards the exit, her new blue dress billowing as she walked. Abbas had arranged for a dragoman – a translator – to let Raya practise transporting. She was to transport herself twice within the *han* and courtyard, then twice again with Oscar, to practise taking someone with her, before transporting back to the Büyük Çarsi – the Grand Bazaar – again with Oscar. She was to go the coffee house, meet up with Musta then return to the *han* and visualize home, or 'home-home' as she now referred to it, finding herself calling the *han* home more and more.

At first, Oscar had refused, *'I TOLD you – I'm outta the game, sister. Nothing but a cat's life for me now.'* Then Bryony reminded him he was already bearing the weight of what happened to Jake on his conscience. 'It's not just about me, Oscar – this is about another young person too, remember.'

The transports in the *han* by herself were a snap. Although she did startle Macide when she suddenly appeared in her sitting room while she was doing some needlework. In her second transport with Oscar she landed in what she thought was an empty stall, not realising a camel had been brought in earlier that morning. She landed inches from the camel's hindquarters scaring her more than the beast who continued chewing in that sideways circular way that they have while giving her the once-over with a big long-lashed brown eye.

'OK, Abbas, I'm ready to go.' She stood in front of him as was agreed, and he would document everything he saw to tell Musta for his study. He looked ever so pleased to be involved in a project with Musta. And she could see he enjoyed this intellectual challenge – running the *han* must be dull work compared to being a janissary. She was glad she could at least give him this.

She closed her eyes, imagined the coffee house. It wasn't particularly vivid, so she walked her way through her memory of when she peered inside and it looked like the inside of a jewellery box. Sweat trickled down her back with all these clothes on and her thoughts went to the baths. She reasoned that it couldn't hurt to start there – it would still be good practice. She saw the third room with all the women lounging and chatting. Wondered if any of them would like a coffee cup reading and POP – she was there. With Oscar.

'Hey, I won't tell if you don't,' Oscar offered. Raya was about to argue his logic, but then thought better of it. She was past the bathing rooms and thought it best not to spend the time it would take to go through the whole process, before going on to the coffee house, but a few readings here couldn't hurt.

'Ah, the girl from London with Light Eyes, the one the Karatays discovered,' a woman said to her friend, when Raya asked them if they'd like a reading. Raya worked extra hard to give a good reading, and to let herself be overheard by the nosey women around. They jostled for their position in the queue but Raya explained she could only do a few more today. A cluster of women formed around her. They were all very curious about her and life in London. What was the weather like? Had she ever met the King? What were the English men like? Oscar snoozed on a couch. This was fun. A lot of fun. She'd been the new girl a million times before, but this time she was the cool new girl everyone wanted to know.

One of the girls in the group shrieked in excitement and dragged another teenager into the circle. 'Helena, here she is – the one you discovered!' It was the Karatay daughter.

'Come on, you knew this was going to happen sooner or later,' Oscar said, apparently not as asleep as he looked.

Raya stared, her smile frozen. *'What do I do?'* she asked the cat, but he didn't answer. She almost started to giggle – unusual for her, not being the giggly sort. But it was so weird for her to be the one with the edge rather than on it, when it came to this sort of teenage girl – one of the über-kids for sure. Then things got weirder. Mrs Karatay appeared behind her daughter's shoulder. From her expression, she clearly had not forgotten how they really met. Raya flushed.

'Work it, baby,' Oscar said.

'Oh, so now you're talking? What? Work what?' Raya was annoyed at having to drag him around if he was only going to be a pain.

'Only you and the Karatays seem to remember what really happened. So YOU can keep the secret, or not – that's power, sistah.'

'*Stop with the lingo already.*' But then she got it. She smiled warmly and cleared off the cup from the last reading on the small table in front of her.

'Mrs Karatay, Helena, how lovely to see you again. I can't thank you enough for being so generous with your kind words. I've done quite a few readings, thanks to you.'

Mrs Karatay gave her a look of wary relief.

'Please, let me do a reading for you – on the house,' Raya said and everyone clapped.

'Oh, Mother, let's have her at my party!' It was Helena.

Her mother worked hard to hide her startle; her stage smile looked well-practised.

'We'd be the first to have her at a party, Mother. Please?' the daughter implored. 'And Rachel, it is Rachel, right?'

Raya nodded.

'It's for my sixteenth birthday. There'll be henna tattoos and women to do our make-up. There'll be dancers, jugglers, musicians, the most amazing food and of course all the girls can use the hammam there,' Helena said. The girl was trying to convince Raya to come to HER party?

Surely the world had turned upside down. But here she wasn't the outsider Goth foster girl with an attitude – the type other kids' mothers warned against. She wondered for a split second how different her life might have been if she'd played it differently. Surely it couldn't be that simple.

'Well, I don't see why not,' Mrs Karatay changed her mind, obviously one with a good nose for self-preservation and status.

Popular – so this is what it felt like.

* * *

After surveying Raya as though she was a wall in need of painting, Mrs Karatay insisted they treat her to a new outfit for the party. Raya played along that this was mere generosity and not a comment on her wardrobe. They hurried into the bazaar with Oscar trotting next to Raya. As time was getting tight now, she needed to find Musta and carry on with her day's assignments, she agreed to the third dress they suggested – she didn't want to seem too compliant. A filmy gold affair with lots of beads and brocade. Amazing, but not Raya's usual sort of thing. Certainly wouldn't go with Doc Martens.

Then they stopped at a shoe sellers and there they were. The leather was as soft as the yellow colour was buttery – the wonderful shoes she'd seen on her first day.

Without hesitation, Mrs Karatay signalled to the seller that she wanted three pairs, one for each of them. Wow, these were those people who SO didn't have to think about money.

'Of course, madam. Three pairs of the yellow shoes for you three good Muslim women,' the seller said and raised an eyebrow at Mrs Karatay. She nodded, and he went to the back of his stall.

Raya gave Helena a questioning look. Helena whispered, 'You're supposed to be Muslim to wear yellow shoes, but no one really cares. The seller's just covering his butt.'

'Helena, please,' Mrs Karatay said, as though her daughter had made some bodily noise in public.

She agreed to meet them in front of a particular fountain the next day before the party. They offered to keep the new clothes and shoes for her, which was perfect. That way Raya wouldn't need to explain anything to Bryony. She thanked them and hurried to Musta's usual coffee house, Oscar running behind her.

Raya hovered at the entrance, with no time for readings there today she didn't want to go in – respecting the no working woman thing. Musta could see she was distracted and excited, but she put it off on getting all this support around her learning to transport. She could see he didn't believe it, but he didn't pry either. She wondered if this is what it was like to have a real uncle. He warned her from getting too caught up in the excitement of being here.

'Be careful, Rachel. It is dangerous to fall in love with any place, the one where you're born, or one you choose. There are good AND bad things about every place and everyone.' He looked hard at Raya. 'Don't get too carried away too soon. You have plenty of time.' Adults were always telling young people 'not to rush' and to take their time. She didn't know what he was on about. Everything was lovely and people seemed really good to each other. Whatever his motivation, he seemed genuine and earnest. And for all of everyone's affection and kindness she was grateful.

'Thank you, Uncle Musta. I do appreciate everything you have all done for me. But I need to get back to the *han*. My auntie wants me to do some more studying after my transport practice.' Musta wanted to see her actually leave, transport, but then another man at the coffee house called him over, to resolve some argument about politics. She waved goodbye and skittered away, bidding Oscar to follow. She found an empty alleyway between two buildings, hugged the cat, imagined the *han* and without any problems, popped them both back 'home'.

'You're late,' were Bryony's first words. Raya landed back in their room as was her aim. Bryony was gathering her few things together. She looked resigned and defeated. Oscar excused himself to check out what the cat ladies might be serving up.

'What's going on?' Raya asked.

'Macide's giving me my own room.'

As odd as it was at first to be living with your social worker, she'd got used to it. This felt crummy.

'Did I do something?' It came out meeker than she intended.

Bryony stopped what she was doing for a moment and looked at her. 'You really have to ask that?' her tone was sour, but she immediately looked sorry and said so. 'It was Macide's idea. She could see there's tension between us, and anyway, if I'm going to have to… to make a life here, I might as well get on with it.'

Raya picked at a tassel on a pillow. 'I'm sorry I'm late,' but she meant she was sorry for everything – for getting them all in this mess. 'I bumped into that mother-daughter pair I insulted the first day, and we kind of made up.' Raya found that partial truths often made for the best lies.

Bryony plunked down on what had been her bed. 'Well how did that go? And how did your transporting go today? Abbas said things seemed to go pretty well as far as he knew.' She was back to normal Bryony mode. Raya exhaled a private sigh.

She spun a version of her day, underscoring that she did transport successfully and on purpose (leaving out that this was to the baths… again), and omitting her agreement to go to the Karatays's party and do a few readings – as a sought after guest of honour. No need to rub it in. She was glad Oscar was out, in case he might have reneged on his oath of silence. But she couldn't see how holding herself back would do any good for anyone, here or in twenty-first century London. Raya wondered if it was hard for Bryony to see a young witch like herself excel so quickly. She couldn't wait until tomorrow.

Chapter 34

Party

The next day, Raya went through her practice transports at the *han*, with and without Oscar.

'Take me!' Abbas meant it, his playful eyes gleaming.

Raya choked on her own saliva. 'Oh no, I couldn't. I mean, I'd be too worried something might go wrong – I'd never forgive myself.' This was the truth. His face fell.

'Then promise to take me before you take Kâtip Çelebi? I know he'll ask.'

'Promise.'

When it was time to leave, she imagined the bazaar and the particular fountain where she was to meet the Karatays. She slowed her breathing, relaxed, but nothing. She tried again, bringing up the smells and sounds and the sights, but again – nothing. She opened her eyes to Abbas and

Macide's expectant faces. She would have excused herself to try from the privacy of her room, but she knew Abbas was doing the 'lift-off' observations for Musta's study, and Macide could talk of nothing else but wanting to see for herself after Abbas's description yesterday. This was all starting to feel a bit much – all this doting attention.

'Hey, you were liking it before. This is part of the package,' Oscar told her.

Oscar was right of course, she couldn't let a little love put her off her game. Transporting all three of them back home would be a lot harder than this. So she tried again, imagined the spot where they were to meet, imagined Mrs Karatay and Helena, heard them gossiping, then BAM – she was there.

Raya held Oscar while she looked for Helena and Mrs Karatay, and after what felt like a long time she saw them walking away from the fountain through the bazaar. Raya rushed up to them like an excited puppy. Mrs Karatay acknowledged her, but seemed bored and impatient. She hurried the girls along, out through a stone arch.

'Why did you bring your cat? Does he help with the readings?' Helena asked as they walked as fast as their skirts would allow.

'Yes, he does – he keeps away the bad spirits.' Raya was relieved to have an easy answer – she hadn't been sure how to explain bringing Oscar along.

A two-horse carriage was waiting for them in the next street and as Mrs Karatay ushered them inside, Helena jabbered away about the people she expected at the party and gossiped about them.

By this time, they'd reached the banks of what looked like a very wide river.

'I don't know about this, Raya. Why don't I wait for you some place?' Oscar grumbled. She held the cat firmly.

'I thought you liked water – remember the baths?'

The cat huffed, *'Um, yeah – the baths and the Bosphorus are just a TAD different, don't you think?'*

'Oh, don't look. Here, I'll cover your eyes,' She tucked his head under her arm. He dug his claws in, through her dress. She was glad it wasn't the fancy one they bought for her yesterday.

They were helped down the steep staircase to the bank by a man in short billowy trousers, cuffed below the knee, wearing a waistcoat but no shirt. Bobbing on the water was a large, ornately painted rowboat. The man who had helped them down the stairs leapt into the boat like a graceful frog and joined another man already in it. Both men were young, tanned, bearded and, of course, turbaned. Their well-muscled arms made long, even strokes that sped them across the water.

'So this is the Bosphorus Strait?' Raya asked. The mother and girl nodded. *Wow, that really would be something to fly over this on wings you made yourself.* It had to be more than a mile wide. It was brimming with wooden boats of all shapes and sizes.

Some of the small boats looked a little weather worn, stacked with piles of fish. And then there were the big boats, huge and beautiful with sails as tall as buildings. Men were crawling all over them. It must have been hard work making those ships sail by the way they ran around, yelling, climbing, and pulling on the ropes.

The men in their boat took sudden, hard strokes backwards, bringing the vessel to a halt. One of the big sailing ships skimmed past, leaning towards them. Raya gasped, thinking it might tip over. Waves smacked the side of their boat, rocking it each time. Raya grabbed the side. The others laughed. 'That's not kind,' Helena said, 'None of us can help where we've come from.'

'*Biatch,*' Oscar said. Raya squeezed him hard, even though no one else could hear him.

* * *

They moored on the other side of the Bosphorus where they got off onto a wooden platform. They ascended steps to the top of the bank. Helena and her mother marched up, chatting away. Raya squinted and shielded her eyes against the incessant sun. There were two monumental, gracious wooden buildings. They were largely square, reaching out over the banks on stilts, with peaked roofs. Large windows lined the walls. The views must be stunning. The entrances were on the inland sides with paths leading out and lush gardens beyond. They looked like two posh hotels. One of the men encouraged her up the steps, a bit unbalanced holding Oscar, while the other tied up the boat. The Karatays and Raya headed to the building to their left and entered a doorway on the side away from the Bosphorus.

It was much cooler inside. Her eyes adjusted as they reached the end of the short, arched entryway. In front of her was an amazing room, some sort of grand lobby. Oscar scrabbled against her hold.

'You can let him down if you like. I trust he knows how to behave?' Mrs Karatay said.

'Thank you, Mrs Karatay.' Then to Oscar she said, '*Stick around except for going to the loo, OK? No looking for* kedi et *around here. There's going to be plenty of food, I'll get you stuff – deal?*' He agreed, almost as gobsmacked with the surroundings as the young witch was. It was heaps nicer than anything she'd ever seen, but then again, she'd only ever been to a Travelodge once with her nan.

It was a huge space with alcoves that led off the main room. The walls were lined with sumptuous couches in wonderful greens and purples, with deep red cushions all along. There was gold braid on the edges of everything.

Above the couches were gigantic windows, giving you views of the magical gardens, the Bosphorus and Istanbul beyond. Above the windows the walls were covered by gilded panels painted in geometric patterns. Raya craned her neck, her mouth open. Above the panels was an equally exquisite ceiling with a dome in the middle. Even the hammam, as beautiful as it was, paled next to this.

Helena sniggered at Raya's sense of wonder.

'Now, Helena,' her mother said, sounding bored. 'Don't be rude. You don't remember the first time you saw the *divanhane*. You were just a baby.'

'So you come here a lot? Is that the name of this hotel? Maybe I could show my auntie sometime,' Raya said.

This brought more giggles from Helena. 'It's not a hotel. It's our house,' she said.

'Actually, it's our summer home, that's what *divanhane* means,' Mrs Karatay said. Then she excused herself to see to the party preparations, but not before reminding the girls to have their baths now, before the guests arrived.

'I'll be here,' Oscar told her and hopped onto one of the couches.

After their luxurious baths, complete with staff to scrub them, Helena went to her room to get dressed. A servant showed Raya to a guest room. There, the new dress and the long-coveted yellow shoes were waiting. The dress was a matching gold colour with small beads and embroidery at the neck, hem and sleeves. Over this was a long, sheer over-dress of the same colour that opened in the front and was edged with a wide band of gold brocade. No veils or headscarves would be needed because there would only be girls, of course.

'Why's that?' Raya had asked when the servant told her this. The servant was a bit impatient with Raya's lack of knowledge. She answered by nodding out the window, towards the other building. 'That's the *haremlik* over there for the men; and this is the *selamlik*, for the ladies.'

* * *

The party was marvellous. There must have been at least three hundred guests, all girls with their mothers, aunties or grandmothers; a noisy, happy, colourful, bejewelled and perfumed bunch. Servants brought endless trays heaped with the most amazing food, both savoury and sweet. They circulated with the sherbet, coffee, tea and juices. Musicians played throughout, sometimes with a singer. The girls danced when there weren't professional dancers for them to watch. There were jugglers and clowns as well.

Raya was given a special table covered with a beautiful cloth. They'd made a sign that stretched between two poles behind where she sat, presumably saying *Rachel of London*, but it was in Arabic, which she couldn't read. She hadn't realised she would be doing quite so many readings. She needed a break. But the staff told her she'd only be allowed ten minutes.

Raya was surprised, but figured she should be flattered. She wandered over to the most recently delivered tray of food and took a plateful when she saw Helena with a group of girls and joined them. But Helena acted a bit funny, like she didn't know Raya.

In any event, this got Raya a lot of attention for her eyes. A number of girls leaned in to get a good look. One even gasped, claiming she could see her future in them, and ran away either shrieking or giggling. This all got to be a bit much, so Raya was relieved to have the excuse of returning to her table to do more readings. But they went on for hours. Oscar sat by her feet, and occasionally on her lap. For every one she did, that person seemed to send two or three more friends.

The sounds of evening birds and bugs filtered in, and the musicians slowed to a gentle stop. Staff lit the jewel-toned glass lanterns that hung on chains from the ceiling. Finally, guests started departing. Raya heard boatmen calling to each other and the occasional clatter of oars. She looked out the windows and saw the last blades of sun slash the Bosphorus. She realised she hadn't looked out once since she arrived. She was tired. The idea of transporting herself back to the *han* sounded wonderful; the quickest commute. Now, to concoct an excuse to disappear. *Or should I show off?*

Mrs Karatay walked up to Raya holding a pretty cloth pouch. 'Thank you, Rachel. You added just the right touch to our party. We received many compliments about your readings. A number of people said they would like to you to read for them again.'

Helena was across the room saying goodbye to some friends while servants cleared up.

'You're very welcome, Mrs Karatay. It was lovely being included in such a won-der-ful par-ty...' Raya didn't realise she was trailing off. She was visualizing her cosy bed at the *han*, a steaming cup of mint tea, and Oscar curled up at the foot. Raya forced her focus back to where she was and picked up the cat. She saw Mrs Karatay and Helena peering at her, concerned. Or was it confused? Mrs Karatay held the cloth pouch and said something, but Raya couldn't hear her, then – POP. She was back at the *han*.

Chapter 35

Should I Stay or Should I Go

Raya landed less than gracefully on her bed. Oscar spilled out of her arms. It was good to be home.

The door creaked open. Macide appeared.

'Well, hello, dear. I thought I heard you in here. I'm afraid everyone's been terribly worried. Can you come out here for a few minutes?' Macide said, then disappeared back behind the door.

'Do I have to go in there, now?' Raya said, really to herself.

'Hey, they know where you live,' Oscar said.

Raya stood up and took in a big breath as though she was about to go underwater, then opened the door to

Macide's. There were lots of those colourful glass lanterns lit around the room. Four worried faces sat looking at her: Macide, Abbas, Bryony, and Musta.

Oh no.

'Rachel, where have you been?' Bryony said, then continued in head chat. *'You locked down your thoughts so completely, I thought you were dead.'* She choked back a sob.

'It's OK. She's safe now,' Macide said.

'I'm sorry,' Raya said meekly. Bryony seemed upset beyond Raya's being her ticket home.

'That was very selfish, young lady,' Musta said.

Abbas's usually warm eyes were beacons of anguish.

Then Raya felt it. Each of them had been truly worried about her: she felt it.

Bryony hugged her. 'I can't tell you how glad I am to see you – in one piece – and how mad I am–'

'That's some dress, Rachel. Where did you get that?' Macide interrupted.

Raya took a deep breath. 'The Karatays.'

'What?' Abbas said. 'I thought you hated them.'

'I bumped into them yesterday at the baths, and they asked if I could go and do readings at Helena's birthday party today. So… I DID transport on purpose with Oscar – and back again.'

'Oh, Rachel,' Musta said.

'Why are you here, Uncle Musta?' Raya said.

'When it got to dinnertime and I hadn't seen you at the coffee house, I came here to find out if you were all right,' Musta said.

Raya groaned. She looked around the room, there were empty coffee cups, half-eaten plates of food, Macide's needlework lay in a heap on a couch. She got a flash of the scene that had been; the four of them keeping vigil, trying to figure out what to do.

'I'm really, really sorry,' Raya said. This felt good, but raw – people caring so deeply.

'Well, you're safe and sound and that's all that matters,' Macide said, giving her a squeeze around the shoulders. Raya could tell Macide was holding off Bryony's anger as much as getting her to bed. 'Come on, let's all turn in for the night; tomorrow's another day.'

* * *

Raya woke up to a soft knock at her door – Bryony. She and Oscar yawned and stretched. Bryony sat on the bed across from them, fiddling with a pillow. A leaden silence filled the room.

'Do you ever think about home, besides for your practice? You know, home-home?' Bryony asked.

'*I don't*,' Oscar said. He jumped down and sat by the door to the balcony, twitching his tail. Bryony opened it for him.

Raya looked away. 'Yeah, I do. Sometimes.' Morning noises filtered in – a camel grumbled.

'Tell me, exactly what do you think about when you think about home?'

Raya felt exposed. 'Um, I think about the Cosmic sometimes, and the fun I had there. About Ian and Emma and of course Pavel…' Her voice trailed off. 'But that usually gets me to thinking about Jake, and well…' Tears filled her eyes, they collected, threatening to plop down in large fat drops.

Bryony reached over and cupped her hand over Raya's. The tears tumbled out and she cried in earnest. She let Bryony sit next to her and give her a proper hug. 'Shh, it's normal to be worried, upset. It's good to let it out.' They were quiet for a moment.

There was a tap at the door and Macide peeked in. 'Oh, sorry. I didn't mean to intrude. Just wanted to tell you breakfast is ready when you are.' She disappeared again behind the door.

Bryony smoothed her dress, the one Raya got for her. 'Raya, I know this is terrible pressure on you. It truly is. No young person should have so much responsibility, and you shouldn't have to be responsible for a grown-up,' she sighed then stood up. 'And for your bloody social worker on top of that, eh?' She smiled, trying to make a joke of it, but there was sadness in her eyes.

Raya thought about it for the first time – what it must be like to be as old as Bryony, probably someplace in her thirties, and have your future depend on some kid. Some mixed up fourteen-year-old. Well, Raya hadn't asked for all this either.

Bryony put her hand on the door. 'Come on, let's get some breakfast.'

* * *

There were two loud knocks at Macide's door. Abbas answered it. It was a groundsman with another man in long brocade robes, white billowing trousers and a turban – a messenger from the Karatay family. Raya looked up when she heard the name.

'I am here to relay a message to Rachel of London,' the messenger said.

Macide nodded for Raya to respond.

'Yes, I am Rachel... um... of London.' She felt funny getting this attention in front of Bryony.

The messenger extended his arm, offering a cloth pouch to Raya, the same one Mrs Karatay had been holding out to her after the party.

'That's not mine, sir. I'm sorry you came all this way,' Raya said to the messenger.

Macide stepped next to Raya and nudged her. 'I think they're trying to pay you.'

'Yes, these are your earnings from your work for the Karatays yesterday,' the messenger said.

Raya blushed and wrinkled her forehead. 'But I thought I was a guest.' Then, everyone but Raya laughed.

'The Karatays have been getting enquiries. They hope you don't mind, but they have been giving out your contact information. But only to the best people,' the messenger said. He gave a brief bow and left.

Raya loosened the drawstring and spilled the coins on the table. Her eyes were wide – this was quite a haul. Abbas manoeuvred back to the table and counted the coins for her.

'You've been paid very well, young lady. That's more than I would have earned in a week as a janissary.'

Raya bit her lip, delighted, confused and embarrassed.

'You have to understand, people such as the Karatays only make friends with people who are very rich and influential. To them, you're a service provider,' Abbas said.

'Yeah, I don't know what I was thinking. That their sort would ever really want to be friends with me.' She pocketed a few coins and put the rest back in the pouch.

'*Come on, don't feel bad. You knew in the bottom of your human heart what these people were like,*' Oscar said.

'*I guess,*' Raya said, still hurt.

'*But hey, it was a good party wasn't it?*' Oscar brushed against her ankles. This was new, the cat trying to cheer her up.

Abbas got up from the table and patted her on her scarf-covered head. 'Being young isn't always easy, is it?' Raya shook her head, but Abbas didn't wait for a reply, 'Believe me, I know how seductive to the soul wealth and power can be.

* * *

After her warm-up transports in the *han*, she sat on one of the stone benches in the courtyard with Oscar on her lap. She imagined the Grand Bazaar in all its glory, smelled the coffee, and POW!

Ah, to be back in the Büyük Çarşi. The sights, the sounds, the smells, the donkeys.

'*Hold that thought,*' Oscar said when she tried to put him down. After two donkeys laden with goods ambled past, she could feel the cat exhale.

'*OK, now's good, thanks,*' Oscar said, and she put him down.

The crowd flowed around them; a few people stared at her.

'Do you think they recognize me from my coffee readings?' Raya said.

Oscar looked at her flatly. *'Get over yourself. You forgot your veil.'*

'Agh!' she said aloud, feeling embarrassed. She reached in her pocket. There was no veil, but she felt the coins she'd taken from the pouch. She stepped into the first stall with veils and apologized for being without one. Good thing everyone could see she wasn't from there.

'Come on, let's go find Uncle Musta. I need to talk to him,' she said.

She located the coffee house and stood in the doorway, Oscar next to her. Soon a waiter recognized her and brought her a table and chairs.

'Ah, Rachel, you and your light eyes are good for business. Like a living *nazarlik* – lucky charm that keeps away the evil eye,' the proprietor said.

She'd always hated her eyes, like dirty sea water. But now they were useful, making her easily recognizable, despite the scarf and veil.

'Thank you. And thank you for letting me read here again. Is it all right it my cat joins me today?' Raya said.

'Of course,' the proprietor said and waved at the waiter, who brought another chair for Oscar and a cup of coffee on the house. She people-watched and thought about a future in Istanbul.

When Uncle Musta came in while she was in the middle of a reading, she felt a wave of relief. He had a coffee while she finished, then suggested they take a walk.

'Rachel, is everything all right? It's not like you to lie to your auntie – your sneaking off to the Karatays's party,' he said as the three ambled down the crowded bazaar street.

'Oh, Uncle Musta, I don't know what to do. I thought maybe you'd have some advice,' she said.

Musta nodded at the many people who knew him. 'About what?' he said.

'About whether I should stay here, in Istanbul, or return to England. My auntie wants to return home soon, but I don't think I want to go,' she said.

'Well then, why don't you stay and she goes? You're old enough. And we're here to help.'

If only it was that simple. She thought for a minute.

'Sure, we could go our separate ways. It's just that my auntie had promised my mother she would stay with me until I turn eighteen, and with my mother dying and everything, it's hard for my auntie to break that promise.' She thought she might as well stick to the story Bryony concocted back in old England.

'Ah, I see,' Musta said. They walked along in silence. Musta stopped by a sherbet seller and bought two glasses. They found a stone bench and sat down. Oscar jumped up and butted his head against Musta, who stroked the cat.

'It sounds like you don't want to be responsible for making your auntie break her promise to her sister who's passed away – that this would feel like a betrayal, maybe to your mother as well.'

Raya nodded and sipped her sherbet.

More people said hello to Musta as they passed. A man stopped briefly. Musta introduced Raya as his niece. She felt a rush of warmth.

'Rachel, as you consider a life on your own, this is part of it, making these difficult decisions, and facing the fact that sometimes we end up disappointing or upsetting people, including people we love. This is for you to decide, Rachel.'

The sherbet seller collected their cups. Musta stood up. 'Alas, dear niece, it's time for me to go.'

Raya stayed on the bench after Musta left, thinking about what he'd said. The light shifted to pastel, the relentless heat of the Turkish summer receding.

Chapter 36
Rachel Nazarlik

'May I be excused? I think I'll take my dinner into my room,' Raya said.

Abbas started to say something, likely that she shouldn't be excused from the look on his face, but Macide interjected. Bryony didn't say anything.

'Of course you can, dear,' Macide said and put more food on Raya's plate before she took it with her. Raya motioned with her head for Oscar to follow and he did – after a huff.

She closed the door with great relief, put the plate on the shelf and sat on her bed. 'Oh, Oscar. I don't know what to do. I mean I'm responsible for getting Bryony back home, and I don't know if I want to go.'

'Oh, you know what you want all right. You want to stay here. That's obvious.' He stood on his hind legs, stretched

up against the wall and sniffed towards the shelf. *'Hey, you gonna eat that?'*

Raya placed the plate on the floor for him. 'Why does it seem like my life is always interrupted for other people and their problems?'

'Yeah, it's not fair, is it?' But it wasn't Oscar responding to her. She recognized the annoying voice of that kitchen jinn from the other day.

Oscar looked up from his plate, and if a cat could laugh, he would have been. *'Boy, that's ugly, even for a jinn. Looks like a cross between a rat, a frog and a bottlebrush. What's he saying?'*

'Tell that flea motel he'd make a good footstool,' the jinn said into Raya's ear. She batted away the tickly feeling. 'Nothing, he's just spouting the usual jinn rubbish.'

Oscar licked some crumbs off his front and walked towards the door. *'Do you want me to go get Bryony, to get rid of it?'*

'No!' she accidentally barked. 'I need some time without her – to try to sort my head out.'

'I'll help,' crackled the jinn.

Raya ignored it and turned to Oscar, 'Stay, Oscar. Help me figure this out.'

Oscar hopped on the now unused bed and curled in a circle. *'OK.'*

Raya talked it through with Oscar. She realised she did want to stay in Istanbul.

'I don't know, Raya. It's different for me to stay here. I am a cat – I mean, you'll live a lot longer. Won't you miss all that stuff back home that you humans do so much, like watching telly?'

'What's "telly"?' the bottlebrush jinn asked.

'It's kind of like a box with lots of moving pictures.'

'Don't talk to it – you know what they're like. OK, what about, the Internet, your mobile? Your friends?' Oscar said.

The jinn asked about the first two, and when Raya thought about it, they were more boxes with buttons and pictures. And as far as friends, really the only ones she cared about she'd only known a few weeks – the gang at the Cosmic, and Angie and Jake. The longer this lop-sided conversation continued the more she found herself agreeing with Bottlebrush. Oscar must have sensed it, or had had enough because he leapt onto the windowsill and jumped out as soon as Raya opened the shutters for him.

She felt another release when Oscar left. She let herself feel it – this very weird and difficult decision. She wanted to stay here in Istanbul, even more than she had wanted to stay at the Cosmic. This felt like home. Now, how to tell Bryony?

'*Why tell her?*' the jinn suggested. '*She'll find out soon enough. You've only got seven more days, right?*'

Raya gasped. 'How do you know that?'

'*Jinn know LOTS of things – we're the beings made of fire, remember?*'

She started to ask him what that had to do with it, but thought better of it. Talking to jinn was like arguing with a spring made of jelly. She didn't know how Bryony did it.

She fell into a dark, dreamless sleep.

* * *

The next day, their eighth in Istanbul, was normal, if you can call practising transporting at the *han*, then to the Grand Bazaar, doing some coffee cup readings, stopping at the baths then transporting home, all the while brushing that nosey jinn off her shoulders 'normal'. The only different thing was her avoiding Bryony. She thought she should tell Bryony her decision to stay – the stand-up thing to do, but she couldn't face it.

'*Who cares? Stand up. Sit down, do the hokey-cokey and turn yourself around.*' The jinn's voice dissolved into a snorting laugh. She was glad he found himself so entertaining, maybe he'd give her a break.

Shortly after she transported back home, Abbas knocked on her door and asked if he could have a minute.

'Here, Rachel, we want you to have this,' he said offering a little wooden box with one of those blue glass eyes they called *nazarlik* on the lid. These good luck charms were everywhere, on all the houses, shops, sewn onto clothes. There were so many, you stopped noticing them.

Inside the box was another one, circled in silver and on a pretty chain.

'You know, people are calling you 'Rachel Nazarlik' because of your light eyes,' Abbas said. He looked bemused. 'I think some of these people actually think you are a living good luck charm. This one's from me and Macide, to keep you safe,' he said.

Raya rolled her eyes. Abbas frowned. 'I see. You transport yourself at the blink of an eye, see the future in the mud at the bottom of a coffee cup, yet you laugh at keeping safe with this well-known power?' Abbas looked serious. Raya decided not to argue about what she thought was nonsense.

She was touched by their concern, but in spite of her getting her head around being a witch, time travel, and other previously unimaginable ideas, this – the idea that a bit of coloured glass could protect her – was hard to believe.

'Thank you, Uncle Abbas. I'll wear it always.' She fastened it around her neck.

* * *

Raya woke up on the ninth day to the sound of birds, the soft padding of camels' feet in the courtyard and the occasional chiding of groundsmen. She opened the shutters to let the strong sunlight in. The warmth still felt good. Oscar jumped from the balcony walkway up onto her windowsill.

'You ready?' Raya said.

'Yessireebob – I'm all yours, kid,' he said and closed his eyes in the sun's caress.

'Where's Bryony?' she was keen to keep avoiding her.

'Macide's taken her to the baths and then they're going to hang out with her friends.' Raya felt guilty relief – maybe Bryony would be OK staying here.

Raya got her veil ready. *'You can come in, you know,'* she said.

'If it's all the same to you I'll stay here. Feeling a bit twitchy – like something's about to happen,' he said.

'A premonition or good hearing?' she asked the cat, an eyebrow hitched up. But he didn't answer. He flattened himself on the windowsill, ears plastered to his head.

Strong footsteps pounded up the staircase outside, then the balcony shook. Oscar gave a small hiss and pressed himself against the window frame. Raya popped her veil on and peered out the window.

Two tall men were approaching, one white and one black. They were wearing the most ornate clothing she'd ever seen. A groundsman was simpering behind them, saying things they ignored except for an occasional nod. Oscar jumped down to the balcony and sidled past them. Raya closed the shutters, pretty sure they hadn't seen her.

She didn't know why, but her heart was thumping. There was a sharp rap at Macide's door. She heard Abbas's voice.

'Greetings, Kizlar Agha and Kapi Agha. To what do we owe this great honour? Please do come in. You'll have to forgive my less than splendid hospitality: the woman of the house, my mother, is out, I'm afraid. Can I offer you some coffee? Some nourishment?'

'No, thank you. We won't be staying. The Sultan's wife, Turhan Hatice Sultana requests the services of Rachel Nazarlik. We will bring a coach here for her tomorrow morning at ten o'clock,' one of the men said. There was a pause.

'Of course, Kizlar Agha, we will do everything in our power to have Rachel of London, I mean Rachel Nazarlik, waiting for you at the gate. But you better than most know how hard it can be to guarantee the behaviour of young women.'

The visitors chuckled. The voice that spoke before, spoke again. 'You have no idea. Yet, we would hate to disappoint the Sultana.'

There was a pause. Raya's heart was pounding so hard, she thought they might be able to hear it.

After goodbyes, the men left, insisting they show themselves out. Raya remained with her ear to the door.

'What an honour,' one of the groundsmen crowed to Abbas. 'A request from Topkapi Palace!'

'With this Sultan – Crazy Ibrahim? You know what they're like, brother killing brother, executing enemies, what they did to my uncle. I don't want her anywhere near that place,' Abbas said.

'But think of all that luxury. And hardly anyone gets into the innermost quarters. I'm sure you could accompany her. Aren't you just a little curious?' the groundsman persisted.

'Over my dead body,' Abbas growled.

Chapter 37

Safe as Houses

'*Oscar, did you hear that?!*' Raya was about to explode with excitement. '*Topkapi Palace? Me? And invited to give the Sultana a reading!*'

'*I don't know. I got a bad feeling from those two – didn't like 'em.*'

'*The groundsman didn't think it was such a big deal. You get things wrong sometimes, don't you?*'

'*Of course he does.*' It was the reedy voice of the bottlebrush jinn.

'*Let me go get Bryony – get rid of this idiot,*' Oscar jumped onto the windowsill ready to leave.

'*No! I mean, she's on her way to the baths and everything. Let her have a nice day,*' Raya said. The last thing she wanted was to see Bryony, between her guilt and now this amazing opportunity that she had a feeling Bryony would be against. And Raya was so excited she knew it would leak out of her, no matter how hard she locked down her thoughts.

Oscar jumped from the windowsill to the bed, hunkered down and twitched his tail like an angry clock. *'OK, but if you go to this Topkapi Palace, I'm going with you.'*

That's all she needed. Bring a cat along with her to a royal visit? She'd look like a right plonker. *'I don't know, Oscar – that's really sweet of you and everything, but–'*

'No discussion – I'm going.' He sat up straight, then narrowed his eyes. *'Or I'll grass on you – tell Bryony what you're up to, sneaking off to the Palace, eh?'*

'All right, all right. You can go.' People seemed pretty blasé about her bringing the cat around with her so far. The excitement was bubbling through her. *'Come on, let's get going. We'll transport to the bazaar – like I'm doing my regular practice – and touch base with Musta. And anyway, I'll need a new dress for our visit to the Palace.'*

'Of course you do.' Oscar was excellent at sarcasm.

She put her veil and headscarf on, ready for transport.

* * *

She stepped into the doorway of Musta's regular coffee house and let Oscar jump down from her arms. Musta wasn't there at the moment, but they thought he'd arrive in about an hour. Too wound up to wait, she decided to go shopping for that dress first and return to check in with Musta later. Maybe she'd get some matching shoes, too.

'So remind me – why do you need a new dress to go to the Palace?' Oscar asked as he trotted to keep up with her as she threaded through the streets of the bazaar.

'I don't want to be easily recognized when I'm waiting outside of the han *for those royal guys tomorrow.'*

'Fashion stealth – I like that,' Oscar said.

Strolling from stall to stall, she decided on a pale rose-coloured dress with lots of beads and pearls sewn on, once again, not her usual style. She still had time and looked for shoes. She found a gorgeous deep rose pair with darker rose beads in a geometric pattern on the pointed toes. Bliss.

When she and Oscar returned to the coffee house Musta was seated at a table with other men. He had his back to the door. He was telling them something in his calm, authoritative voice. She waited in the doorway as she wasn't working there today.

One of the other men nudged Musta.

'Hello, dear niece. How nice to see you, and of course, your fine cat companion,' he said and crouched down to give Oscar a stroke. 'How are your studies going?' He crooked an eyebrow. This was how he referred to her practising transporting and any other magic she might know when he was in earshot of other people. From what she could tell, it was more to do with him wanting to keep these wonders to himself until he was ready to publish them, rather than worrying that others might disbelieve.

Raya was dying to talk to someone about this amazing opportunity – someone besides a cat and a jinn. It was one of the few times she really missed having a friend her own age around here. She also wanted to make sure Abbas's concerns weren't grounded, and for that, Uncle Musta would be perfect. If only she could steer the conversation in the right direction without telling him, because he'd be sure to tell Abbas and the others.

She reached up to bite her nails, but her veil was in the way.

Musta laughed. 'Are you all right, dear niece? You seem distracted, burdened. Let's take another walk.'

As they strolled through the Grand Bazaar, she listened and hoped for a chance to steer the conversation to the Topkapi Palace. Then one of his mates stopped him to talk politics – one of Musta's favourite topics. After a brief chat about what each thought of the current Grand Vizier, apparently a shameless kiss-up and yes-man, they said their goodbyes and parted ways. *Perfect.*

'So you actually KNOW the Grand Vizier, Uncle Musta? Does that mean you've been to the Palace?' Raya said.

Musta darkened. 'Yes, my good friend, Kemankeş Kara Mustafa Pasha used to be Grand Vizier. He got me into the second courtyard of Topkapi Palace once...' He trailed off.

'So, he's named Mustafa, too.'

Musta came back from his thoughts and chuckled. 'Ah yes, it's quite a common name. But never mind about that. Topkapi Palace – beauty beyond your imagination, young Rachel. One thousand times more beautiful than any grand mansion you've ever seen.'

'Even nicer than the Karatays's *divanhane* on the Bosphorus?' Raya was more and more intrigued.

Musta bought two sherbets from a passing seller and handed one to Raya, as had become their habit. 'Oh, dear niece, that place is like a nomad's tent in comparison. The Palace is a self-contained jewel of a city in its own right,' Musta said. He made sweeping gestures as he described the glorious furnishings, the sumptuous scents from the twenty kitchens, the musicians playing, and all the marvellous clothes people wore there. He went on to describe the three courtyards, the splendid park-like grounds and more.

Raya wasn't foolish and she knew that Abbas's uncle was executed by the Ottoman rulers, if not exactly by this Sultan, so she pressed on to make sure she'd be safe as best she could without asking directly.

'Uncle Musta, I know Abbas's uncle was executed by a former government. I mean, is that common?'

Musta threw back the rest of his sherbet and gave their empty cups back to the seller. 'I don't know if the Ottoman rulers execute more than other royal leaders do. They all do this to some extent. I'm not saying it's right – and a lot of times it isn't. Like going to war – there's always a lot of questionable death.

They walked along some more, Oscar at their feet. She thought about this. She was aware enough to realise that modern governments, including from her own time killed people, sometimes designated bad guys, sometimes their own citizens, and of course plenty of regular people got killed in wars, too. Maybe this wasn't so different. When she thought about it some more, she figured there were probably more murders in some place like London, or certainly in New York, and people still went out and had fun. It couldn't stop you. You just had to be careful. And like Musta had been saying the other day, part of becoming independent, an adult, was making these difficult decisions for yourself.

Chapter 38

Don't Lose Your Head

Raya listened at the door to Macide's for Bryony to leave after breakfast for her jinn work.

'I think you should talk to the girl – I agree she's been avoiding you,' Macide said. She must have been stirring her tea. There was the rhythmic clink of metal spoon against glass. And as much as the velocity of Macide's stirring was a gauge of her emotional state, she seemed a bit stressed. That her relationship with Bryony would affect other people hadn't occurred to Raya.

Bryony was pretty good at thought reading and now with her increasing ability to understand Turkish she could often fathom the gist of what people were saying. She must have pantomimed her response – probably shook her head and shrugged her shoulders to say, 'What can you do?', because after a beat Macide said. 'Well, you know her best. I only hate to see this invisible rock between you two.'

After Bryony was through the front gate, and Raya heard the carriage leaving, she ventured into Macide's for breakfast. More to keep up appearances; she was far too excited to eat. She excused herself explaining she was going to transport to the bazaar first today, and practise her transports within the *han* later this afternoon, although these seemed too easy to bother with any more. Macide didn't question it, and Abbas had gone out to the mosque.

Back in her room with Oscar, she changed into the rose-pink dress, headscarf and veil. Then Rachel Nazarlik and cat companion transported to a spot in front of the *han*, about fifty metres away from the entrance. Veil on, perfumed and ready at a quarter to ten on her tenth day in Istanbul, waiting to meet the Sultana – not bad for a foster girl from east London. A carriage pulled past her up to the entrance, and one of the two men from yesterday got out and started towards the gate. She ran up to him.

'Yes?' the man said.

Raya didn't know if these guys were royalty themselves, or what to do exactly, so she gave a small curtsey but then tripped on her dress. He caught her by the arm.

'I am Rachel Nazarlik. I believe you've come for me.'

The man did a double take, then stared at her eyes. 'Oh yes, so you are.' He didn't smile. He opened the door. 'Please, get in. I'm Kizlar Agha, Chief of the Girls, and my colleague here,' he gestured towards another man inside the carriage compartment, 'he's Kapi Agha, Lord of the Door.'

Raya nodded as she got in and Oscar hopped in, too. No one said a word about the cat. She could only suppose these two saw much odder things in their time.

It looked like Cinderella's carriage before it turned back into a pumpkin, but on steroids. She sat on the red-and-gold velvet seat. The walls were painted with intricate flower designs lined with more gold. The Chief of the Girls was black. He settled on the seat across from Raya, next to the Lord of the Door guy who was white. They made a stunning team, both tall, handsome, and dressed resplendently. From the way they interacted, it seemed the Chief of the Girls was the higher up of these two. She took a second to memorise their titles. After hearing about what Macide's brother went through working at the Palace, she wondered where these two might be from and what they might have gone through, too.

The Chief instructed the driver to go. Raya glanced out the back window as the carriage jolted forward. Other carts and carriages were getting on with the day's work – two, a fancy yellow one and a plain one stopped at the *han*. The guard at the gate was talking to one of those drivers. Great. It looked like she had got away. The ride was bumpy on the cobbles.

'Turhan Hatice Sultana will be delighted you could come,' the Chief said.

The carriage continued rattling along the maze-like winding and hilly streets of Istanbul.

The Chief turned to the Lord of the Door. 'This one looks a little like Turhan Sultana, don't you think? A bit younger, of course.' The Lord considered Raya, then asked her, 'Where are you from? Turhan Sultana was from Ukraine, originally.'

'Me? I'm from England,' she said. Oscar burrowed next to her, pushed his head under her arm.

'I'm not liking the vibe, Raya. I don't think they're being straight with you. I can feel it in my tail.'

'In your tail?'

'Ah, that will make you the first one from England. The girls are from all over. But none from England,' the Lord of the Doors said.

She looked out the window. *Girls?* People turned to look at the carriage, some nodded, others gave little gasps of awe – quite a different reception than the carts of accused witches got in Colchester. After about twenty minutes, the carriage slowed and turned again. Raya glimpsed through the front window and around the driver – a grand marble gate. People, on horses, camels, or with donkeys, and many more on foot poured through the gate in both directions. It felt busier than Colchester, what now felt like a lifetime ago, and here it was in Technicolor compared to that drab time in England.

On the other side of the gate was a vast park. Just as Musta described, it was like a whole town, loads going on. And like in the rest of Istanbul, all shades of humanity from across the planet milled about. Everyone but them stopped and dismounted their horses and handed them over to staff. Their carriage drove on through the park.

To the right was a high wall around the park. To the left was a mosque. There were statues and fountains. A clutch of people stared up at some marble pillars.

'Oscar, do you think that's like Nelson's Column?' she said.

'Umm, I don't think so.'

Then she saw it, human heads on top of the columns. *Boy, those are realistic.*

The Chief followed her gaze up to the heads. 'It doesn't pay to be on the wrong side of the Sultan.'

'So, those are real?'

'Oh, yes,' the Lord said. 'That first one, that's Kemankeş Kara Mustafa, the–'

'Grand Vizier,' Raya finished the sentence. A hot flush rushed through her.

The two men nodded to each other, made comments about her being better informed than they'd thought. But it sounded as though they were underwater. Her heartbeat thundered in her head. Everything started to look very far away. She clenched and unclenched her fists repeatedly.

'I knew this wasn't a good idea. Now, breathe, breathe, Raya,' Oscar said. He sunk a claw through the delicate fabric and into her thigh.

'Thanks, that's helping,' she told him through head chat. She fought the transport with all she had. She could feel herself being pulled, like the other accidental transports, and who knows where this one might take her. She was gaining more control, she reminded herself. She dug her nails into her palm – strong sensations in the here-and-now to help hold her in place, like Bryony had taught her. She was about to see the Sultan's wife, as an invited guest. She wasn't going to miss this for the world.

* * *

The carriage came to a halt in front of another gate. She struggled to stand up – she was still a bit dizzy – and stepped out.

This gate looked like the pictures she'd seen of Disney World, and for a moment Raya wondered if the Ottomans had copied it. It had an arched entryway in the middle with fairy princess towers with pointed roofs on each side. Big, muscled guys stood around it. They were deferential to Raya's chaperones, so the two she was with must be pretty high up, even though they weren't royalty themselves. She would have been chuffed, if nausea from what she'd just seen hadn't taken over. *'Oscar, I'm scared.'*

'That's the smartest thing you've said for a while.'

When they walked through this fairy princess gate, another, more serene park opened in front of them. There were rows of tall trees. It seemed cooler, but she wasn't sure if she was fooled by hearing the breezes caught in the treetops.

There were fewer people, all well-dressed, and purposeful, like staff, not visitors. There were animals grazing, something like deer, but not quite. There were lots of large birds walking around. She almost tripped over one, who then opened its tail up into a fan of gorgeous big feathers. Peacocks.

Wonderful aromas floated from a row of low buildings with chimneys.

'Might as well check it out while we're here.' Oscar started off towards the kitchens.

'*PLEASE stay with me,*' Raya said. Oscar trotted back to her, not looking his happiest.

The two men walked straight ahead along a marble colonnade. More columns. Raya's stomach turned. She stole a look at the tops. The first man reassured her that only the columns in the first courtyard had heads.

'*Oh THAT'S reassuring,*' Oscar said.

'*Shut up,*' Raya retorted, grateful for head chat.

When they reached the third gate, the guards didn't want to let Raya through. The Lord of the Doors was not shy in telling them it was Rachel Nazarlik of London, the famous fortune teller with the lucky eyes, making her appointed visit.

'Well why didn't you say so in the first place,' the lead guard said as he stood back and let them pass. The Chief and Lord with Raya right behind made an immediate left, so that she didn't get to see much of this third courtyard. She was ushered into the women's quarters, the harem. Again, Musta was right. The décor was miles beyond anything she'd ever seen. Every inch of the walls and ceiling was covered with intricate patterns that then made other larger patterns when put together – geometrics, flowers and plants. There would be one design to about as high as your waist, then a band of tiles with Arabic writing, or a vine design, then other patterns above that. The pale marble arches to each room provided some visual relief amongst all the swirls and patterns. The ceilings, many of them domed with sky lights were also covered in designs. Intricately worked metal lanterns hung along the walls.

Raya glanced into rooms when she could. Lush Oriental carpets covered many of the floors that were otherwise done in the same cool marble as the arches. There were plush couches, fine wooden cabinets, and delicately etched metal tables. The windows stretching towards the high ceilings had decorative iron grates across them, their patterns complementing the many others. She wondered who they were keeping out. They passed an open passageway to a smaller courtyard where a number of young girls in sheer white, baggy trousers and long hair plaited with cords of pearls were playing with a ball – tossing it to each other and chatting. They were not wearing veils. A few of these young women looked at her before returning to their game. Servants went back and forth carrying all sorts of things.

'Excuse me,' Raya said.

'Yes?' The man glanced at her without breaking stride.

'Aren't we in the harem, the women's quarters?'

'Yes, we are.'

'So why are there men here, like you two?'

Lord of the Door answered matter-of-factly, 'Snip, snip, my dear.' He made a scissors gesture with his hand in front of his crotch.

The two men continued along the maze of hallways. She hurried to keep up, and Oscar had to run. The Lord glanced over his shoulder towards Raya. 'Don't worry. It's one way to move up in the world here at Topkapi.'

The Chief, hustling her along, said to Raya, 'Come along now, Turhan Sultana's expecting you.'

Chapter 39

The Sultana

Raya was brought into a large room and Oscar followed. Every surface was exquisite, but the room was empty except for a sofa on a platform and a couple of chairs. The Chief stopped; she did the same. She'd never felt so nervous.

'The Sultana has requested that we look after your cat while you have your audience with her,' the Chief said.

'Oh,' she said, clutching Oscar, 'I'd hate to bother you. I can look after him, he won't be any trouble.'

The second man, the Door Lord swooped the cat out of her arms, surprising both the girl and cat. 'It's no problem. I assure you he will be fine. You see, the Sultana prefers no other energy in the room when she has a reading,' he said and walked out with the cat. Raya's stomach dropped, she swallowed hard.

Raya was bade to follow the Chief of the Girls to where the Sultana was waiting. They wended their way through another few turns down more hallways until they reached another room, smaller but just as decorated, where a young girl was sitting, not much older than Raya, maybe seventeen or eighteen. She was slim and fair, with hazel eyes, long dark blond hair and a delicate oval face. She was very pretty and knew it – she could have been one of the über-kids from Raya's old life. Another woman stood at a doorway at the opposite side of the room. Raya wondered when the Sultana would arrive. Her nerves were jangling, her ears buzzing. The Chief stood at attention upon entering the room and signalled for Raya to do the same. She took a few steps back to stand next to him.

'Turhan Hatice Sultana, I bring you Rachel Nazarlik of London,' he said.

The teenager nodded. 'Thank you, Kizlar Agha. That will be all.' The Chief left the room soundlessly. The Sultana asked the woman by the door to bring the coffee now, enough for both of them.

Raya stood planted on the spot. Turhan clapped her hands and jumped up and over to Raya the minute the woman servant left the room. She leaned into Raya's face. 'Yes. Your eyes ARE the colour of a *nazarlik*, just as they say. Oh, you must be good luck then, and I hear your readings are absolutely brilliant...' She prattled on, not unlike any teenager, except that she didn't wait for Raya to say anything. She seemed to be used to doing all the talking.

The servant returned with a brass tray with two cups of Turkish coffee and a plate of pastries. The Sultana sat down on the high-backed, cushioned chair she had been sitting on to begin with and gestured for Raya to sit on the less ornate one across from her. The servant put the tray down on a table between them.

Raya, already full of adrenalin, didn't want any coffee, but she felt she couldn't refuse. Turhan chatted away. She asked Raya a few questions about herself. The Sultana, too, had come to Turkey from elsewhere. To her credit, she was interested in Raya and where she'd come from. But she also reminded Raya of the spoiled Karatay daughter.

Turhan finished her coffee, she nodded towards Raya, reminding her to start the ritual. Raya did her most thoughtful and dramatic version. She could see that the Sultana was testing her. Turhan would do things a bit wrong, start to turn the cup in the wrong direction, this sort of thing, then eye Raya to see if she caught it.

After they put the saucer on the cup, turned it a suitable number of times in front of the Sultana's chest anti-clockwise, they placed it on the table. The Sultana snapped her fingers, and the servant waiting like a statue stepped forward with a gold coin. Not silver, but gold. The Sultana handed it to Raya and asked her to look at it for a good few seconds with those lucky eyes before placing it on the upturned cup. Raya tried to make her words sound like an incantation.

'May this coin dispel all evil and bad will towards Turhan Hatice Sultana, her future and her heirs.' The Sultana closed her eyes; she seemed to like Raya's style so far.

They waited in silence for the cup to cool. Raya realised the Sultana was waiting for her to start, so she took a deep breath, closed her eyes, and tilted her head as though she was checking the cosmic weather.

'Let us begin.'

Raya was grateful to have had all that practice at the Karatays's party – a dress rehearsal for today. As she started out with her usual patter about how the reading was done her mind was drawn elsewhere. The shapes in the cup came alive into violent scenes – including murder.

She hadn't realised it, but her voice had trailed off as she stared into the cup. The Sultana touched the back of her hand.

'Rachel of London, are you all right?' the Sultana said. Then to her slave, 'Please bring us a jug of sherbet and maybe a cool towel, Çeren.'

Çeren nodded, stepped out of the door, and spoke to someone else. Raya heard footsteps receding down the hall.

Raya blushed, mortified to have lost control of the process in front of the Sultana. But the Sultana seemed pleased, clapped her hands. 'My goodness, you certainly DO see things in those coffee grounds don't you? Tell me everything.'

Then two young men slaves entered, one carrying a small table, and the other carrying a tray with a jug, cups, and a bowl piled with folded towels. They placed these within reach. The Sultana thanked them and they left. Çeren poured two cups of sherbet. Raya gulped hers down. She hadn't realised how thirsty she was.

'Tell, me, what do you see?' Turhan prompted.

Raya took a deep breath organising what she was going to say to this young Sultana, blinking back at her.

She'd been sold into slavery by the time she was eleven, then bought by the Topkapi Palace at twelve, when the Sultan's mother, Kösem Valide Sultan gave her to her weird, creepy son. The mother was hoping this would keep him busy while she ran the show. Ibrahim's mother, Kösem, was some bossy cow, all right. And that Ibrahim sure was one big bucket of weird.

Other images appeared. Ibrahim had been locked in a windowless prison cell as a child. One of his brothers killed all the rest – all the rest, that is, except for Ibrahim.

Boy, these people were something. Ibrahim wasn't released until his early twenties, messed up for good. He did horrible things to women and servants. No wonder his nick name was Ibrahim Deli – Crazy Ibrahim. Raya felt sick.

She looked up at the young Sultana, her face open and hopeful. Raya saw her in a different light. She was not simply a spoiled rich girl. Raya gave her a wan smile but didn't say anything yet. She wanted to see the whole story before she spoke.

Raya saw that Turhan had become Ibrahim's favourite concubine, then his wife, and that she had a baby boy, Mehmed. Being the mother of a male heir to the throne – now that was job security in this place.

'I can see you are a very strong person, Turhan Sultana. You have come through many trials and horrors already. You were taken from your mother when you were still a child, stripped of everything you knew, even your name. Then, you were sold to the sultanate here, far from your homeland. Sultan Ibrahim's mother paired you up with Ibrahim, to keep him happy. You gave him his first son.' Raya paused to look at Turhan, to see how this settled with her. The Sultana flushed, but quickly put that in check. Impressive.

'Yes, you see my past clearly,' the Sultana said. Raya took this as a request to go on. She looked away from the coffee cup, filled her eyes with the intricate patterns on the tiles lining the walls, then looked back at the cup, turning it this way and that, to see if the same visions appeared. She wanted to make sure.

What lay ahead for Turhan was beyond anything Raya could have imagined. In a few years, Ibrahim would be strangled by the Janissaries. Loads of people were fed up with him, he was so strange and messed up.

Raya looked up for a moment and could see that this young wife wasn't the squeamish type. In fact, it might please her, putting her young child in charge, which would mean SHE was in charge of the entire empire. Raya's expression must have told it all.

'What? What do you see, Rachel with the Lucky Eyes?' the Sultana whispered.

Then Raya saw that the Sultana was not only a survivor, but a murderer. If not by her hand, by her order. She was going to have her mother-in-law killed.

After Ibrahim was executed and their child, Mehmed, rose to the throne, Turhan would become the Valide Sultan – Large and In Charge. But her mother-in-law, Kösem, wasn't going to give up without a fight. Not after being boss lady for over thirty years. But it looked like it hadn't occurred to her she might lose.

The Sultana's gaze held steady and cool. A chill slid down Raya's back.

'Çeren,' Turhan said softly, 'please lock the door. Then come here and let's hear what Rachel has to say.'

Raya didn't hold back, she told her everything: Ibrahim's execution; her mother-in-law, Kösem, trying to take over from Turhan; Turhan ordering Kösem's execution and; Turhan's struggles and successes in ruling the Ottoman Empire.

Turhan Hatice Sultana smiled. 'Excellent, Rachel of London. You certainly live up to your reputation.'

'Thank you.' Raya blushed.

'But I hope you didn't think I brought you here merely to read my coffee cup.' the Sultana intoned, all girlish notes in her voice gone.

'Pardon me?'

The Sultana signalled for Çeren to pour more sherbet and took a sip before continuing. 'You must appreciate that I have the best spiritual advisors in the empire available to me. Your reading WAS right on target – matches what I've been told before about my future.'

Raya was baffled. Had Oscar been right – was this about something else altogether?

'I'm sorry, Sultana, I don't understand…'

'I think you do, Rachel of London. After all, we know you're from the future – we've been waiting for you,' Turhan continued.

'What?' Raya dropped the formal tone. Gobsmacked didn't capture it.

The Sultana and her servant laughed.

'I was told by the great spiritual advisor, Cinci Hoca that a young woman from the future would come – would help me like no one else could. I have people placed all over, as you can imagine. Some of them in the baths spotted you right away – on your first day here.'

Raya shook her head, not comprehending.

Çeren looked to her boss for permission to speak. 'We were waiting for the girl from the future. We were told she would seem like a desperate refugee, but would be carrying a live jewel, like nothing anyone's ever seen before–'

Raya gasped, 'My mobile!' With everything that had happened that day, barely missing getting hanged, she realised she'd lost track of it. When the workers at the baths didn't return their dirty, tattered clothes, she hadn't thought much of it. She wasn't even sure her phone was still in her trousers pocket. It could have fallen out in the transport for all she knew.

'Ah, so you admit it – you ARE from the future? You CAN travel across time.' the Sultana leaned forward.

'Yes, ma'am,' was her automatic response despite their being close in age.

The Sultana spoke quickly, conspiratorially. 'I need you to go back in time a few months and do something for me.'

'I… I don't know if I can, I mean I don't have very good control over this yet–'

Çeren opened the door and stood aside. The Sultana led Raya down the hallway. She stopped by a window where a carriage waited outside – the fancy yellow one she saw stopping at the *han* this morning. The Sultana nodded to the man standing by the carriage door.

'This may inspire you,' the Sultana said. Raya's heart was pounding. The man opened the carriage door and pulled out Macide, Abbas, Bryony and Kâtip Çelebi, Uncle Musta, all of them gagged with their hands tied behind their backs.

'NO!' Raya screamed before she could stop herself. Her voice echoed down the marble hallway. 'LET THEM GO – THEY HAVEN'T DONE ANYTHING WRONG!'

'We know.' The Sultana smiled again. 'You have to understand, Rachel Nazarlik, governing is not for the faint-hearted. I need a little insurance that you will do this one small favour for me,' she said, but still did not say what it was.

Raya's blood pulsed, she flushed hot. Everything slowed down, her senses heightened – she saw each stitch on the

Sultana's elaborately embroidered dress, she smelled the hibiscus in the courtyard, she heard a mother peacock and its babies somewhere on the grounds. She felt like a coiled panther, watching, readying for the perfect time to strike, to save her friends. If only she knew how and when.

Chapter 40

Against the Ruled

'Are you crazy?' Raya blurted out, 'Kill your mother-in-law? I CAN'T. I can't do that!'

Çeren pointed out the window to Raya's four friends still standing next to the carriage, bound and gagged. Abbas and Kâtip yelled things, but she couldn't make it out. Raya tuned into Bryony as best she could – she never had to do it while also being frightened out of her mind.

'Don't do it – you have to let us go, Raya,' came from Bryony. Could that be right – Bryony telling her to let them perish? That was what the Sultana promised – their deaths if she didn't comply.

'Bryony – NO! I can't let you all die!'

'Raya, you HAVE to. You can't do things that change history – it could lead to many more deaths than just four. Believe me.' She paused then added, *'It's part of our training...'* Bryony sounded sad beyond measure, afraid, and resigned.

Raya couldn't believe Bryony could be so brave and selfless. This was not the muddled social worker she knew. What kind of training WAS it to become a proper witch? But she couldn't bear the thought of their deaths. She tuned Bryony out. It was either that or faint, and her instincts told her that would only make things worse. She glared at the Sultana. Her breathing was laboured as though she'd been running, her cheeks were hot.

'I'm not asking you to do the deed, of course,' the Sultana purred. 'You'll contact my trusted advisor, Cinci Hoca, he's expecting you in whatever time he might meet you, and he will arrange for the, um, "action" to be carried out, and the disposal. You just bring me proof. This removes me from the deed by one more step as well – should help with my popularity in the future, too. But the real reason I need your help with this is that I missed my chance. I need to keep my mother-in-law, Kösem Sultan, from appointing that worthless Grand Vizier, Sultanzade Mehmet Pasha – nothing but a corrupt yes-man. I need

MY man in there – so I can REALLY make my mark on the Ottoman Empire.' She paused looking into the middle distance as though she was imagining her future reign. 'Yes, soon they will be speaking Turkish across all of Europe – even in England!' Then she focused on Raya. 'Well, as soon as we get rid of Ibrahim, of course. But all in good time.' Killing her mother-in-law and even her husband were nothing more than necessary business moves for her.

'You need to go back to approximately the twenty-seventh of January of this year. I worked it all out for you,' she said, pleased with herself. 'That's four days before this idiot Sultanzade gets sworn in. Should be plenty of time–'

'What would you consider proof that your mother-in-law's dead?' It sounded like someone else had asked the question. But it was her own voice she heard. There was no going back. Staying here made no sense, so she had to move forward, even if that meant going back further in time.

* * *

Without knowing how, and all on her own, without Oscar or Bryony, she did it. She transported back to the twenty-seventh of January, 1645. She'd felt her entire being, heart, body and mind focus with laser intensity on this one aim – and then she was there, in the Grand Bazaar, seven months prior.

The usual splendours of the bazaar radiated a creepy funhouse feel now. She pressed through the throbbing humanity along the cobbled streets towards the coffee house the Sultana told her to go to, to meet this advisor, Cinci Hoca. She stopped at the doorway. A young waiter served coffees to a table by the door when he noticed her.

'Can I help you?'

'Yes, I have been sent to speak with Cinci Hoca.'

'I'm afraid he left about a half-hour ago. Won't be back until tomorrow.'

She hadn't thought of that. That would leave her with one less day to get all this figured out and finished.

She wondered about walking over to the *han*, and seeing if she could stay there. But the thought of seeing Macide and Abbas, before they ever knew her broke her heart and put her mind in an unhelpful loop. Instead she walked to the baths, and languished there for as long as possible. Finally, in the third room, after she'd had endless cups of sherbet one of the staff came up to her. A young woman she hadn't seen before.

'Are you Rachel Nazarlik?'

'Yes,' Raya answered.

'We were told you might show up and need a room for a night or two. Come with me.' Raya didn't question it – one of the less weird things to happen today so far.

She was given what looked like a room usually used for some sort of beauty treatments. They left her with a clean sarong wrap to sleep in. Without appetite for food or ability to sleep she lay on the narrow bed and listened to the sounds of the last bathers, and the staff closing up for the night. They showed her how to open the door to leave should she want to, and then they left. The place went quiet – a cavernous sort of quiet.

Raya woke to the sounds of women's voices and splashing. She must have dozed off after all. She was immediately filled with dread and adrenalin. This was her eleventh day in old and slightly older Istanbul.

She returned to the coffee house and Cinci Hoca was there this time. He was a big man, in his fifties with a neatly shaped white beard. His clothes were brocade and ornate.

'Rachel Nazarlik, I've been expecting you,' he huffed with his bulk. Drops of sweat dotted his brow below his white turban. He pulled a chair out at a table just on the outside of the coffee house. 'Please have a seat.' He gestured to a waiter who sped off.

She sat and looked at him, not sure what to say. How did this work? Did you say this stuff out loud? He seemed to be waiting for her to start. She was exhausted and wired at the same time. The waiter returned with two cups of the thick coffee and a couple of pastries. Raya figured she should eat something and forced the too-sweet square down. The muddy, bitter coffee was a welcome contrast.

'I suppose you know why I'm here,' she tried.

He nodded. 'I believe so.'

OK, so HE'S not going to say it, she thought.

'So, I'm here to… to make sure the "action" is completed.' She thought she might as well use the Sultana's terms.

He nodded again. But they could be talking about buying a tablecloth or walking a dog. She'd better be clearer.

'Um, I will need proof of course, that the honourable Kos–'

'Yes, yes, that the honourable person is no longer troubled by these daily struggles,' he cut her off and raised an eyebrow. Of course, they had to be careful, they could easily be overheard.

'And how do I get my, um, proof?' she raised an eyebrow back.

'Return here in four days and I will give you the item requested,' he said as though he was talking about a tablecloth, rather than the treasured jewellery taken from the dead Valide Sultan Kösem – something she would never part with voluntarily according to Sultana Turhan.

Raya suppressed a gasp as best she could, four days would be her fifteenth in old Istanbul, too late to transport home to London.

'I'm afraid that's not possible. I need to return to my boss, no later than two days from now. I'm under strict instruction.' She held the older man's gaze.

He didn't seem like any big clairvoyant, empath or integrator to her. He seemed more like a businessman. He didn't question Raya's edict – that was one reason she doubted his skills.

He shrugged. 'If you say so. Then you'll need to get our "customer" to take their delivery sooner. Let's see, how could we do this?' He stroked his beard and looked out onto the bustling marketplace. 'I know. Why don't we tell her you're my protégée, learning how to do your coffee cup readings and that I've sent you to read hers.'

'You work for her too?' Raya asked.

'Why yes, of course,' he said as though this was nothing unusual. Nothing unusual in arranging a murder as though it was a haircut. Nothing odd about getting paid by the murderer AND the victim. And nothing strange in meeting with someone who recently made a jump in time.

The fat man continued, 'In the reading tell her you can see she is in great danger, and that she needs to go the third dock north of her mother's summer home, her *divanhane*, on the Bosphorus. Tell her to wait there at three in the afternoon the day after the reading, and that someone she knows and trusts will come and take her away, in a boat to safety.'

Raya took in a deep breath. 'OK, so how do I find her?'

Chapter 41

More of the Truth

There weren't any secret words or knocks needed to find Kösem Valide Sultan. Fat old Cinci Hoca simply took Raya to her. Well, to her staff at the Palace, to be more precise. Raya didn't see the Sultana Turhan, and didn't know what would happen if she did, besides her head exploding. Would this Turhan of seven months ago know her? Would she know that her future self sent Raya back here now?

The staff had them wait in one of those amazing, overly decorated rooms. The woman servant came back. 'Kösem Sultan would be delighted to have a reading by your new protégée,' she said, 'You know how she loves a good reading. She's made room in her schedule for tomorrow, at eleven in the morning.'

Raya took a deep breath and held it to keep herself from saying anything stupid. Tomorrow would be her twelfth day in Istanbul.

She and Cinci were given rides in royal carriages to wherever they wanted to go. She was glad the young woman at the baths had said it would be OK for her to stay a couple of nights, although she hadn't seen the need at the time.

She was starving after eating nothing besides a few pastries for the last two days. She rushed in and found the same girl worker. She said Raya had enough time to go and get some food before they would close up. She returned to the baths with her dinner where she had another surreal night of avoiding her own thoughts and listening to the sounds of water in empty rooms.

Raya woke in the wee hours – no sun through the skylights yet. She felt sick. How did she ever get herself in this situation – needing to trick someone into the arms of their assassins in order to save her friends? The Sultana was going to have Kösem killed eventually anyway – Raya tried to reason to herself. And if she didn't go through with her part, she would have to live with the knowledge that her four friends died as a result. Four of the best people she'd ever known. Bryony even risked her life to try to help her in old England, although it hadn't worked. Bryony. How could she do it – tell Raya to let them die in order to save a load of other people none of them ever knew? She realised that would be the right thing to do, if you knew for sure all those other people were going to die. She went to the toilet and threw up.

By that time the baths were open and she decided she could do with one herself before meeting Cinci Hoca outside at ten o'clock as agreed.

* * *

Another ride in another royal carriage. None of it had the shine it did a few days ago. They stopped inside the first courtyard, the one that was the most like a small city in itself with throngs of people, conducting business or just sight-seeing. Raya and Cinci walked casually, blending in to the crowd. Cinci made sure Raya remembered the location to tell Kösem – which dock on the Bosphorus, and reminded her in staccato whispers to act horrified and upset when she 'saw' Kösem's future in the cup. Like she needed reminding, or needed to act. She wanted to tell him to shut up. She wanted to be safe and sound with everyone back at the Cosmic Cafe – a fairy tale for sure.

Finally it was time for her appointment with Kösem Valide Sultan, the Mother of the Sultan and de facto leader of the entire Ottoman Empire. Cinci Hoca went with her – the proud mentor launching his prize student. This would douse any possible suspicions Kösem might have, according to Cinci. The more she got to know this royal bunch, the more being paranoid seemed smart.

After the formal introductions and Cinci's hyperbole about her skills, the door closed and she was alone with Kösem Valide Sultan and her servant. For a moment, the horror of the situation melted away and she saw a regular woman in her fifties. Regular except for the authority she carried, the power she had, and of course her amazing clothing – bedazzling and bejewelled. Raya thought of Ms Watts, Macide and the various women world leaders she learned about at school. She saw Kösem fitting right in there with them, on her own page. She swallowed hard and smiled.

It was as though someone else was doing this, the reading for Kösem Sultan. She heard the words she said, and saw her hands move the cup through its ritual, but it didn't feel like she was doing any of it. For a few seconds she saw the whole scene, including herself, as though she was hovering against the ceiling. The Valide Sultan asked some questions. Raya answered them. She asked some more, 'How long will I remain in danger? How will I know when it's passed? Who is this who wants me dead?'

Then it happened. Raya cracked. She trembled and tears ran down her cheeks.

The Valide Sultan gave the smallest motion with her head, and the servant left the room, clicking the door conspicuously. She reached across the small table and took Raya's hands.

'Tell me, dear, what's troubling you.' Her voice was calm, steady – a mooring for Raya's storm of emotions.

'Valide Sultan, I beg your forgiveness – I've told you the truth in that coffee cup – you ARE in danger for your very life. But it's not exactly the way I said.'

'I see,' was all the Valide Sultan said, as though she heard this sort of thing all the time. Maybe she did. Then Raya told her more of the truth.

'Someone DOES want to kill you, but you can't go to that dock on the Bosphorus – that's where the killers will find you. I'm SO sorry. I've been forced into this. They have four of my... family.'

The Valide Sultan lifted Raya's chin with her finger and looked into her eyes. 'And they'll kill them if you don't send me to my assassins?'

Raya nodded.

'You still haven't told me who has ordered my death. Anyone I know?' her tone was world-weary sarcastic.

Raya didn't want to tell her, although she got the feeling she had a good idea.

The Valide Sultan leaned back in her chair, folded her arms across her chest. 'So what sort of proof does this person need?'

'Jewellery, something very personal to you that you never take off–'

The Valide Sultan laughed. A big, open-mouthed, head thrown back laugh. Boy this woman was strong. 'You mean something that wouldn't come off, unless I LOST my head?' She pulled out an old, gold, Greek cross on two chains from under her dress. 'Two chains to keep from losing it. It's from my homeland – and a secret I keep – shall we say, "close to my heart"?' She unclasped the two chains holding the cross, pooled them into Raya's palm, and closed the girl's fingers around them. 'How long do I need to hide?'

Chapter 42
Good Advice

On her thirteenth day in old Istanbul, Raya snapped her laser focus onto her memory of the Topkapi Palace; on the hallway outside the room where she first met Turhan Hatice Sultana. With an ear-splitting whine and a flash of heat against her skin she was there, seven months forward, in late July 1645. This razor sharp ability to transport had come on with her last desperate need to go back to January. She didn't know if it meant she had this skill for good. But she hoped with all her heart it would work at least once more, to get her back 'home-home' to twenty-first century Britain.

Something had shifted. It was as though a cog inside her had moved and meshed perfectly and powerfully with another gear she hadn't known was in there. Twenty-first century London was where she wanted, where she NEEDED to be. And not just her, but her friends, too. She could no more part with Bryony, Macide, Abbas or Musta, than she could willingly part with a limb. She had no idea how she was going to make this happen, if it was allowed, or even possible, but like a missile on countdown for launch, there was no stopping her now from trying.

She had definitely transported to the right place, to the long marble hall outside the room where Turhan had first received her, but maybe this was the wrong time. Servants raced through the hallways, yelling and clutching clothing, household goods, even furniture. She had to duck into doorways to avoid getting mowed down.

'What's happening? Where's everyone going?' she yelled out but no one answered. They pounded past, their eyes like spooked horses.

'Get out! It's over!' a servant girl she recognized screamed as she raced past, clothes spilling out of her arms.

'What's over?' Raya shouted back, but the girl was gone. Raya dodged through the stampeding hordes to a window. And then she saw it.

Mayhem clogged the grounds of the Topkapi Palace. Janissaries fought soldiers in different uniforms. They were attacking each other with swords and knives. Others shot bows and arrows, or muskets. Some were on horse-back. They were toppling statues, ramming buildings with logs. Dead bodies were strewn across the lawns. Others tried to carry them away, but it was useless, more dying by the minute. Camels, horses, and donkeys charged around frantically.

A young slave boy hurried down the corridor. She grabbed his arm. He swung around, fear in his eyes until he saw it was only a girl. 'What's going on?' she asked him.

He looked at her like she must have been under a rock. 'They've all joined forces – all our enemies. They conquered Istanbul a few days ago. And now they're taking the Palace. Where the hell have you been?' The boy tore away down the hall.

Raya slunk further along. She opened doors to the once glorious rooms, now littered with smashed furniture, tiles and lamps.

She had to find Bryony, Macide, Abbas and Musta. She made her way through the fleeing throng, and stood in the doorway to the courtyard. She smelled blood and rotting bodies in the hot sun. Someone had killed a bunch of peacocks seemingly for the heck of it. The prison blocks were in the second courtyard, and the harem where she was, was in the third. She didn't want to transport there, didn't want to land on a sword or soldier.

She pressed against the wall and surveyed the situation. Other servants and slaves slunk along, then ran across areas where arrows were flying. She scurried like a rat against the wall to the first 'safe point', imitating what she saw the others doing. Occasionally a soldier grabbed a servant girl and hauled her off. When she saw it happen again, she hiked her dress up and ran like hell, thinking at least one soldier already had his hands full. It worked, or she was lucky as she got to the second gate, now abandoned by any guards, a clutch of servants and slaves huddled underneath, eyeing their chances of getting out of the Palace altogether.

She spied the prison block in the centre of the second courtyard, where the Sultana had 'promised' her friends would be when she returned. She fingered the Greek cross on the two chains around her neck. Useless now. There was a terrible clash of swords and shields to the right of the cell block. Other soldiers threw themselves onto the pile. This seemed to be her chance if you could call it that. She stared at the door to the cell block, saw nothing else but that door, then POP – she was right in front of it. It was open. She dashed in. The iron grated doors to the cells creaked on their hinges – all open. One door lay on the floor. Empty – the cells were empty.

Standing alone in the abandoned prison was a cool

respite. But she wasn't protected from the sounds of swords against shields, muskets firing and the screams when they found their marks. She thought about the *han*, the pink rendered wall around it and the gate until that was all she saw and BAM – she was there, too.

But like everything else in what had been her beloved city, it wasn't the same. Soldiers with weapons filed out of the *han*. Carts piled high with supplies and goods from the bazaar rolled in. Two soldiers with metal breast plates and helmets stood guard with very long muskets. She pressed against the wall to stay out of their direct line of sight. They spoke in another language – not Ottoman Turkish, and not English. Transporting inside might not be a good idea. She had nothing more to lose. She adjusted her veil and headscarf, took a deep breath and walked up to them.

'Excuse me, sirs, but this is where my family lives – lived. Do you know where they are? Are they inside?' she asked in Turkish, thinking it more likely they might know a bit, rather than English. The first guard sighed, as though a scared girl was the last thing he needed. The second guard said something to him, pointed inside, then trotted off. The first guard gestured for her to wait and she did, watching the flow of soldiers and supplies going in and out.

The second guard returned with one of Macide and Abbas's groundsman. Raya burst into tears upon seeing him. He spoke rapidly to the guards in their language and then to her in Turkish. His eyes were kind but frightened. He hugged her tight, even though they had never as much as shook hands before.

'They're all right, Rachel. They're upstairs gathering their things. They bribed the Venetian soldiers to let them escape. Every piece of gold and silver they had. The soldiers had already taken over the *han* – we couldn't stop them,' the groundsman shook his head. 'They're all up there gathering as much as they can before they leave. Go – go now!' He turned and hurried off to whatever his next assignment was. She didn't have time to thank him, or say goodbye. She raced across the courtyard, a few soldiers looking at the unusual sight of a girl amongst them. She took the stairs two at a time and thundered down the balcony flinging the door open to Macide's apartment. Everything was strewn everywhere.

Macide, Abbas and Bryony turned from their frenzied packing to look up. Bryony and Macide burst into tears. Abbas came towards her with an enormous grin, eyes brimming, 'Rachel! You're alive!'

Kâtip Çelebi, dear Uncle Musta came through the door from her old room. 'Did I hear you say "Rachel"?'

He gasped upon seeing her. 'It's God's will – you're alive!'

After hurried hugs and more tears, the adults returned to flinging things into sacks while explaining what had happened.

'Now that Turhan Sultana got the Grand Vizier she wanted, history's changed, and it's crashed into the present,' Bryony explained and she stuffed things into a canvas bag. Her spoken Turkish had come on, and from the nods from the others, it seems that time travel was no longer a secret.

'I don't get it,' Raya said as she tried to help, but mostly got in the way.

'Are these the saucepans you wanted?' Kâtip asked Macide before stuffing them into a sack, then continued, 'It's like when two tectonic plates crash into each other and cause an earthquake. But with this, it's time and possible histories crashing into each other instead.'

That was Kâtip Çelebi down to the bone, always interested in things, regardless of the circumstances.

'But the mother-in-law, Kösem, she's alive!' Raya protested. This isn't my fault!' Bryony gave her the briefest look – it was more, 'you don't understand' rather than a telling off.

'What?' Raya said.

Abbas tried this time. 'We know. She's come out of hiding, but it's too late. She couldn't stop her daughter-in-law Turhan who's off in Europe overseeing the invasions. Last we heard about Kösem, she'd gone to try to broker a treaty with the Habsburgs.' Abbas shook his head and sighed before continuing. 'But she was hidden away long enough for Turhan to make HER man Grand Vizier, instead of that idiotic yes-man Kösem had in there. And Turhan's man more than lived up to her expectations – they call him Amansiz Pasha, "General Ruthless". He did what she wanted, increased the fighting on all fronts, bringing the Ottoman Empire into the rest of Europe.'

Raya nodded. She remembered the Sultana saying all this. 'That was fast!'

Kâtip gave a rueful laugh, 'Turhan promised they would be speaking Turkish in England before the year ends.'

'But's it's just been a few days,' Raya objected, while piling folded clothes into a sack for Macide.

'But now, it's as though history WAS rewritten, with Amansiz waging horrendous attacks for the last seven months on all the Ottoman fronts – Transylvania, the Venetian and Habsburg empires,' Kâtip Çelebi said.

'So it's like history gets redone?' Raya stood still, uncomprehending, a pillow dangled from her fingers.

Abbas snatched it away and tossed it back on the couch. That's when she noticed Oscar huddled into the corner of the sofa.

'Hey, mate, missed you,' Raya said to the cat.

Oscar merely meowed.

Kâtip continued, 'After about six months of Turhan's Amansiz Pasha in charge, all of our enemies banded together – the only way they could realistically push back the Janissaries.' He went into the kitchen and collected some cutlery.

'And push back they did,' Abbas said, arching an eyebrow.

Raya dropped the clothing she'd been holding, staring gape-mouthed. 'Oh no, you were so right, Bryony. By saving you guys – I've DONE all this?' She plunked down on the floor. 'But I couldn't… I couldn't let you guys die…' Sobs heaved her shoulders and her face crumpled into her hands. 'What have I done? All these lives… the *han*, my wonderful Istanbul…'

Bryony crouched by the girl and brushed her hair out of her face. 'Oh, Raya. It was a truly impossible situation. This is Turhan's doing – no one blames you.'

'AND *there's no more* kedi et,' Oscar moaned. Bryony laughed.

'So what do we do now?' Raya asked.

Macide stepped up to the girl. 'We leave. That's what we do. People are getting onto boats on the Bosphorus as fast as they can and they're sailing out to whatever shore will let them land.'

Raya gasped.

'Oh dear girl. You can't be shocked by this. You've moved before, I've moved before – we can do it again,' Macide said. 'It could be worse, eh?' She sounded like she was trying to convince herself.

Raya felt awful, she felt layers and layers of awful. 'Uncle Musta – what do you think we should do?'

He stopped packing. 'I can't leave, dear niece. I know my advice to you was not to get too attached to any one place, but as I've learned, it's much easier to give good advice than to use it.' He shook his head. 'I can't leave my Istanbul. I guess part of me hopes I can help somehow.'

The sounds of men unloading and loading carts, metal clanking, and horses nickering came through the window from the courtyard below. They continued packing, all of them except Raya. She stood still, inhaled the warm air laden with the scent of sun-baked earth, animals, and warm metal. Something was growing inside her. Something infinite but weightless, enormously strong, but could be dashed by a single word – something you carried with you always, once you had it – love. Like a vine, it grew feet and yards, became her heart and veins. She felt tall and new, ancient and miniscule.

'Raya, are you all right?' Bryony asked. Raya was laughing and crying. She turned in circles, her arms outstretched looking at each of her friends' faces, including the furry one, again and again and again, as she spun with increasing speed. And then – POP.

Chapter 43

A Wonderful Shock

Pavel called Integrator Headquarters with the news. Raya and Bryony were ordered to the Integrators' Reintegration Unit in north London – a must for all witches after a mission, whether it included time travel or not. It was where integrators recuperated, made sense of what they'd experienced, and got treated for any diseases they might have picked up, like the bubonic plague.

It had been quite a shock – a wonderful one, but a shock nonetheless for everyone when Raya transported them back to the Cosmic Cafe in twenty-first century London. She even did it with twenty-four hours to spare. Ian had ushered out the few gobsmacked customers with some lame excuse about 'foreign customers mistakenly coming through the back door', given their seventeenth century Ottoman outfits. But the biggest surprise – and complication – was that Raya had transported Macide and Abbas with them. It was just as well that they had both been told about time travel.

Bringing someone from a different time was the greatest infraction of the Integrators' Code, along with altering history. Although you couldn't really separate moving someone to a different time FROM altering history. And Raya had done both. It wasn't clear what repercussions might await her. They couldn't take away her Integrator Accreditation, as she'd never had it, not to mention she didn't even know it existed. Plus she was too young. You had to be at least eighteen to be an accredited integrator, although twenty-one or -two was much more common, after you completed academy.

They took all of this quite seriously as evidenced by the quick arrival of a bureaucrat from headquarters called Mr Bliss who sat with endless forms for them to fill out before they were allowed to leave the Cosmic Cafe for the Reintegration Unit.

'But what about Macide and Abbas?' Raya asked. 'What happens to them?'

That was a murkier area. The short answer was no

one knew what might happen long-term. Ms Sonya Watts had arrived along with Mr Bliss and talked them through the possibilities. From their readings at IHQ, it looked like transport back to old Istanbul wouldn't be safe due to the ongoing war there, and it wasn't clear it was even possible.

Raya felt indescribable guilt about her part in causing 'these changes in history', she couldn't bring herself to think she had caused a 'war'. But she couldn't, and didn't even try to hide her happiness at having brought Macide and Abbas back with her, even if it meant she would never become a fully accredited integrator.

'Love can be selfish, like that,' Oscar offered without being asked.

Of course they would take care of Macide and Abbas, find them a place to stay, an integrator family who spoke at least modern Turkish, and they would set them up with English language lessons, and support of various sorts. But 'time refugees' were very rare, and there were no set protocols in place. After all, how could you possibly prepare for travellers from every past time and place?

'But why can't they stay with me?' Raya asked.

Bryony looked at Ms Watts who tried to answer. 'Well, maybe eventually, but let's just get everyone settled and see how things pan out. Plus, you'll be in the Reintegration

Unit for at least a week. Macide and Abbas can't sit here and wait for you, now can they?'

Raya took a few deep breaths before responding. She felt like she was being talked to like a child, in spite of all she'd been through. 'But I can see them, right?'

Ms Watts smiled, 'Of course you can. We not only encourage it, we support it – train or bus fares – that sort of thing. We really ARE on your side, Raya.'

Raya knew they were, without a doubt. She dropped the attitude.

* * *

The Reintegration Unit was lovely; a refurbished, rambling old mansion with a large garden at the back. There was accommodation for integrators and their familiars, mostly dogs or cats. One young woman had a rat and one man had a goat.

Everyone had their own room and a Program Coordinator who helped them pick and choose from the array of possible groups and meetings. There were mandatory daily debrief groups. You had to choose at least one from each of the three categories: Expressive Arts and Music; Integrator History and Science; and Physical Fitness.

There were ten people in Raya's Debrief Group. Three of them had been on missions in the present, but in different places. One had been to Mexico, one to Syria and the other to the nation of Georgia. Missions were a type of public service always aimed at helping – humanity, animals or the planet. Jake pointed out that people ARE animals when Raya told him about it. Most missions were set in the present, because it was very tricky going back in history with the aim of improving things, but without changing the course of events.

Raya was the youngest at the Unit, something she'd expected after all of that palaver with the forms from Mr Bliss.

'Does anyone ever go to the future?' Raya asked on her third day there.

'That's an excellent question,' the leader said. 'Not that we know of.'

'Does anyone from the future ever show up here, in the present?' the boy who'd been to Mexico asked.

'That's the other side of the coin, isn't it? We've had a few cases where people have claimed to have travelled from the future, but so far it hasn't been true.'

Bryony went home on the third day. She'd been through this a number of times before. She took Oscar home with her.

That was something else they worked out with the help of the therapists – who Oscar wanted to live with and what he wanted to do. Although a stray life on the banks of the river Thames was still on offer as promised, he'd changed his mind. He too felt more attached now and appreciated not all witches are selfish, after his first unfortunate assignment.

Raya loved the Free Dance group, and also tried the guitar, and pottery. But mostly she talked, and asked questions.

Raya was relieved when headquarters found a good match for Macide and Abbas – a Turkish integrator family in London, only a forty-five minute train ride from South Nutfield. Their English language classes would start next week. Meanwhile, Pavel brought them in every day to see Raya and Bryony. Everything was new and amazing to them – the cars and Tube trains seemed particularly spectacular, and the jets flying overhead.

They asked in her debrief group why she brought them back. She started with the obvious reasons about saving their lives in a time of war, but the crooked eyebrows and knowing eyes in the room wouldn't let her off with half-truths. She loved them too much to let them go. She realised it was actually selfish, and probably not the most mature decision, but at least she was aware of why she did it. It had been hard enough letting go of Uncle Musta, but she could see he would be too heartbroken to leave 'his' Istanbul.

'I know it's not forever,' she said to the group.

'You mean they're going back to their time?' the boy who'd been to Mexico had asked.

'No, I mean in the whole scheme of life kind of way. They might want to move away, I might, people eventually die...' she said and looked at her feet. She was wearing her new Doc Martens, a gift from Ian. She smiled.

The group went on to discuss other people's experiences in this area, but Raya's mind was elsewhere. Like a ribbon, she felt the events in her life connect up: her grandad, nan and mum; her experiences in foster care; her adventures this summer.

One day at the Unit, Raya said to Bryony, 'You know, I think I'd like to visit my mum more often.'

'That's a lovely idea,' Bryony offered, still her social worker.

It was great seeing Pavel again, but it also made her miss Kâtip Çelebi, and boy, would they have got on great. She told Pavel all about the time she spent with Musta. He was well impressed – he was one of Pavel's heroes. It was unbearable to think she might never see Uncle Musta again.

Emma and Ian came in most evenings after he closed the Cosmic and Emma closed her new bakery, usually with some of Emma's newest concoctions.

Jake came in twice during that week, along with Angie – as he was living with her again in South Nutfield. That was the hardest reunion. At least she found out beforehand that Jake should have no permanent problems, other than setting off metal detectors with a couple of pins in his arm. She sobbed terribly when she first saw him, but Angie calmed her in time to hear Jake prattling on to Pavel about the history Raya lived through.

Raya realised she would like to return to Angie's if she'd have her. It was time to choose her GCSE subjects. She picked law, history and sociology. The adults were delighted. She would have been surprised herself not that many weeks ago. Bryony enrolled her in pre-academy integrator lessons – twice a week after school, which meant tutoring with Bryony or Ms Watts. Her future never looked as interesting to her before.

Chapter 44

Jiggety – Jig

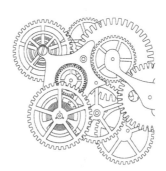

Jake concentrated as he carried a plate of köfte to the table then ran back to the kitchen. Raya finished laying it, and Angie placed a flower arrangement in the middle. 'That was nice of Ms Watts to drop this off, wasn't it?'

Raya nodded. She patted her hair. She had the top parts combed over the newly shaven underneath; her new flexible hairstyle.

Jake returned to the table with a huge salad and added this to the array of böreks, stuffed grape leaves, and pilaf.

'This was fun, making all this, all of us together,' Jake said and beamed. His hair completely covered his scar now. Raya smiled at him. Her happiness at seeing him was starting to outweigh her guilt. The sound of footsteps crunching gravel came through the open windows on this warm August afternoon.

'They're here,' Angie sang out. She wiped her hands on her apron and opened the front door. Pavel, Bryony, Ian and Emma, and Macide and Abbas piled in. Macide and Abbas were all excited about their train ride from London – their first.

There were hugs all around, gifts given, and exclamations of Happy Birthday to Raya. News was noisily shared and celebrated. Bryony was going to teach part-time at an integrator academy starting in the autumn, and hopefully move to full-time in another year or two, after she'd had time to see her social work cases through a bit further, including Raya and Jake. Her experience with Raya made her realise this was what she wanted to do as well as giving her the confidence that she did have something to offer.

Seeing Jake through his accident and recovery, Pavel was finally able to move forward and stop punishing himself for the road traffic accident that had taken his wife and daughter five years before. He hadn't been able to forgive himself, a fully accredited integrator, for not seeing this future before it was on them. But now, he could let himself connect to others again, and be part of the world. Raya wasn't the only one with problems in this department. He was rejoining the Police Integrator Unit.

Emma brought out the birthday cake in one of her new official bakery boxes. And Ian had won 'Best Veggie Chilli of East London' just last week. Angie had decided that in a few years, when Raya and Jake no longer needed her, she would travel around the world. This was something she was always going to do with her husband, but he died before they got the chance. And in the meantime she was going to look into being a non-witch volunteer for the integrator service.

Just before they sat down to the sumptuous Turkish meal, Bryony asked Angie if it was all right to open a back window for Oscar.

'Of course.'

Bryony reappeared in the front room and took her place at the table. 'He wanted to come but was running a bit late, so I told him he could catch us up.'

There was lots of passing of food and eating more, loads of conversation, usually a few happening at once. There was a thud, followed by a few garbled swearwords and a knocking from inside the toilet door.

'I told him the KITCHEN window.' Bryony disappeared down the short hallway. She and Oscar returned, arguing like an old married couple.

Bryony patted the empty chair stacked with thick books, next to her. Oscar jumped up and nodded his hellos because he was holding something in his mouth. He dispelled the contents on the table, a jumble of chain.

'Raya, happy birthday. I was trying to wrap it, but it's hard with paws. Hope you don't mind.' He tapped the heap with a paw.

Raya repeated what Oscar had said for the benefit of those who didn't understand cat. She untangled the necklace. A *nazarlik*, the good luck eye amulet on a silver chain. Abbas and Macide laughed the loudest. Raya burst into tears.

The party wound down, after more food than any of them needed, and Emma's scrumptious carrot cake. Pavel, Emma, Ian, Macide and Abbas headed back to the train for London. Bryony walked home across the field, but Oscar decided to hang out with Raya and Jake a little longer.

* * *

Raya docked her phone in the living room and turned on some 'good washing-up music'. They had a great time, belting out songs and wiggling around as they did they washed the dishes. Oscar bopped his head. As Angie put some leftovers into the fridge she said, 'I see we're out of milk. Raya, would you mind nipping down to the shop and getting us some for tomorrow?' Of course Jake was going too – this was the Chakmas' shop – where he worked before and now after the accident. Oscar decided to *'come along for the ride'*.

Ice ran down Raya's back. She hadn't thought about Tony in ages, and now she was about to face the poor couple he terrified so badly that they sold the petrol station and reopened this village shop instead. She took a deep breath and followed Jake and Oscar who had already trotted ahead. Once she caught up, Jake rattled on about how he'd told the Chakmas all about her and her natural talents, but not the time travel part because Pavel told him that was the one thing they tried to keep amongst the professionals, 'and me of course', he said with a proud grin. 'Come on,' he said and ran ahead.

As they neared the shop, Raya recognized two old schoolmates, a girl and a guy, leaning against the wall. One was drinking an energy drink, the other was smoking a cigarette. They nodded their hellos. She couldn't believe she used to hang out with these guys – they looked boring to her now.

The bell on the door jangled as Jake and Raya entered. It was empty except for Mr and Mrs Chakma.

'Oh my goodness, Piyali, look who's here,' Mr Chakma said to his wife.

Mrs Chakma leaned forward across the counter. *Does she know I knew Tony? Does she think I had anything to do with that horrible idea?*

'You must be this Rachel Jake keeps telling us about,' Mrs Chakma said. She extended her hand.

Raya used all her integrator skills to read Mrs Chakma and the situation. But she couldn't get a thing, not her thoughts, past, or future, not what she had for lunch. Nerves.

Raya shook her hand and smiled meekly. 'Very nice to meet you. I've heard such lovely things about you. We're all so grateful for what you've done for Jake,' she said but was interrupted by Oscar rubbing her ankles. 'Oh yes, and for Oscar of course.'

'Oscar! Where is my furry friend?' Mr Chakma said coming out from behind the counter rattling cat treats. Oscar meowed his sweetest. What an actor.

Mrs Chakma tilted her head and looked warmly at Raya. 'Our son, Genko, he has integrator skills too,' she said conspiratorially. 'Not like you from what I hear. I understand you'll have the option of academy when the time comes – congratulations, young lady.'

Raya's splutter was genuine, her blush honest. 'Oh thanks, but well, it's all new to me really.' The sparkle in Mrs Chakma's eyes and her warmth, as well as her age made Raya wonder if she'd be a nice friend for Macide, if they could ever move down here.

'Stop it, Piyali, you're embarrassing the poor girl,' Mr Chakma said.

'Don't be silly, she's not embarrassed. Are you embarrassed?' Mrs Chakma asked but didn't wait for an answer. 'Like I was saying, our Genko's a lawyer in London now – uses his skills in that too – human rights law,' she beamed.

'Oh wow – I'm doing a GCSE in law!'

'Well, you'll have to meet him sometime – I'm sure he'd be happy to tell you all about it.'

'That would be great,' she said. She had to look away and swallow a few times to check the tears that had welled up. The Chakmas were so kind and open to her. To think that all this was right here all the time baffled her. She must have been running so fast, the scenery had blurred.

Mr Chakma was paging through a stack of old science magazines showing Jake the articles he thought he'd like.

'And their daughter Nima's a proper engineer, like I told you,' Jake said without looking up.

'I remember. I hear she's the type that builds bridges – right up Jake's street, as I'm sure he's told you,' Raya said and rolled her eyes.

Mrs Chakma laughed. 'Oh, just a few times.'

They finally remembered they'd come for milk. Mr Chakma gave them each a chocolate bar, then walked out of the shop with Raya, Jake and Oscar.

Outside, Mr Chakma made a fuss over the moggie once more.

'Watch out – that cat will probably end up in a curry.' It was that girl, the former friend against the wall.

'Yeah, do you want cat Korma, or cat Jalfrezi?' the boy chimed in.

Jake stood up straight, clenched and unclenched his fists. Raya watched carefully.

'Just ignore them. That's the best way,' Mr Chakma whispered.

'But–' Jake said.

'Shush. Can you imagine if I reacted to every stupid comment? Go home you two. I'll see you soon,' he winked and went back into the shop.

The boy classmate left his spot on the wall and towered over Jake. 'Paki lover, you are. We see you over there all the time. Wish you WERE one, don't you?' the guy said.

'Yeah. Bet you want to wear pyjamas all the time like they do, too,' the girl said.

Jake stared straight ahead, his eyes brimmed tears. Raya knew he was no good at fighting, and was on strict orders NOT to, given they'd recently opened up his skull.

'You're not going to let them get away with this, are you, Raya?' Oscar asked from his perch on the fence top, fully coiled, tail twitching.

'Come on Raya, you big old witch, go ahead – turn me into a toad, why don't you?' the guy said, leaning too close to her.

The girl stepped up to them, circled Raya like she was sizing her up. 'I dunno, Raya. If you're so powerful, why don't you make yourself better looking? Give yourself a decent pair of tits!' The girl guffawed.

'Do something! Don't just take it!' Jake pleaded.

A man walked by with his dog and averted his gaze. A sedge warbler sang its staccato song from a field. Raya thought about it. This would have been just the sort of opportunity to mouth off she used to relish. But more to her surprise was that she used to consider these kids friends – think this sort of rubbish was OK, even funny.

Then she thought about all she'd seen and been through this summer. The powers she didn't used to believe in, but now has. The people she'd met, the new family she'd formed. Then there were the things she'd done, even if they *were* by accident. Some she was proud of, and others – she didn't know if she could ever forgive herself. She wondered what she might be capable of doing – on purpose.

'Come on, Jake. Let's go home.' She started off down the road, with Jake and Oscar in tow. She ignored their protests about her lack of action. The two former friends continued to heckle them. She paused, turned towards the two kids once more.

'It's Rachel. Just call me Rachel.'

Thank you for reading!

Dear Reader,

I hope you enjoyed reading *Being a Witch, and Other Things I Didn't Ask For* half as much as I enjoyed writing it! I'd love to know what you thought, what you enjoyed, or even hated. And let me know if you'd like information on any of the historic figures including Kâtip Çelebi, Turhan Hatice Sultana, or Matthew Hopkins. You can write to me at *info@sarapascoe.net* and see more about me and upcoming projects on *www.sarapascoe.net*.

A lot of people ask how I came up with the story. It all started with a skinny, balding stray cat in our village. He was so shy, I thought he was feral. Then, one day as I was gardening, he came up to me and gave a very sweet meow for such a large cat. That was that, he was ours. Although this was in a small English village where everyone knew not only each other, but each other's animals, no one knew who Oscar belonged to, or where he'd come from.

So, my husband came up with a theory: 'He must have fallen off a witch's broom as she flew over the field next door.' Thus, the seed was planted. At the time, I was working in my former profession, as a psychologist with children, and the plight of foster kids has always gripped me. But rest assured, besides Oscar, all non-historic characters are completely fictitious.

Finally, I need to ask a favour. It would be great if you could post a review online, especially on Amazon (links provided on my website) or Goodreads. Good, bad or neutral, getting reviews can make or break a book – it's in your hands!

Thank you so much again for spending time with Rachel, all the other characters, and through them, me.

With warmest wishes,

Sara Pascoe

Printed in Great Britain
by Amazon